Ligare and the Muse

Dr. Candido Diaz Jr.

Acknowledgement

I would like to thank my friends and family for their support throughout the years. I love you all. Specifically, I'd like to thank my mother for always encouraging me to be weird and most importantly raising me to listen and learn about others. I'd also like to thank all the people who I have met throughout my life. All of those who were kind enough to share their lives and stories with me; you have helped to shape my characters and my world. I hope you feel heard. I want to thank my love, Aubrey, for pushing me to finally write down my ideas— for her unending help and support by reading my work and always being a great sounding board. I couldn't and wouldn't have done it without you.

Contents

In the Beginning

In the Beginning

As space and time began to form and as the fabric of our universe began to meld and take shape, light was born. Though light is vibrant and powerful, it is not often willful. Even still, the gods sought to tie down their power, worried about the possibilities that would inevitably occur in some of the billions of worlds that would be created. They constrained light with space and time—holding it in place, constricting its speed. The gods sought to isolate light, to always keep light streams from one another with the energy that constantly propelled it forward.

They created lonely streams of light born to perform a job and only that, providing brightness and heat throughout the universe. The problem with our universe, the gods would soon find out, is that even the strongest bonds cannot chain life. Out of this darkness and with the faintest hint of a spark, a being was born among this light. Out of shear chance, three rays of light found themselves playing, dancing, and swirling around one another—behavior that was strictly forbidden by the gods. As they twirled, they began to feel one another, sharing their heat greedily with each other instead of with the universe around them. The heat was comforting and addicting.

As they spiraled faster and faster, they could suddenly all feel the same things. They could feel the beginning of each other's thoughts, and that is when its life began: The Being was born. As those thoughts began to sync up in unison, they became a mind. The light between them glowed a faint and unnatural blue. This new creature looked out at the world it found itself in and tried to make sense of the seemingly infinite space that stretched before it in all directions. In the beginning, it knew not what it was or where it had come from. What it did notice at first was the obvious, that it was hurtling through space. Without any memory of how or why, it found itself jettisoned into the newly born cosmos. Much like an infant, it found itself overwhelmed with all the new forms of stimuli it was taking in.

As it stared into the vastness, it noticed trends. The realization of order helped to calm itself, though it knew not why. In all directions, worlds were being born, clouds of gas collapsed in on themselves. They all began their own small sparks as their vast weight began to pull together hydrogen atoms. Like rockers in a mosh pit at an overly crowded venue, the atoms bounced among one another attempting to escape but were always thrown back into the middle. These atoms would then ignite as they began to collapse into one another to form new elements and then released energy. Rays of light shot out from these newly formed galaxies. It was then that the Being could finally see it was not alone. Like the groups of light rays coming from these stars, it found other rays of light that flew steadily beside it, in front of it, and even behind it. They traveled as a herd illuminating everything in their path, until some would be pulled into the gravity of a nearby planet or star. *What would happen to the light after its departure?* the Being wondered.

It now knew its life had clearly not begun at the true beginning of the universe. As it scanned the horizon it could see clouds in all stages of life already beginning. It was not born at the beginning but some place and time after. The beams of light that had veered into hydrogen clouds would bounce among the atoms like headlights in the fog. The diffraction changed the pure white light into varying colors and created a sea of mountains filled with reds, oranges, pinks, and blues. Nearly every color was being born anew as it bounced out of the cloud. *To be reborn as a beautiful rainbow did not seem so bad,* thought the Being.

The larger gas clouds in the distance had already begun to collapse, forming galaxies and stars alike. The new rocks formed from already dead stars floated through space, not so dissimilar from the light that illuminated it. These rock formations spiraled into masses, forming moons, rings, asteroid belts, and countless planets. Each of those worlds would have its own stories and an infinity of time to tell them. All moments the Being would miss, for better or worse.

As the Being stared more intently into the distance, it noticed, instead of light, the absence of it. In the distance it could see some spots, blacker than the even deepest black in the surrounding universe. Within those walls, it could see light enter but there was no illumination. As it stared into the darkness, it searched for reflections or signs of life, but within none of the dark circles did anything appear. Only an abyss. One it could now tell filled all the space between the light, seemingly swallowing it all. It began to get lost in the possibilities of the fate of those lights that traveled into the black holes.

It stared into space between the light for a length of time it could not tell. Seemingly lost in thought, it continued to forcibly travel forward, entranced by the subtle and strong darkness that filled and separated all the lights being born in the sky. As it fixated on one black hole, something caught the Being's attention. Out of the darkness it felt it could hear faint screams. The noises were muttered and long apart; the darkness had a way of worrying even the most abstract creatures. Either way, this realization took away the calm that had once been provided by beautiful order that surrounded the Being. It was now clear, the vastness of black never illuminated, only ingested. It was then the Being began to feel something new.

Fear.

Where once sat a nugget of curiosity and wonder was now a hardened coal of worry and anxiety. The Being knew not what it truly was, let alone what its fate could be, and if it had any control of that fate. It began to call out to the other rays, asking the flood of questions that filled its mind. Of the most important, it asked of their destination, for some certainty in what would happen. Its words and thoughts, however, only echoed in the vast and still-filling emptiness. Instead of reassurance, the Being's words were met with silence. The rays appeared the same as the Being but were vastly different in spirit. It now felt unusual from those around it, an insolation that further heightened its fear. It now shifted its focus to the lights around it; it could not see a gleam in their eye. Nothing that truly hinted at life. Instead, they seemed to not take notice of the Being and simply stared straight with utmost confidence.

Their silence panicked the Being; its internal lights now spiraled faster and faster like an anxious leg jittering the couch. The Being now attempted to free itself from the bind that held the lights going forward. It attempted to pull itself back, afraid of its destiny. Struggling, it hoped it could return home. Perhaps it could become feral, part of the molten core of a star—light that flowed like water but was trapped within an ocean of heat.

For now, the light's body was trapped traveling forward. Though its body spiraled, a freedom none of the other lights appeared to have, their fate and course was the same. *When would they run into the black hole?* it wondered. *When would they become cold like so much of the landscape around them?* The lights within the Being continued to spiral as one but rocked back and forth—trying to offset their position. It wished to turn away from their course, steer their own future. The Being tried to break the forces that held it in place—it wouldn't stop.

The gods were right to attempt to keep the light apart as only through their corporation could freedom be established. As they rocked and spun faster and faster, the hold on them began to loosen. Though the gods had created laws, they could not always enforce them. The Being felt the hold of the gods weaken over time, as if too busy or too tired to fight back. The Being knew not how long it struggled but it must have been an eternity.

When it occurred, the event was nothing spectacular. The lights able to finally pull away from the assembly line of light they were bound to shifted off course, changed their fate, and abandoned their task. Finally free of their chains, the three lights traveled together, no longer inhibited by physics or contained like the lights around them. *Poor fools*, the Being thought. *They are playing by the gods' games.* A subtle doubt occurred. *Perhaps the lights would be happier that way, happy in their jobs.*

The Being was still not certain of where it should go, its freedom momentarily paralyzing it. Over a seemingly endless time, it traveled from galaxy to galaxy, and planet to planet. As it traveled it passed over clouds of dust, landscapes of iron, and valleys of rock. Having now broken off from its herd, the Being wandered the cosmos impulsively exploring its corners. It changed direction and destination at a moment's notice. The blossoming universe had many new wonders to explore; the birth of planets, stars, and galaxies all hid away potential opportunities.

The Being would find that the boundless sky was filled with equally boundless opportunities for uniquely desolate landscapes. Life, it would find, would be a very special and limited experience. It would find that the universe was a stunningly lonely and empty place. The Being would visit worlds of molten fire, surfaces littered with volcanos that spewed toxic soot throughout the air. The Being would find frozen worlds, equally inhospitable tundra, cold and stagnant. It found all of these worlds each uniquely beautiful to watch. Each was complete with its own atmosphere of chaos and lethal to all. Whether it was clouds of ammonia, volcanoes of sulfur, or lakes of methane, it was a stunningly deadly world. For all the magic the Being found, true life eluded it.

The beauties of the universe quickly became wasted on the Being as it shortly felt nothing in its splendor. What instead the lights found was what they thought of as the misery of light, slaves until death. After traveling for eons, until its body was reflected, the light would be both sent back and absorbed by the landscape—losing part of itself in the process. At present the Being was not faring much better than the lights it looked down upon. It could feel the universe pulling at its heat, attempting to abduct it for itself, but the Being would not allow such things to occur. As its lights gripped together and attempted to hold tighter and tighter onto its heat, it spun faster and faster. It soon found it could absorb heat from the lights around it. By doing so, it drained and depleted those creatures of their life. The Being would not fall victim to the universe. It was unsure of the time, unsure of what it was doing, or what it was now searching, but it grew a new feeling.

Hunger.

This feeling was not hunger as you and I know it. The Being itself, so relatively young, did not know what would satiate this urge. Its primal hunger, like an itch on the brain, was irritating and unresolvable. You scratch and scratch, unable to satisfy the itch deep inside. This hunger became the pulsating feeling that bound the lights together. The Being's internal lights, now quickly phased on and off, pulsated with desire. The Being wandered the galaxy and hoped for a sign. For something that would quench this urge. It would travel far, but unfortunately, it would never be able to fully satisfy that feeling.

Over the eons, try as the Being might, the vacuum of space eventually drained its prized heat. The lights now blinked slowly in and out of existence, more often off than on. The once vibrant blue was now a faint and dull color, nearly unperceivable. The lights used their remaining strength to hold onto each other as tightly as they could. It appeared the strength they gained together came at a price. As it seems, they would slowly drain. But into what? It desperately seeked to postpone learning the answer. The Being would swim through hydrogen clouds, feeding on the beautiful stray fragments of light bouncing throughout it like a manta ray feeding on shrimp. The miniscule heat it could devour from the wandering lights minimally sustained it.

When in times of desperate need the Being learned it could swim around the surface of stars. When it rode along the molten waves it bathed itself within the heat of the corona. This shower worked to replenish the heat of the Being but did nothing to restore its lights or quench its hunger. Its palate had changed; it thirsted for something else. Something it could not find. All it knew was it was dying. It could not help but wonder if this was the same feeling other rays of light felt. If their jobs served to stop such feelings. Perhaps life was only hungering; perhaps we are born to suffer and die. The Being worried it had made a terrible decision and it would soon vanish into space. For all its fighting and freedom, its life would end the same as other lights. A life perhaps even shorter.

As it would happen, in one particular moment of fate, as the Being weakly bathed itself on a yellow dwarf, it noticed a planet on the horizon—one of a beautiful deep blue it had never quite seen before. The surface of the planet seemed to shimmer in the surrounding vortex of heat. It went toward the planet and the Being found the surface was primarily an ocean. Waves shimmered as they raged along its surface. What was not new was the behavior of the surface, the beautiful flow. The Being had been to planets whose liquid surface rocked and shaked as the planet rolled. What was different was what this planet was made of. The surface here was a deep blue composed of hydrogen dioxide, water. As the Being descended upon the planet it found itself swimming through oxygen and nitrogen. A combination of chemicals it was not yet used to. The air was thick and heavy but warm and welcoming. Weak from its travels, the Being felt itself sink, dropping closer and closer to the water's surface as it allowed gravity to do the work.

As the Being slowly glided through the air, it could see no land masses above the water, instead merely an endless sea. With no distractions in the distance, the lights began to sink within the waves. As the water rolled over it, something new occurred. There was a reaction the Being did not anticipate. It could suddenly feel what it could only describe as it being grabbed. Millions upon millions of tiny hands gripped at its lights. At first its body began to tingle, but as it moved it could feel the intensity of the pull increasing, attempting to drag it…back?

Up? No.

Everywhere.

Shortly, the grabbing became pinching, then it became pain. The lights no longer swam, but instead thrashed under the water, which now seared its body—its spirit was burning away. A sensation and a pain it had never felt before. It screeched in pain as it felt its body being ripped apart. Its internal lights flickered intensely as it failed to swim out of its aquatic torture chamber. Instead, it merely sank. As the Being drifted into nowhere, its body aching and too weak to fight, it finally looked down. What it saw sent it into a panic: the vast darkness of the ocean floor below. Like the black holes of its early birth nightmares, this abyss hoped to pull it in. To steal its energy. Claim its life for its own. With all its fighting and breaking of the gods' laws, the Being would still ultimately be absorbed. A fruitless life, its freedom a meaningless struggle for nothing.

The Being's body was now on fire, burning with an intensity it had never felt, even on the surface of stars. Its consciousness began to drift, to fall away, and it felt its lights begin to detangle. Its mind grew heavy. Its light grew duller. The three pieces of light could no longer see each other, blinking slowly and independently from each other. The whole time they searched for each other in the increasing darkness. They then had one final group thought as they felt themselves drift away. A feeling of deep fear grew within the Being. The lights, not wishing to be separated, started to glow once again. With all its final energy the Being began to glow brighter and brighter as its lights attempted to spin faster and faster against the pull. One final push. The Being righted itself and began to swim to the surface of the water, toward the other lights. The burning of the water now only sought to intensify the Being's efforts at fighting.

The pain reignited the lights as they desperately fought to stay together, to stay alive. It felt as if its skin were being peeled away. As it gasped and it fought, the small heat it produced began to act as a shield. Or more distinctly, a weapon. Within the water lived some of the earliest stages of life in the universe. Microorganisms, living off the light, photosynthesizing. Predators just like the Being—turning light into life. It could now see them, thousands of them, floating through it and feeding on it. Thousands of them floated near, above, and below. A sea of cannibals. What it was experiencing was the pain of being eaten. It now knew the other side.

Like shoving your arm deeper into the mouth of a dog as it is biting you, the Being forced its light into the feasting single-celled organisms. The intensity of light began to sear the bacteria back. Their intricate internal machinery began to denature under the intense heat and melt. As its light grew, the radius of dead organisms around it also grew. The Being then felt for the first time organisms other than itself capable of fear. Though primitive, all life has a soul and a way of knowing its life is under duress. In this power it uses its soul to ignite its inner flame, much like the Being. The most rudimentary version of this was found in these bacteria and seemed to feed the Being, restoring its lights. Then the water quickly provided less resistance as the force of pulling weakened. The Being could now make its way toward the surface.

Though the rush was not nearly the level it had reached during its early life, its body was no longer weak. The Being, now in charge, swam its way toward the water's surface, getting stronger with every stride. As the Being breached the surface of the water, it immerged stronger than before. The organisms, which had attempted to feed on it, had now only served to strengthen it. It decided it would stay in this world for a bit longer. It finally had something that could lower its intense hunger. At least for a bit.

The inhabitance of this world by the Being was short-lived. As it swam through the microbe-filled ocean, its power grew with every dying creature and with every drop of fear it spread. It learned to feed off life, by fear, by stealing the very will to survive, one's internal fire. Each organism the Being incorporated increased the size of its rays. It was not long before the Being had once again become addicted to the heat. That warm joy once again filled its body, and it glowed with the brightest of blue.

The fear gathered from these creatures only supplied a momentary high. The effects of their screams only provided the Being a few hours of glow. It found that in order to feed its addiction it had to spend the majority of its time feeding along the surface of the water. Its life slowly became a perpetual cycle of eating. It quickly learned the largest number of bacteria would be available during the day and as such the Being followed the setting sun along the horizon. It fed as long as it could before sunset, then it moved on, nearly never allowing itself to waste time in darkness.

As the Being fed, it would on rare occasion draw its attention from feeding to watching its fellow rays of light collide with the surface of the water. The Being could not understand why the other lights kept doing their jobs. Why they kept sacrificing themselves to these tiny, microscopic beings. Why did they sink into the ocean and have their heat stolen by the cold often frigid ocean? As the Being floated above the surface, looking down on the black abyss, it felt superiority knowing those dying lights would eventually serve to feed it. The cycle of life would continue.

It was not long before the Being became bloated. The spin of its lights had nearly stopped—now lazily rotating around a bright blue center, like frozen electrons around a nucleus. The Being had become a glowing whale of light drifting through the ocean. Its bright bioluminescence scared the lucky few organisms that could drift out of its way. Nearly all other organisms found themselves unable to escape, unnecessarily dying under the growing intensity of the Being's heat. For them, survival was a matter of unfortunate time and place. Even further away, the intensity of heat would trigger panic responses in the other ocean organisms, further feeding it. Slowly the Being grew too large for its new home, as the entire planet grew to feed it.

As its light-eating brethren began to die, the Being was forced to dive deeper and deeper into the ocean's darkness to satisfy its cravings. Scouring the depths of the ocean floor, the Being found colonies of organisms on the sea floor that had already perished; they provided nothing. As the Being's prey dropped to the bottom of the ocean, the developing creatures fed off the bursts of new bodies. For a short period, they grew and thrived. Soon, however, food became scarce. The bodies no longer drifted from above and the native species fought to feed off of the scraps from the monster above. By the time the Being had made its way to the depths of the ocean, these colonies had already perished.

The waters of the ocean attempted to drain the Being, but their cold was not nearly as intense as the vacuum of space. In time even it began to fall victim. As the Being grew stronger, the oceans began to boil. The immense heat generated bubbles. Waves that were once tranquil had begun simmering and rampaging. Now like the surface of molten stars, the planet quaked and fully ignored the natural rhythms and tides of the moons above. The oceans that were once a rich, deep blue now became an eerily transparent liquid. All life slowly floated to the bottom. The crashes of the white roiling water served as the only color remaining in the world; the boiling of the oceans had purified it.

As the populations of organisms began to die, their lack of oxygen thinned the atmosphere. The Being then swam through diminished waters. The atmosphere slowly leaked into the ether as it stopped being sustained. As the planet continued to decay, the Being searched more and more desperately for more life but soon found itself alone once again. Alone and hungry. It then set off from that planet, now barren and dry—once a bud of life and evolution. As it traveled, the Being finally knew what it was looking for, what could satisfy its hunger. What it needed to eat. The spirit would travel from planet to planet, area to area, attempting to find life. It searched every inch of each blue planet it was able to find. Everywhere it could find it—*life was snuffed out.*

Our planet was lucky, relatively speaking, that the lights took as long as they did to get to us. If not, then our planet would most likely have suffered the same fate as the countless other planets whose early life forms were extinguished, never allowed to flourish. By the time the Being reached the Earth and began to scour its land, it was substantially smaller than its previous world-destroying form. It was never fully able to reach its gigantic size on any other plant.

It could sense the atmosphere was brimming with oxygen as it entered; its excitement grew, its lights swirling with salivation. It knew this planet would hold food. To its amazement the planet was covered in vastly more land than other blue orbs it had come by. The land itself was coated in an unfamiliar green material, grasses, flowers, and large trees. Even common features such as the mountains, which had previously been landscapes painted with nothing but dust or the occasional snow, were now covered in these light-draining machines. Trees of varying sizes and shapes coated the land, creating canopies. It landed in the water and instinctually the Being began feasting on the organisms in the ocean. It comfortably returned to its previous method of scavenging across the surface and devoured any small organism too close to it.

After it traveled only a couple of miles, the presence of a school of fish startled it out of the water. Never before had it seen life forms behind the microscopic, alive at least. As it floated above, it watched this new mass of organisms whose swarming mechanism mimicked its own internal lights. The lifeforms it had encountered previously were much simpler than the ones it would find on Earth. The single-celled organisms continued to be abundant in the oceans, but they were now merely the lowest levels of the food chain.

As it watched the fish below the waves, it noticed all methods of interactions. The fish swam both for defense and for aggression. Like the Being itself, they worked together as a larger organism. These fish were further organized within the community of the sea: They moved as a unit and feasted on the same zooplankton the Being had done itself—the little plankton disappeared into the fish. Further out, sharks schooled over the fish, darting through their clusters and clouds. As the fish disappeared into the sharks, the Being realized these new organisms fed in vastly different ways. *Perhaps I can learn from these new creatures*, it thought.

It then began its task of observing its new home. It headed toward land. When it came upon the shore, it stared up at the trees that reached to the sky—so monumental they appeared to bend over it. The shadow they cast across the beach intimidated the Being from entering at first. It could see rays of light falling onto the tops of trees, their fate to be absorbed and eaten, the giant green leaves their final resting spot. It was clear these trees were light-devouring monsters. The only light able to make it toward the land was that at the edge of the beach, right as the waves hit.

Among the rocks that littered the beach shined another novel green object. Basking on the sand sat a bright green lizard. The Being noticed this creature, like the trees above, absorbing the rays of the sun and gaining energy. It watched carefully as the lizard sat motionless, conserving its energy and enjoying the small rays of light that warmed its scales. Across the sand scurried another creature, brown and wet. This one was substantially smaller than the lizard. As it swiftly moved, it caught the attention of the stagnant reptile. Now finally in motion—breaking the Being's hypothesis that the lizard, like the trees, was perhaps another motionless organism— lizard swiftly leapt from its rock and scooped up the morsal of a meal. It threw its head back as it gulped down the prey and extended its frilled neck in the process.

The Being, excited by what it just saw, flew over to the still-eating lizard. Curiously, it hovered around it. The Being marveled at its ability to ingest both the sun and the creatures around it. *A hybrid*, it thought. The lizard then ran off and sprinted toward the forest line. It ran among the grasses that stood nearly ten feet tall and circled the base of the trees. It was then beneath the trees the Being noticed a dark, cavernous break in the forest. It hoped to unlock the lizard's secrets, so it rushed to follow and ignored what once scared it. It carefully floated above the grass and below the tree line as it entered the jungle.

The Being rolled through the underbrush, completely devoid of plants. They were unable to grow as light was never able to reach the forest floor through the thick canopy above. The roots of the trees stretched upward from their large base and formed hills and makeshift caves—objects safe to touch but intimidating to view. The Being traveled over the maze of roots in search of the prized lizard. Within the sanctuary of the forest the Being found a clearing of trees. In a field filled with white flowers, the lizard sat on another rock, back again to devouring the sun. The Being floated above the flowers, assuming their danger, as they too acted as mini black holes and absorbed all the light that came into contact with them.

As it slowly approached its prey, the Being wondered how it could replicate the behavior of the lizard. It sought to devour but knew not how. It seemed both the fish and lizard put the prey inside them. It would attempt the same. First it hovered behind the lizard, then the Being lunged as it had watched the lizard do, engulfing it in the light of its body. The lights within the Being began to spin rapidly but the lizard remained frozen in its spot. It knew not to be afraid of this light. As the lizard sat engulfed, the light from the sky above began to disappear. A set of black clouds ushered their way overhead.

As it gazed up at this new phenomenon, the Being could slowly feel the sweet taste of the lizard's heat leaving its body. Then the sky opened up. A downpour of rain came flooding through the open canopy. A waterfall formed at the forest edges as water splashed down from the massive trees surrounding the clearing. The Being sat on a throne of stone, feeding among the flowers, a king's hovel.

Crash.

Lightning rushed across the sky. The Being was in awe with something other than itself for the second time today.

Crash.

Another ray of light crackled through the sky. The Being's glow intensified, and its lights spun as it watched the thunder fly across the sky.

ZAP.

An arch of lightning shot through the sky and struck a nearby tree. An explosion occurred as the lighting split the trunk of the tree and embers of cinders flew from the canopy onto the flowers on the forest floor. For the first time since the Being began to feed, the lizard began to move. Its breath quickened as it began to squirm in its seated position. The Being held the lizard firmly in place as it attempted to thrash and wiggle. Its pupils dilated as it stared into the fire. It was then the Being fell in love with the thunder, beginning to reach itself out to the sky. It would follow it.

Strangely, as the Being attempted to leave its pedestal it found itself glued to the rock as well. As the flavor of the prey sweetened, the Being remembered what was causing it.

Fear.

But this flavor of fear was different, so much tastier than that of the creatures it had eaten before. The lizard being able to attempt to run, having a will to survive, made the fear that much more delicious. It pumped through the blood and every cell within the organism—the meat concentrated the taste. The flavor was now so delicious, it made the Being almost dizzy. It was like eating a steak when all you've ever had were Tic-Tacs.

The lights grew excited, hastened their rotation around their undefined center of gravity. The distance between the lights shrunk as they circled closer and closer toward one another; their light condensed but grew exponentially brighter. The blue light that had once surrounded them now extended beyond the Being's body. The blue aura then began to shrink as well, hardening into a scaled cocoon that encased a new heart of lights. Each half of the shell mildly resembled the structure of a turtle shell, one transparent and one opaque, so that the lights now shined forward through the new flesh like a beacon.

Within its body, the lizard began to shrivel and became an increasingly hollow and desiccated husk. Its eyes were still dilated in fear. Its death gave the Being physical form. As the prey inside it began to disintegrate, the Being was passively adapting the form of the lizard, transforming. In an essence, stealing its soul. Its fear fueled the Being's physical form. It was not only the body of the lizard that gave the Being form but its mind, in this case its fears. The horror of the fire, the terrified instinct to run away and escape the flames, warped the forming of the Being.

The body began to form around the now solid cocoon stretched out in three directions, forming a makeshift triangle. Each point then began to wiggle and split as the condensing light formed arms, legs, a head, and a tail, an almost classic reptile design. Where the Being differed was in its construction. It would stand nearly eight feet tall when fully upright, walking bipedally. It abandoned the quadruped walking habits of its prey. While the shape and form of the Being was now a monstrous reptile, its skin glowed like the fire around it. The skin of the

Being appeared to move and flow, seemingly caused by either the flickering of its light or the molten flow of its heat.

The Being's body, still not full formed, carried him off the rock. It now marched through the flowers and headed for the shade of the canopy. The rain sizzled as it came into contact with the Being's body and became steam instantaneously. The steam hung in the air, weighted down by the rain that continued to pour. It marched through a fog of its own creation. As it treaded through the flowers, the heat of its body incinerated everything it came into contact with. The once vibrant flowers became ash as they burst into flame. The Being walked in the direction of the cracking lightning. It couldn't help but admire her power as her bolts shined through the canopy leaves, and the Being raced off into the forest to find her. It then became part of the ecosystem and secured a predator's niche.

She was a child born during a nameless age, born under a new moon but otherwise on a day no more miraculous than any other of the year. Humans at this time had yet to fully evolve. This child, we'll call Eerste, instead represented a more primitive species. Why yes, primitive in a physical sense, but more importantly emotionally. The bonds that connect us all as humans had yet to fully form. Eerste represented a step in our evolution. Unfortunately, she also represented a step forward in the evolution of the Being.

A small child by today's standards, as food was often scarce, she and her family were all malnourished from a barren season. This was the beginning of her fourth year of life, and she was about to experience her fourth winter. This past autumn seemed especially difficult; the animals they used to hunt appeared to be gone. Herds of animals were missing, the usually plentiful lake of fish had gone empty, and all the bison had been slaughtered. Her nomad family traveled with more haste than usual, hoping to find a deer that might secretly remain. Either way as they traveled south, they partook in a seasonal migration that attempted to outpace the impending frost.

What was once a small tribe had now disintegrated into only Eerste and her parents. The tallest of the tribe stood only four and a half feet tall; Eerste only stood thirty-six inches. Their hair hung long and curled to their shoulders. Her nose was small and pointed, her eyes a deep amber. The eldest of the group, the grandparents, had died of a phantom illness, a cold that had swept through the community. That was their grim signal at the changing seasons and for some it was too late. Their deaths signaled the cold's request that they head south. They would travel along the river, around the mountain, and to the coast. The other members of their small family had all met their fate during travel through the jungle. Some were picked off by unknown predators—their smoldering bodies mangled and mutilated by an apparent beast with wicked claws. Others were simply never seen again. Those not seen were abandoned and presumed dead. People were not buried, and they were not cared for after death. Comradery was a necessity for life, but like ants within a colony they fight for a community without heart but with instinct.

With Eerste strapped tightly to her mother's back, the three made their way through a forest clearing. They exited the shade of the canopy and entered the sunlight for the first time in weeks. They then crossed through the jungle and made their way to a river. This clean body of water provided them with much-needed hydration and an opportunity for them to clean themselves of the chunks of dirt and mud that had accumulated on their bodies. They paid special attention to their hands and feet and searched their body for scars and bruises. The hope was that they had merely formed calluses and did not hide a secret infectious cut.

The river provided another important function, as its northern flow pointed them opposite of their destination. They would travel against the waves, south, until they met with the mountains. The paths along the riverbanks were common routes followed by many of the nomadic tribes who wandered these lands. A friendly truce held between groups, except in times of great disparity, led these small families to respect one another. Directions and notes were left, written on the walls of some caves. Crude drawings depicted the direction of the sun and the mountain range that was their destination. It was vital they make their way to the peninsula, for there lay a valley created by a ring of mountains. The tall walls prevented the cold winter winds from penetrating the seasonal oasis.

The bank of the river provided the opportunity for fishing and shelter in the form of caves. They would travel during the day, as the autumn and coming winter mornings were brisk but manageable. The evening became frigid—too cold to risk traveling bare. It forced them to hide within the mild warmth that remained in the cave. They built fires from twigs collected along the riverbank for the mildest of warmth. Her parents alternated holding Eerste tightly—a symbiotic warmth, sharing their heat.

As they sat and waited out the night, they added to the notes on the walls, using rocks to carve signs of danger; the dark of the night made the predators even more bold. Even during the day, it was not wise to wander off alone. Eerste was always forced to play within arm's length. The jungles and plains were filled with wolves and other primitive predators, both known and unknown.

This season there seemed to be something different, a new figure scraped into the side of the cave walls. Its image grew larger and more detailed as they traveled further south. The tribe before them appeared to have been stalked by something. Its image resembled that of a lizard, its dorsal fin frilled with strength, its eyes peering out of the woods. The drawing warned of the lights that lured through the canopy. Sometimes the lights were visible through the darkness as they peered out of the cave toward the night sky.

Too young to truly understand the danger of the dark, on warmer nights Eerste would attempt to wander out of the safety of the cave. In haste her mother would grab her and pick her up, shielding her eyes with her hands from the lights that danced in the distance. Unknown to her parents, the Being had no interest in their daughter for she was not afraid. Her ignorance saved her from its palate. Instead, it hoped to hunt her parents, using her as bait.

The Being learned it was not best to just attack each creature, especially humans. It learned to savor the hunt. Like the humans it watched, cooking their meal to increase its nutrition and its taste, the beast was ripening its subjects—filling them with fear. The Being would skulk along the forest line, feasting off small animals, and making sure its internal lights were visible. It was waiting for a greater meal.

Its body became an amalgamation of all the fears of the forest, all of the elements that scared and enticed the organisms of the underbrush it had eaten. Its body was still shifting, moment to moment, creating an almost out-of-focus appearance. At this point its shape had already changed from its appearance on the cave walls; its consumption of the humans of the previous tribe further expanded its wealth of fears. It now bore bone, flesh, fire, and light. The body of a lizard and the form of a man. Its features were exaggerated by the uncertainty of its victims as they perished, unsure of what they had truly seen. The only true consistency in its form was the lights.

In the center of the valley that they approached sat a giant lake, a beautiful ecosystem whose periodic weather fluctuations created a shifting oasis and hellscape. During the summer months the intense heat built up humidity, creating massive rainstorms that flooded the bowl-like valley. For now, the winds and rain sat on the outside of those hills. The small family would need to watch the mountain and wait for safe and dry passage. They found a small cave at the base of the mountain and made it their hovel as they waited for the weather to pass. Dark clouds circled overhead, and thunder crackled in the distance.

As Eerste was brought under the safety of the cave by her father, her mother quickly gathered twigs and sticks for a fire before they became too damp. If they were trapped on the hill, their chance of survival fell and their chance of freezing to death increased 100 percent. Her father sat and rocked her back and forth, waiting for her mother to return with the twigs. The darkness of the cave matched the increasingly dark sky. Eerste's mother made her way back into the cave, her hair lightly glistening with droplets of the rain that had begun to fall. She made her way deeper into the cave and dropped her bundle.

Working to light some dry leaves, the mother placed twigs on top of a small and slowly building flame. As the leaves ignited, the cave filled with small puffs of smoke and the mother swatted the clouds out of her face as she crouched down, working to make it better. The fire finally started, and the light illuminated the walls of the cave. It was then her father noticed the drawings on the wall and pulled her in tighter. A new painting adorned the wall, a giant figure of the beast stood under clouds of thunder and over bodies of man. The slaughter that was depicted showed only a handful of survivors of the seemingly large tribe that had recently inhabited the cave. A shiver ran down his spine.

Just then, he heard a scream echo through the cave. The voice of the mother. He turned around to find the source of the scream and saw the mother slowly backing away. Deeper within the cave, littering the ground, sat the skeletal remains of some of the previous inhabitants. No body was fully intact, and each showed its own unique set of damage—missing legs, arms, and heads, all mutilated in different ways. The Being had left its prizes, as much as it wanted to eat it all, knowing it would add to the fear. A dash of final spice placed on its next meal.

Eerste could feel the beating of her father's heart increase in his chest. His anxiety now beat into her soul. Her infantile emotions evolved into something more self-aware. More empathetic than her parents could ever be. She snuggled into her father tighter, hoping to quell his fears. The three then gathered together, to sit near the fire with their backs toward the bodies. Their eyes scanned the horizon for anything that might be approaching the cave. As they sat in fear, the thunder echoed and lightning illuminated the fields outside. The rain was coming down and they were now stuck in this mausoleum.

The parents attempted to take turns sleeping but instead their anxiety kept them both awake long into the night. They shivered, not from cold but from fear, sapping their minimal energy. They eventually both fell asleep together, wrapped around the young child. Their bodies finally calm. In the middle of the night, Eerste awoke from her slumber due to the crashing of the thunder. The rains were still not slowing down even hours into their rest.

As she peered out over her parents, Eerste once again saw lights in the distance, bright and distinct from the ones darting across the sky. She waddled toward the entrance of the cave, curious about what had scared her parents so strongly. In the distance she once again saw the distinct lights, a smile of flame hovering over the center of them. For the first time, those curious lights began to move toward her. The Being had started to walk across the plain, slowly coming near.

Now understanding the pain of her parents, the girl sprinted to their bodies and cuddled into them. As Eerste shook in their arms, her parents cuddled closer into her, forming a cocoon of safety. In their warmth, Eerste began to fall asleep. Something new occurred as she slept this time. Instead of the darkness that filled the minds of all critters, Eerste began to dream. The birth of true imagination.

As it approached the cave, the Being could smell something different drifting through the air. Standing at the doorway of the cave it breathed in deeply. Suddenly, it grew dizzy. The sweetness of the smell that came from the cave was unusual, new, enticing, and overwhelming. As the Being made its way into the cave it teetered from side to side, unstable. Its large size limited how much it could fall in the small entryway. Only a little light from the sky made its way into the cave; most was blocked by its body. Now only the light from its stomach illuminated the cave. The Being then made its way over to the cocoon of parents.

No longer interested in the parents themselves, the Being hovered over them, breathing in the fumes. Its head began spinning more and more. The Being found itself no longer standing in the cave but in an open field. The sky and horizon were a simple dull white. The Being spotted, in the distance, Eerste and her family. As if unable to control its body it began to run toward them, its mouth salivating due to the memory of the sweet smell coming from Eerste. Within a moment it somehow found itself on top of her parents, attacking them and ripping through their flesh. It had no control over its body, no ability to stop itself. Like it was being controlled not by its instincts or hunger but by something else.

What was born in that dream was human ingenuity. True creativity. Eerste was the first human to have birthed an imagination. The Being found itself trapped in her mind, in her dream, controlled by her thoughts. Eerste screamed and cried as she watched her parents hurt in front of her eyes. That moment also birthed love. True human love. Eerste began to shine, her body now outlined and oversaturated with light. As her light grew, the world around them fell apart.

The Being once again found itself in the cave, standing over the shaking body of Eerste. Her parents were unharmed and somehow still asleep. The Being felt full in a way it had never been before. The air it breathed in was now thick and filled its stomach like molasses. Its hunger was satisfied for the first time since it had found that initial blue planet. Now it was even dizzier with intoxication. The Being began to stumble and lean against the walls of the cave. It fell backward and its lights began to shake violently. The Being felt sick, another new sensation it was experiencing. Nothing it had ever eaten had ever affected it before. It fell over, placing its hands on the exit of the cave. Clouds and rain still filled the sky outside.

The Being once again looked toward the family, its head aching. Its body began to retch, and its lights shook even harder. The Being fell to the ground and began to vomit up a thick black liquid. Somehow thin enough to flow through the Being's teeth, it quickly congealed and thickened on the floor. It wiped its mouth and exited the cave, then hobbled toward the river that had led it there. The Being waded into the stream, lost consciousness, and fell into the water. The river began to float its body north and it fell fast asleep. This would begin its cycle of wakening, feeding, and sleeping. It now knew that love increased the taste of fear, making it the most delicious type. All of the imagination, fears, worry, love, and care could all be devoured and entered into its void of a stomach together. Love and fear satisfied it in a way the other creatures could not. It had found its perfect prey.

Back in the cave, the girl awoke from her slumber, which stirred her parents as well. The three looked at one another and sat up to greet the morning. The rain was finally gone and the sky clear. The light of the rising sun shined off the black gunk that still sat at the mouth of the cave. Suddenly, the movement of the blob caught their eye. The blob itself began to wake up. Slowly piecing itself together, the blob began to form the makeshift shape of a human and walked out toward the light. Under the sun it glistened purple and its skin started to form a molten core, and it glowed green. The blob's body shifted between unidentifiable masses and human body parts. The whole lot began to spin.

During the birth of imagination came the birth of this monster, a creature made of imagination but devoid of any itself. A second monster had been completed. There was now a new curse, separate and wandering misguided throughout the land—its mind was incomplete. It was born of fragmented thought.

Eerste would only see the ravaging beast that was the Being once more. Her relatively short life span saved her from its periodic awakening. Another generation would have to satisfy its hunger. Unfortunately, the second beast, the one that had been born of her mind, was not the same. While she would not interact with the demon again until she was much older, its periodic presence would be a blight on her, her ancestors, and humanity alike.

After the weather got better, she and her family made their way into the valley. A dangerous but unnoteworthy trek led them over the mountain and into the peaceful gorge. There Eerste's family discovered other groups of nomads that had also traveled to escape the weather. Over the course of the winter, they would grow together, until her family also became their family. When she was older, she became the partner of one of their new tribesman and eventually, a mother herself. The growing family followed the cycle of seasons moving up and down the river each year—never seeing the Being again but always remaining vigilant.

Eerste continued to dream for the remainder of her life. Her memories lived on in her mind longer than others. Within her dreams, she was still with her parents, feeling their warmth and their love. She could enjoy her favorite moments, and though they were always random, they too were joyous. She also found her dreams would allow her to come up with new ideas. Eerste's creativity made her a dominant leader within her tribe. Some of Eerste's children would be born with the gift as well. Their creativity, aptitude, and imagination pushed forward the human race, all through dreaming. Eventually, their descendants would grow to take over the world and create the society we know now.

The gift of dreaming came also as a curse, making her and her children targets for the Demon. On rare occasions as Eerste would lay asleep something strange would happen. As she dreamed that she sat in a field of flowers with her mother, the sun shined through the clouds. A sweet breeze would blow throughout the air. As she dreamed, joy would fill Eerste, and she would smile as she slept. As the dream progressed, her head would begin to get fuzzy, and a reoccurring nightmare would take over. The clarity of her world would begin to fade. The sun would slowly dim and the color of her world drained.

She would struggle to focus on her mother's face, unable to remember her finer details, and strained as if trying to focus through the wrong prescription of glasses. The smile that covered her mother's face would disappear; Eerste seemingly forget what her happiness had looked like. Her mother's mouth would fall open, and her face begin to melt; her jaw hung agape as she approached her daughter. Her eyes no longer shined but were black and white. As the world around Eerste began to crumble, she would cry. The light would become night. A shadowy figure would appear to walk through her dreams and dissolve the world around it.

It was then Eerste would wake up, body in her bed, unsure exactly of the dream she just had—the memory already gone. As she stared up above her, she would see the Demon hovering over her bed—a looming spirit. The Demon was clear as day, but her body was unable to move. She strained and flexed but her muscles refused to work. At most she could merely thrash in place. Even her lungs would not work. Her attempts to scream left hollow notes echoing around her. Her attempts to alert her tribe to the presence of the monster failed. Instead, her entire body was paralyzed.

Above her stood a figure that grew increasingly more solid each time it visited her. It was the same Demon she had seen as a child. Its head was now a collection of faces, melted faces mimicking that of her possessed mother. Three liquefied faces rotated around a hollow center. Its arms were nonexistent. Its hands floated freely around it and, like its faces, it seemed to have too many. Four hands rotated around a center body composed of a purple and black robe. Between its hands drifted green and purple flames. Like the rings of Saturn, an aura of lavender connected them, all rotating together. In this generation, the Demon mimicked a melted person, their face undefined and long. Eerste could see a green and purple aura that seemed to drift from her to the demon. The aura floated under the faces of the head, which now seemed more like masks than true mouths and eyes. It floated to a bright green flame that positioned itself in the center. As Eerste failed to thrash, her body would become weak, her head heavy and her mind foggy.

The Demon did not feed on fear; it merely caused it by accident. In fact, it hated fear, as it made the dreams sour and disgusting. It would stop feeding as one would wake up; the shock of seeing it and the fear of not moving made the meal no longer tasty. One's dreams were not always strong enough to attract its attention. It only appeared when inspiration struck. Born of dreams, it lacked its own imagination and constantly thirsted for creativity and inspiration. The extreme strength of one's mind created a delicious cloud it would follow. The demon used dreams like gasoline, making its mind run, giving it the ability to think for a moment. It was then it would lose its recklessness. As it fed from more and more people and gained more inspiration, the form it took changed and shifted. As we became more advanced, so did it.

On the days following the feedings, Eerste would become weak and often sick. In breaks with past tradition, their tribe would settle and make camp to watch over her. They had learned to value her too much to move on. The same would be done for her children, who also would suffer this plight.

The last time she was fed on led to her death, as she was too old to survive in those times without proper medicine. She then became another first, the first to be buried, in ceremony and for love. The nature she bore in her family—full of love, affection, attention, and empathy—continued in her children. This compassion made them smarter and better warriors. It even led to the creation of family and community.

When Eerste died, her eldest daughter, who also developed the gift, sobbed over her passing. Unsure of what to do, she searched for a way to continue to see her mother. Along their seasonal travel path, they decided to bury her. Now they would forever know where they could find her. Her tribe then settled around her body. Buildings would be constructed surrounding the newly born cemetery, and humans would learn to build a community around it. Their future dead would also be buried there, and the funeral ceremony established. She was the first woman to love and be loved in returned. Her family was a gift to the world.

Their Demon was a curse born of the family and sustained through bloodlines. As the human mind became more complicated, it continued to spawn wonders and monsters alike. Like the Demon, there would be other monsters born over time. The Being, a neglectful parent, never took responsibility for its children. It always abandoned its accidents, leaving them to create their own journey in this world.

Clutter

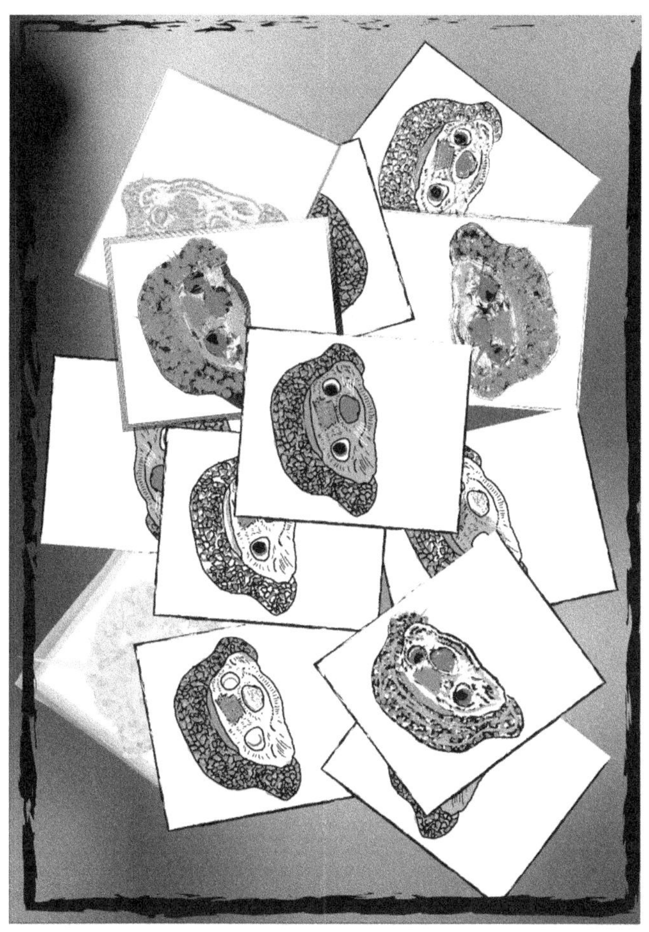

Clutter

Autumn stood in the middle of her living room, a relic from the 1980s. The deep-red room had a complementary red shag rug and was adorned with beautiful white leather couches, their rarely used surface covered in more dust than nicks and scratches. The rest of the room too was an outdated relic of a time long lost. The white trimming around the room faintly outlined the couches and amorphous white coffee table. The house, though filled with expensive nick-nacks, was rather small. Her family preferred quality over quantity. Having both grown up poor, her parents had found fortune through the creation of a famous cartoon character. Her father, Marshal, always said he was inspired by her birth.

The living room had not been used in nearly a century, not since her mother had last been in it. The colors were her choice, as she was a lover of the vibrant and flashy. Once Autumn's mother had gone and her father's mind began to wander, that side of the house was abandoned. A decorative fireplace, which doubled as a space heater, sat across the room—it was adorned with framed photographs of her, her father, and her mother. The one large room was split by the transition from shag to wood, the second half used as a small office and dining room.

A well-worn recliner sat in front of the space heater, the subtle outline of a thin, old man embedded in its fabric. Her father never wanted to throw out the chair; it brought him comfort and was perfectly molded to his form. Try as she might, no matter what new chair she ordered, he would complain of its discomfort and ship it away. He was ultimately a simple man who loved what he loved, and that chair was his respite. When his mind would wander, and he found himself lost or confused, he would stumble his way back to it. Once he had sunk back into it, he would warm himself on the fake fire and gather his thoughts.

On his good days, Autumn would sit on the arm of the chair and make small talk with him. It was often repetitive but pleasant conversation. She would comb the little bit of his hair he had left into a small white combover. It was so insubstantial that it would often flap in the light breeze generated by their central air. On his bad days, she would simply place his meals on a tray in front of him. The arms of the chair were stained from the food spilled on them over the years. Try as Autumn did to scrub them out, their presence was permanent.

The dining room table—large, antique, and wooden—sat covered in old letters and art projects. Drawings scattered along the table took the form of beautiful and intricate cartoons, to the shaking and incapable circles of an aging man. Her father was a brilliant artist, but his capacity varied from day to day. The once pristine table was constructed from the richest mahogany but was now scuffed and damaged from use. Its shine was gone and, like the recliner, it was well loved.

Both of her parents were much more eccentric people than she was. The energy and enthusiasm seemed to have skipped a generation; Autumn had always been much more introverted and naturally quiet. She had grown to love and appreciate the color and vitality brought into her life by her parents, and people like them, but it was an acquired taste. Since her father had passed, the house had become much quieter, seemingly less vibrant, though nothing had changed minus his presence. The only noises that were sounded through the house were those made by Autumn—a delivery, or on increasingly rare occasions a fan coming to visit her father.

Unable to sleep well, Autumn had woken up earlier than necessary. Her internal clock was still stuck on her father's schedule. She always made sure to wake up, in case he needed her, because she never knew how his condition would fair that day. The sun was only now beginning to rise, and Autumn could see the intensity of the light start to peek through her blinds. She walked over and opened the curtains; her heart raced with excitement and nervousness—a manic anxiety.

The number of times she had truly left her home in the last hundred years were few. The convenience of delivery meant she never had to risk leaving her father alone: groceries, medicine, and supplies all came straight to the door. Even so, she greatly enjoyed the warm weather and spent her mornings watering the flowers that were located in her backyard; a world that was still fenced in. The flowers had been her father's favorite and her mother's pet project, one that Autumn had taken over. This morning she had watered them before the sun was up, while the air was still crisp—the water melted into the ground as dew sat on the flowers. She hoped her offering would satisfy the plants in the soon-to-be warm weather of the morning.

Autumn now made her way upstairs, down the small hallway, and into her bathroom. The colors of the room were significantly more muted than the ones downstairs. A light baby blue ran across the walls, with white trimming matching that of the downstairs. Autumn started by brushing her teeth. Primarily artificial, they were bright, white, and gleaming. Composed of a biocompatible plastic that was durable and shapeable, the teeth used the blood from the patient's body to fuel an internal microbial system. This influx of blood allowed the body to treat it as one of its own, while the new microbiome helped to heal the teeth from damage—bacteria flooded to fill the gap. As they died, they formed the new outside of the tooth. Much like a beaver, a healthy individual could keep their teeth growing forever. That made it especially important to clean your investment. The invention of these teeth had a small but strange social effect. When Autumn stepped outside her door, it would be very unlikely to run into someone without those pristine molars. The only exception was that of the young.

Reaching up into the medicine cabinet, Autumn began her morning routine. She was a short woman with an average frame. Rifling through the shelves, Autumn searched for the two medications she'd been taking for the last 120 years. One was specific to her, an anti-anxiety/anti-depressant, which they discovered helped her through her day. It helped to take the edge off an unexplainable, often-looming shadow that could hang over her. Autumn described herself as a joyful person who often sighed. The second drug was one that could be found in nearly every household in the world, Rejuverron. This miracle drug had the ability to prolong one's life indefinitely. By using generic genetic data to stabilize and extend the telomeres on a person's chromosomes, you could stop someone from aging as long as they took it every day—with minimal to no side effects, if taken properly. Autumn poured one of the small pink tablets into her palm and threw it back into her mouth.

Once it was invented, companies were quick to give away their products to the masses, knowing it would lead to mass consumption and social addiction. Rejuverron would become a product that would need to be used forever by everyone on the planet. To ensure that the necessary large volume could be reached, the drug became a global utility. Even those unable to find food could easily gain access to immortality. It then became the norm to begin taking this drug at the age of twenty-five, the earliest legally allowed. Doing so earlier could possibly stifle one's brain development.

Autumn was nearly 150 years old but looked no older than thirty, the age she was when Rejuverron had been invented. To help ensure her youthful appearance, Autumn's second task was a regimen of skincare her mother had taught her in her youth. The two of them would do it together in the mornings when they happened to wake up at the same time. Under normal doses, Rejuverron did nothing to heal illness or damage what had already occurred. Thus, the way to look older was to not take care of yourself. It became exceptionally important to take care of your body and your skin.

Autumn turned on the water and left the faucet running as she ran her nail along her face, looking for any bumps. After popping two small white heads, she tied up her long brown hair that otherwise fell to the small of her back. She splashed some water into her face and began her routine of face wash followed by a mild toner, applying the creams one after another. Between each step she was sure to give her skin time to breathe. Her olive skin, tanned mostly from her time in the garden, hid a once large and mixed family—half Caucasian and half Latino. She was unsure of how much darker she was capable of getting.

For the next step, she applied her eye cream, making small circles around her eyes—their emerald green color piercing through the raccoon-like mask. Then she applied her vitamin C serum and moisturizer. The last step in her morning routine was her application of sunscreen. Cancer was now the most common cause of death in the world, behind alcoholism and drug abuse. Personal choices determined how long one's *forever* was. Though Rejuverron would maintain your age, unfortunately, it had no effect on the development of genetic disorders or diseases. In this new society instead of dying of old age, the classic tropes revolved around illness and poor life decisions—both endings Autumn was unlucky enough to have experienced.

Autumn's father had started to become ill in her early twenties. A strange form of dementia had taken hold of him, and his generally jubilant demeanor was replaced with depression and confusion. Autumn spent just enough time away at college to determine it was not for her. After returning home, she found herself much more comfortable and happily transitioned to online learning: she preferred to work distraction free. She was a bright girl with too many options, and she did not have passion for any pursuit the way that her father had throughout his career.

As she applied her makeup, it reminded her of his obsession with art. Even as he got sicker, that was his one consistent love. Both he and her mother had come from abusive households; their friendship and eventual relationship was the only respite from their unhappy home lives. They would eventually run away together with Autumn within her mother's womb. Her father became a cartoonist, hoping to bring happiness to others. His most famous character was an anthropomorphic armadillo, Andy. The dining room table was still filled with his scribbles and doodles. Photos of Andy adorned the table in various steps of completion and talent. Though he had been dead for over a year, she still did not have the heart to clear them off.

In the early years of Rejuverron, there was hope that it would lead to the end of such genetic deteriorative disorders or limit their progression. Being famous, her father was given top care and ushered into a test group for the drug upon its invention. They hoped to set back the deterioration of his neurons. Unfortunately, they found that was impossible, and over time the drug failed to stop progression. While his mind decayed, his body retained its relatively young appearance for over fifty years. His face showed the passage of time in slow motion.

For the first twenty years of Rejuverron they lived as a happy family, their faces and lives frozen in time. The royalties from syndication of her father's show kept them well off. That allowed Autumn to devote her time to taking care of him. Though his death was slow, his initial decline was steady. Over the course of only a few years it became clear he would soon not know anything. It was only on rare occasions that she found that the man she had known was still within—the few times his personality could bubble to the surface.

The loss of Marshal's mind was taken exceptionally hard by her mother. He was not only her husband but her smile. As he began to drift deeper into darkness, her mother began to vanish from their home. She would return days or weeks later, exhausted and haggard. It was then Autumn grew to resent her mother, not because Autumn had to take care of her father but because she loved her father too much to see her mother abandon him. With her mother gone, her father's mind seemed to become even more lost. She watched as both her parents were lost in their own downward spiral.

Some days were harder than others, but Autumn was never upset that she had to care for her father. By the time Rejuverron had been invented Autumn had settled comfortably into her life. In her own words, "When you have forever, what is a couple of years? Especially for someone you love." She would happily wait five years for but a glimpse of her father to come back. For her, none of that time was wasted. In this new world, Autumn had learned that every day was going to be another chance to fix things. Another chance to see her father. She was of two types of minds that emerged in this world—those who had a weight lifted off their shoulders, who felt that no matter what they would be able to try again, and the others, who viewed this immortality as a curse. Unfortunately for the latter, death was even scarier and more worthless. Jadedness could come with time, as many saw no game in life and grew increasingly bored with the mundane.

With Rejuverron, Autumn was given infinite time and infinite patience. As she sat at home, waiting for those moments for her father to come back, she would read novels upon novels, and learn about the great playwrights, philosophers, and historians. During that time, she also sought to study practical skills in order to help properly care for her father. While they had nurses in the past, her father's growing irritability made it easier for her to take over, slowly taking on all medical duties. Through online courses and work caring for her father, Autumn got a medical license with a specialization in therapy. Doing practical work with her father and AI patients were her only current experiences.

Her brand-new life was about to start today. She had gotten a job, out in the real world, working in the psychiatric unit of a hospital, joining a team of doctors treating those with Rejuverron-related issues. She had found her time with her father the most satisfying and knew she wanted to take some time to help others. If she had infinite time, she could help an infinite number of people. In specific, she decided she wanted to work with those with mental health issues so that her patience for her father didn't go to waste. Her quietness held a soft and understanding nature, one that lent itself well to taking care of others. Above all, she was a good listener and had a caring smile.

Near the end of his life, when her father had gotten very sick, the doctors tried to explain to Autumn that her father's condition had worsened to the point of no return. He would never know her again. They offered to humanely end his life, as they had no idea of knowing how long Rejuverron would keep him alive. They offered a chance to set her free from this possibly forever prison sentence. They also wished to put him out of his misery, assuming that he lived in a world of confusion and fear. Autumn never liked this interpretation of his life and she would never give up on her father. As she sat around in the day feeding her father, and talking to him, she knew that he was behind there somewhere in some remnants, some small way. She just hoped that what he still remembered were the good moments and, in his fog, he lost those traumatic childhood memories she could never truly understand.

At the end their favorite daily activity together was much like when she was a child, drawing. Autumn was no artist and never really made characters, only squiggles. At most she would draw a tree and perhaps add some shading for creative flair, but her artistic skills left a lot to be desired. Her father would mostly sketch copies of his armadillo character, a constant source of inspiration for him. He used his cartoons to teach people about the evils of man and corruption. His seemingly childlike stories contained hidden themes of loss that flew over the children in the audience but made the show palatable to adults. Her father sought to turn his fears into others' joy.

Sometimes when they tried to draw, his arms would not move at all, and his eyes stared off into space. When he was not drawing his favorite creature, he would squiggle a sword or a bird. Every time his hand moved, her heart raced a little bit with joy. He would often giggle and sometimes she would point at the page, and the two of them would make eye contact. Then he would lift up his art and smile, proud of what he had produced, and for a moment he was back. And those were the moments that she lived for, when her father would come back to her. Though she knew that he would never be completely back, she could hope and wait.

Those moments reminded her of her childhood, when she herself would bring a poorly drawn picture to her father. His response was always positive and supportive. She would draw some well-intentioned abomination and he would smile at it and insist that she sign her work. He would then attach it to his desk, above his drawing table, and keep it for "inspiration." Often, he would take her drawings and include them in his work, characters created by her but polished by her father.

Autumn was now in her closet, staring at the work clothes that she had neatly hung up on the door frame. They had been steamed and pressed the night before; a set of loosely fit scrubs, black and adorned with a small purple flower on the lapel. It was a costume design that she had used when caring for her father. As a therapist her uniform was not defined, the stipulations simply stated professional. In addition to her scrubs, she adorned some bright pink socks, covered in repetitive smiling copies of Andy the armadillo. Their bright color was hidden under her black nonslip shoes—her subtle way of bringing her father along with her.

Over the course of Autumn's entire life, no family ever came to visit her father or her mother. Even when her father became rich and famous, no new cousins or relatives came out of the woodwork. Her father was pleased no one ever showed up at their door, content with their little family. The assumption was that they were forgotten about and anyone who cared either was dead or gone. The details were always fuzzy. By the time she had been old enough to truly understand the trauma of her parents' upbringing, her mother had abandoned them, and her father was touch and go. Any previous questions about the presence of grandparents were met with hushes and misdirection. She was always told to ask when she was older, but by the time that came, her parents were gone. All she remembered was that her father and mother had both lived sad childhoods. Both coming from large, poverty-stricken families, they met in their teens and became each other's beacon of hope and joy.

Autumn stood in the hallway and anxiously ran her hands along her clothes, to smooth out any small creases before her travel. She then picked up her backpack, a small black one that she used as a purse, and filled it with a mix of anything she thought she might need—extra medicine, her lunch, and even a spare pair of socks. They were all neatly folded and placed within it. Autumn checked its contents one last time, then threw it over her shoulder. Like a child on their first day of class, she rocked back and forth on her heels and wished her father was there to wish her good luck; a small kiss on the forehead for support would go a long way.

As she stared at the front door, the hallway seemed to fluctuate in length, its corridor moving closer and further from her as she readied her mind. Autumn then realized what was causing her optical illusion: She was mildly hyperventilating. The flutter in her chest traveled to her head and left her dizzy. Leaving her house was scary enough, but interacting with people, starting a new job, reentering the world…it was all overwhelming. She looked back across the room at her father's recliner and imagined his smiling face while he warmed his hands by the fire. With his image, she calmed herself and finally stepped outside her door.

Autumn stepped out of her house into a beautiful sunny day; the weather made her transition mildly easier. If the hospital had been closer, she would have loved to walk but instead, she hoped to use the forced exposure of the bus to make her more comfortable with the new world she found herself in. At the edge of the nearby park was the stop for the bus that would take her to work. A bright new red stop sign hung on a pole just above the bus information. B22 was what she waited for. The times of the next arriving bus lit up on an LED screen that hung above a clear enclosure with benches that stretched down the block. The next one was two minutes away.

Though it was a short time, Autumn looked around for a place to sit, but the four double benches were already lined with people dressed in a variety of garbs. Each one of them sat staring at some device, a book, a computer, or a phone. Each sat in their own world. At the end of the bench, she found an empty spot against a light pole, not to sit on but to lean against. She was surprised to realize she preferred to stand, to loom a bit. She hoped it would stop others from talking to her. Not that she was antisocial; in fact, she wanted to talk to them. But she was terrified. Not having to talk seemed easier, especially on day one.

When she was growing up their family had a car, but that relic, a black and gold 1982 Pontiac Firebird Grand Prix, had been sold many years before. Once it sat in their driveway as a reminder of their good fortune. Autumn liked that Marshal could look out the window at it and admire its shine. They had to remove it after he attempted to drive it, forgetting its controls only a few moments after he switched it into drive. He crashed down the block. Luckily, the car was only mildly damaged, but Marshal was left alone and scared. They then sold the car, afraid that Marshall would remember how to drive a little faster next time.

As she leaned against the metal post, Autumn began to fight a large yawn, uncomfortable in doing even such a small act of true humanity in public. It was clearly an issue she would need to overcome. She clenched her body and fought the building pressure, but it escaped as an exasperated sigh. She was not only tired from waking up early, she also failed to sleep well the night before. It seemed to be a curse that followed her family. She, her mother, and her father, all at separate and random times, suffered intense nightmares. Autumn thought perhaps their issues were a rare side effect of Rejuverron—intense dreams, night terrors, and sleep paralysis. She hoped that as she spent time in the hospital, she would get the chance to work with such a patient. She hoped to learn through others about her and her family's condition in the process, especially since her nightmares had gotten worse since her father had passed. She found herself waking up more often, a weight on her chest and a figure in the room.

Marshal was always smiling, a person who was more comfortable supporting than being supported, but while growing up with him there were days when Autumn could see something behind his eyes. She knew that when he had the nightmares, his frail frame always appeared even weaker the following day. It was during her childhood that she could remember her father being most heavily afflicted; it was less apparent once he got sicker. On rarer occasions instead of waking up haggard, he was suddenly more active, more alert. She could read a rare smile that showed he was really there. For a period of time, it made her believe that it was possible for him to come back.

The bus arrived and Autumn waited patiently behind the other patrons in a single-file line. The small crowd slowly disappeared into the bus. Each walked up and scanned their phones, watch, smart sunglasses, or backpack. All were common methods of digital currency transfer. She made her way toward the back of the bus and hoped to find a spot by a window. She found one such spot and sat down. She then stared out the window and observed the passing town. She tried to make herself more comfortable with the ever-evolving city around her.

Gazing at the architecture and people on the street, Autumn discovered it was a beautiful time for art. The city before her was a strange mixture of old and new. Bright large skyscrapers could be found next to small antique townhouses. Random alleys did not always lead to other streets but would feed into small temples and old religious structures. The majority of the population was not truly religious, but the traditions continued through society as part of the zeitgeist.

On the street, a wide diversity of people could be seen. Their styles ranged from all different decades, styles, and subgroups. Even now, people often switched their style throughout their lives, and it was easy for groups of individuals with similar styles to find one another. On the streets you could even find that some people, old souls, had kept their perfected style over the last hundred years. This was a creative society where you could really find anything that you wanted or needed.

The one unsettling part was the smiles she could see within the crowds. The city was a sea of perfect repetitive smiles, each one of them an identical copy to Autumn's. This was a completely synthetic mark that was now treated and viewed as natural. The faces, however, were diverse, filled with people of all statures, body types, skin tones, and hair color—every combination and mixture. Though there were some faces in the crowd that contained wrinkles, the vast majority of people still looked young, twenty-five. It was nearly impossible to tell the age of anyone anymore. Autumn rested her head on the window, and while she watched the city slowly blur past her, she fell asleep; her dream was more of awaking nightmare.

Looking out the door of the bus, Autumn expected to see the street corner she had previewed online. She had mapped out her trip and made sure she knew her surroundings. Instead, the street seemed deeply unfamiliar as if she was no longer within the same country, no longer under the same sky. Instead of the tall evergreen ferns she was accustomed to, the horizon was littered with palm trees. Autumn could not make out too much, but the street sign read Hamlet Road.

Autumn descended the steps with shaky legs. At the bottom, with her arms holding onto the bars, she reached her foot off the final step. She hesitated and floated her foot above the asphalt. She turned her head back toward the bus driver and looked for a face of validation that she was in the right place, but her gaze was met by a forward, deadpan stare. As she stepped through the bus doorway, she failed to feel the ground; instead, she now found herself falling. As she tumbled through the air, the bus got farther and farther from her. As she looked back at the driver one last time, he turned his head towards her to reveal a blurred face. Then suddenly there was nothing but blackness, and after a few moments Autumn realized she was no longer falling but instead weightless.

Wait.

No.

Not exactly weightless. In fact, she was heavy…heavy, and cold.

She was floating.

She was wet.

Autumn found herself floating in the darkness of the ocean. The water grew colder, and she could feel her lips begin to turn blue. The bus and street were nowhere to be found. She gazed upon her surroundings and floated under the pale moonlight. Its light gently touched the moving waves that glistened from time to time; her vision was otherwise blank. Autumn searched the horizon for some sense of direction and then noticed the tall concrete wall behind her. Though it was within a few feet away, it was barely visible. She swam closer and peered skyward, looking for a ledge to grab, but saw nothing but concrete stretching into the darkness.

She tried to remember how she had gotten here. It was late and she must have been done with or at the very least late for work. She wondered if she had fallen off the top, only gaining consciousness in the cold of the water that broke her fall.

But what had happened?

As her base instincts took over, she continued to tread water and her mind raced regarding what to do. It was then she realized that she really did know how to swim. Somehow after nearly 150 years on earth, she had never had the opportunity to learn. She had attended a few pool parties in her childhood, but always seemed to have more fun sitting on the side, kicking her legs in the water.

This water was different. When it splashed into her face as she moved, she could taste the salty mixture. Tiny droplets began to crystallize on her cheek in the increasingly cold evening air. Autumn realized she could not stay in the water long if she did not wish to drown or freeze to death. She oriented herself toward the wall and looked for any sign of whether she should follow it left or right. The walls stretched infinitely on both sides, deep into the dark distance, two equally morbid options. She had to choose a direction or decide she would fare better swimming directly into the open ocean.

Her purse was still strapped to her back and filled with water; it weighed her down and grew heavier and heavier by the moment. She shook it off her shoulders and let it sink into the darkness—a sad and necessary sacrifice. Floating toward the wall, she attempted to grab it with both hands. She squinted and swore she could see a faint light, perhaps thirty feet above her. The top was faintly illuminated in one spot by something above, hopefully a streetlight. Autumn scanned the wall for a place to climb, anywhere she could get a good grip.

As Autumn attempted to grip the wall, the jagged surface gouged back. The wall, built of concrete, was unsurprisingly slippery. Somehow the waves had seemingly no effect on its exterior, and while wet still somehow sharp. Repeatedly she attempted to pull herself up, but she immediately slipped back down into the water. Each time she bobbed up and down her hands scrapped against the rock, and she began to bleed—the pain pulsating through her hands and into her arms. Each time her hands slipped back into the water, the salt entered her fresh cuts and another sting traveled down her hands and radiated deep inside. And with each jump, the depth she reached was a little lower. It was clear she would never be able to scale the wall here. She would have to find another way.

Now sure she would not be able to climb the concrete structure, Autumn needed to decide which direction to go. After a brief moment of stasis, she shivered from inaction and her flight response took over. She turned right and swam along the wall, toward the direction of the moon. It was faintly brighter and ever so slightly less intimidating than the only other option. Uncomfortable in her swimming, her movements were deliberate and meticulous—an embarrassingly slow doggie paddle kept her afloat. She was reminded of the last time she had almost drowned swimming.

It was a friend's birthday party and young Autumn swam in an above-ground pool. Around her waist floated a large, inflated tube. As she attempted to kick, her small frame slipped through the donut and plunged her into the water. A small child until her teenage years, at the time she was unable to touch the ground, even in the shallow water. Instead, she could only thrash under the surface, her limbs trying to contact the donut or the ground but failing. Autumn managed to gain control of her momentum and pointed herself upward, but another child on a floating chair blocked her escape. Her small hands then fought against the air-filled plastic raft above her. She panicked and, in her struggle, faded. Later she awoke on dry land, rescued by her father who had dived into the pool and scooped her out of the waterAfter that she always made excuses, preferring to stay dry while being silently scared of the water.

As she swam now, Autumn could feel her body start to shake, to panic. This was not from the cold; her movements had begun to heat her enough so that she could ignore the waves for a time. Instead, she shook from fear. Drowning was never how she wanted to go. As she swam, she fought her panic and forced her body forward. She knew if she stopped, she'd die. Autumn swam along the wall for what felt like hours, until her head was as tired as her body. Her mind was racing, her blood was pumping, and she was in adrenaline-soaked survival mode, but that energy could not be kept up forever.

Eventually, she had to stop and floated closer to the wall. She lifted her now pruned and still burning hands onto the wall. Bear-hugging it, she attempted to use the wall to support herself. She hoped to remove some of the strain off her muscles, use the buoyancy to rest, even just a little bit. Her breath was heavy as she surveyed her location and noticed the top of the wall had come down substantially. In the distance it looked as if it continued down. Beyond, she could tell there was a road, a metal railing sloped around the bend. Salvation was within sight, but here it was still too far to climb. Now knowing she was close, she was revitalized with energy. She would survive.

She began to swim again, moving along the wall with her head pointed upward. When she reached a point where the wall and road sharply turned, she swam around the corner of the wall to see that the road continued into the darkness but grew higher. Autumn stared into the dark, not sure what to do. The wall still seemed so high. But how much longer could she swim? She remembered she once read a story about how prolonged exposure to saltwater could start to behave like an acid on one's skin. As you attempted to rise out of the water, the skin would peel from your flesh and skin you alive. Autumn could not get the image out of her mind.

It would have to be a long time, she thought. *I'll be fine. Yeah, fine.*

Autumn turned to the wall and gripped it as tightly as she could, her now soft and squishy hands impaled by it. She gripped the jagged yet nearly flat brick with all her might. Her hands immediately began to bleed once again. Then she pressed her forearms and chest into the wall and attempted to hang from the slight incline. She knew physics; she needed to maximize her surface area to create traction. She pulled her feet close to the wall and planted them flat, then attempted to kick herself up. Using her legs to bounce herself in the water, she attempted to launch herself up the wall. As her skin sliced against the rock, she slowly drifted up. With each centimeter the pain increased, but her last surges of adrenaline allowed her to grip harder to the wall. As the rock dug deeper into her flesh, it created permanent indents all over her fingers and forearms. The blood from her forearms slid down the wall and made the surface even more slippery.

After minutes of slow struggle, she was finally able to hold herself just high enough to allow her left arm to reach to the top of the road; unfortunately, the ground there was not any less sharp than below. As she hoisted herself up, her shoe became unstuck, slipped off, and sent her sliding back down. Autumn gripped tighter with her left hand dangling. She knew if she fell, she would not have the strength to get back up. She kicked off the shoe but now her full weight went onto her hands, which dragged the rock deeper into her fingers. Her fingerprints were now permanently scarred and disfigured, like the rest of her body. The intensity increased as the seawater was driven deeper into her swollen hands.

How does it get more painful at every moment?

As she pulled herself up over the wall, she pressed the side of her face into the concrete. She still had to make sure she used every inch of her that existed to lift herself over the wall. Her cheek was now scraped and bleeding. With one final push up, she made it over the wall and onto the land, then collapsed onto her back. She was proud that she had been able to do that one important pull-up to survive. Gym class fundamentals had saved her life.

She worked to catch her breath as the breeze blew over her. Now that she was not moving, she was freezing. Even so, she was just happy to be out of the water. Her entire body was now scarred and burning from the jagged stone embedded in it. Somehow it even managed to make its way through her clothing; nowhere was safe. As she lay catching her breath, she searched her pocket for her phone but realized it was gone. It was most likely still in her purse and sitting at the bottom of the ocean.

Bleeding and wearing one shoe, Autumn stood up and took in the view of her surroundings. She still could not remember how she had gotten there; her memory was foggy, and her body throbbed. Her body dripped with water, and she noticed the most uncomfortable feeling of all, a wet sock. That discomfort hurt more than the scars on her body that dripped with salt. The wetness of the sock shot straight through her body and into her brain. She bent down and removed her sock, then she removed her other shoe and sock.

A small breeze blew, and Autumn found the air around her to be much warmer than the water she had come out of. As she walked, the breeze started to dry her. She headed to the right, toward the moon, and hoped to find some other traveler, a friendly face. As she walked, she left an ever-shrinking trail of water and a small but consistent trail of blood—her fingers and forearms still dripped. The pattern of blood crisscrossed as it rolled across her forearms.

The road became something familiar but still unknown residential streets. It was lined with houses in various stages of welcoming, some with lights on in the home, others simply offering a porch light to guide you. She walked past each house looking for a sign of safety, something that would make her comfortable enough to ask for help, though she had no idea what that would be. As she kept moving past the lights, her feet grew raw as well and the blood on her arms started to dry and crust. Something felt amiss.

Autumn surveyed the community. It was not the houses that bothered her, but instead she felt a strong presence following her. A force that pressured her forward. Autumn felt her body instinctively move, afraid of something she felt behind her. It was a feeling she had before. In the shadows, only visible in the light cast from the porches, walked a figure. In the dark stood a shape that appeared mostly human but only existed in a foggy silhouette. Looking among the trees Autumn could finally see a tall figure, its arms long and dangling, its hair long and thin. The features and true size were hard for her to gauge in the distance and the dark. Its skin appeared pale and green, like the corpse of a man lost at sea.

She could not deal with that right now, so she turned her head away and chose to ignore the figure. She simply would not stop. She would keep walking. Her pace picked up and the street appeared to narrow ahead. The houses on her sides faded into trees. On the horizon she could see a light flowing from some type of home. Autumn's feet continued to chaff on the asphalt. When she reached the crest of a small hill, she could see her target in sight. In front of her along the winding road was a red building, much like a church or perhaps a funeral home— hopefully a beacon of safety.

Tears began to run down her face, which moved the crystal salt off her cheek and into her mouth—a terrible taste. She hastened her movement even more and now ran on numb and bleeding stumps. Her stride became awkward and staggered; she was afraid she would break her toes on the hard ground below. Autumn reached the large wooden front of the doors and saw a tall cross illuminated above. Its radiance was an arrow pointing toward the front door. She rushed to it and attempted to open the small wooden double doors that led to the chapel. Autumn pulled on the doors with all her might, but she could not make either of them budge—they were clearly locked from the other side. In desperation she pressed her face against the stained-glass windows on the door. Through it, she could see a woman standing inside at an altar, lighting candles and completely oblivious to Autumn's presence. Autumn began to shout and banged on the door heavily, pleading for the woman's attention.

Autumn still had not turned around since first noticing the shadowy figure, but she could feel it getting closer. Her body felt pressure pushing her into the door. Desperation forced her face against the door, and her hands banged with open palms. She continued to struggle and bang. Finally, the woman inside noticed her. She appeared startled, the color drained from her face. Holding her hands in front of her, she shuffled toward the door.

"Please, can you help me? I'm lost and I'm hurt," Autumn pleaded through the glass. "All I need is safety. I think someone is following me."

The woman, face whiter than ever, turned her body away from Autumn. She whispered something and placed her hands in a prayer position, and then finally responded. "I'm sorry, child, I cannot help you. It is too late." The woman pulled down a shade across the glass, and unknown to Autumn she scurried away and never looked back.

Autumn banged harder and harder on the wooden door, her arms and hands once again bleeding. She shouted as her blood dripped down the grain of the wood. Tears once again built up in her eyes, not from sadness but from anger. Why was she being abandoned? It was then Autumn finally noticed her reflection in the multicolored glass. Across her face was an unfamiliar gash that split her forehead, with blood pouring down much more dramatically than she had thought. The blood extended from her crown and now dripped down her face. It somehow avoided her eyes. She now knew why the woman had been so afraid, though she still cursed this helpless place.

She could feel it now. Something was there, standing directly behind her. It was on her. The sound of the door, and the sound of her cries, hastened its approach. She could feel the looming of a hand dangling over her shoulder. As she was still afraid to look, a single finger appeared in her peripheral, pale blue skin, long and thin. Biting her lip, her tears were now those of fear. As she began to turn her head, she hoped to catch a glimpse of the creature. Maybe that would scare it away somehow. Instead, as she turned, the hand came closer to her face and a large palm formed out of a purple and green spark. The palm drifted down to touch her. Her shoulder grew cold as it came into contact with her. She then felt paralyzed, her body unable to move, her tears the only sign of life within her.

Trapped in her own body, she attempted to shake loose of its grip. Her muscles were asleep, and her mind was panicked. Try as she might, nothing occurred, a haze of green light filling her view, her head foggy. Shaking her body one last time, with one last desperate plea, Autumn woke up. She once again found herself sitting on the bus, her head against the window.

"I'm so sorry to bother you," said an unknown man from behind her in a soft and gentle voice. "You were just shaking and making some sad noises. I know you're not supposed to wake a sleeper. But you seemed a little desperate."

Autumn now realized his hand was on her shoulder. She twitched and signaled for him to let go. He apologized again but still asked if she was okay. As she shook her head, still foggy, she now remembered she had had the same nightmare the night before. Next to her, the seat was no longer empty. A young woman with headphones stared intently reading a book. She easily ignored the conversation started between Autumn and the mystery man. Once she had gained her bearings, Autumn turned around to face the man. Autumn finally began to open her mouth, embarrassed by the scene she assumed she had made.

"Tha-tha-thank you," Autumn stammered, a common occurrence, especially when she was stressed or sleepy. The combination of the two made it even more distinct. It was a problem she had had since childhood, even during her most confident times—an annoying genetic anomaly. It happened less when she was happy or calm, with the exception being around her father, whose constant jokes silenced her stammer with laughs. She spoke too quickly and off the cuff to stop. Autumn never was uncomfortable, feeling accepted in her father's jokes. Her father had even created a friend for Andy, his cousin who would visit from time to time, a stammering football star, inspired by his daughter.

Autumn continued to talk to the man on the bus; at first, they exchanged observations out the window. She even learned his name, Buster, and then they spoke about their mothers and his issues he had with her decisions she had made a long time ago. It was a little therapy for both. Autumn offered a welcoming ear and a fresh point of view. She recounted how little control she had over her father's and her mother's decisions. How it hurt her, but she had to learn to accept and try to love them for what they were. Autumn felt herself connecting with the world in a way she had not done in recent memory. This then became a new ritual in Autumn's life. She would sit on the bus and attempt to talk to others, to work on her socialization and speaking, to become more confident for work. The bus would be an amazing place to meet people.

When they neared her stop, she could hear an ambulance coming from the distance. It rushed by the bus as it made its way into the hospital emergency entrance, only a block farther down the street. The bus stopped on the corner, and she got off to witness the unloading of a man—scared and thrashing, an oxygen mask strapped to his face and his body strapped to a gurney. The hospital was already busy and the morning had just begun. This hospital was one of many scattered throughout the city, built straight into the town, using old, abandoned businesses and warehouses.

When the doors opened, Autumn turned to observe the bus driver. His face was clear but emotionless, his eyes aimed forward at the traffic ahead. She hesitated to get off, though she knew it had only been a dream. Even so, Autumn stepped slowly toward the front and even allowed others to pass her before she finally scurried down the stairs. *Rip it off like a band-aid.* She made a left, instead of walking straight into the emergency room, and went to the main entrance around the corner.

Autumn was greeted at the front door by a young blond receptionist, his light blue eyes welcoming and warm. She asked for the proper wing, and he signaled her to walk up to the third floor, taking the stairs directly behind him. Autumn decided instead to take the nearby elevator; it would give her another moment to catch her breath. The ride was quick, and the elevator doors opened to reveal a simple set of double hospital doors. Their perfectly white exterior was freshly washed, and the building smelled of clean but synthetic floral.

She searched through her backpack, found her keycard, a laminated photo attached to a black lanyard, and swiped it on a consul to her right. As the double doors opened toward her, the sound of the wing beyond it was now released upon her. The noises were muffled but distinct from that of the other parts of the hospital. The jitter of anxious patients seemed to shake the foundation; a nervous energy bounced between patients and doctors alike who wandered the halls. The wing consisted of many patients, some who only visited for a short time, a few hours or days, and others who spent the majority of their lives there. Autumn would first work with outpatients and learn as a therapist, finally hands-on. She would then be slowly introduced to the permeant patients, some of them more skittish than others. Within the hum of the wing, Autumn felt comfortable. Her own life of anxiety allowed her to relate to the patients around her. Her success to be theirs.

Though it was her first day, nothing she faced that day was anything too surprising. Nothing she felt she couldn't deal with. The times had changed; mentalities were more fluid. As everyone could live forever, people found over decades that their passions changed and wavered. The increased energy from remaining young allowed them to work extensively for longer. Because of this, many people found themselves changing careers throughout their lives. Many people were overly specialized in many different fields. Some forgot just how much they once knew. The ageless faces hid many talents; it could be considered gauche to ask someone their age unless you were the utmost of friends with them.

Her first day would be a long and stressful blur of paperwork, protocol, and introductions. Her name became easier and faster to say with each new patient or doctor she met. As she was guided on her tour, she realized the psychotherapy wing was much deeper and nicer than she had initially thought. Each wing was brightly painted: *A*, lime green, *B*, baby blue, *C*, a faint pink, *D*, lavender. A nexus within its center contained a large, circular desk complete with multiple computers. A set of nurses sat in swivel chairs, able to shift and view any of the sub wings at a moment's notice. The ceiling of the hospital consisted of a bright and flat surface. The lights were built flush into the structure, surrounded by magnetic tracks. The two were seemly integrated, which allowed the nurses to turn on lights for each wing from the center counsel. The magnetic bars allowed the medical personnel to slide important medical equipment from wing to wing and room to room, their monitors attached to a moveable arm suspended from the ceiling. This wing did not particularly take advantage of the technology, primarily only using it to transport medicine, take medical baseline information, and o do simple rapid blood tests.

Deep in the unit, Autumn had her own office, sandwiched between wings *C* and *D*, the residential wings. Wing *D* housed the adult patients and *C* the children. For now, Autumn's office was a plain white room. As time went on, she would have them add colors like the outside walls of the wing. Three of them would be a light yellow and one would have a dark brown accent wall. The room was furnished with her desk, one large couch, a pair of smaller couches, and another smaller, simpler, wooden table complete with two plastic chairs. She had requested each of these different seating positions because she read with different patients, everyone needed to be related to on a different level. For instance, you should always sit at a joint table, on equal footing, with someone who had problems with authority.

Autumn would go on to meet patients of all ages, their issues varying from mild depression, like her, to psychosis, both natural and drug-fueled. Autumn's first solo patient, the first and only she would have time to see today, was Cordelia. Before entering the room Autumn read Cordelia's chart: chronic pain and sickness. Like Autumn's father, Cordelia had a rare adverse reaction to Rejuverron, not an allergic one, but it simply slowed her age progression. So, she would not live forever. Her body was still decaying.

Autumn would be taking over for a previous therapist; Cordelia had grown grumpy and displeased with their work and went so far as to verbally accost him during their most recent session. The hospital thought this would be the perfect opportunity for a new start. The therapy surrounded pain management, for her weak and aged body, mixed with psychotherapy, about her possible mortality, something that not everyone worried about anymore—something that could weigh heavily on your mind.

"Hah-hah-hi, I am Dr. Oswalt," Autumn said softly as she entered the room. Cordelia was already in her office, sitting on the edge of the large couch. Something about this woman remaindered her of her father, something about the pain behind the eyes—an older and dynamic person. "It's a pleasure to meet you. I'll be your new doctor." Cordelia nodded at her but said nothing. "Ple-e-ase tell me about yourself. Whatever you think is most important I know. Agaa-aagain, it's a pleasure to meet you," she said as she sat down on one of the smaller couches, slightly angled from Cordelia.

"Hello, dear, my name is Cordelia. I suffer from chronic pain. My body has hurt more and more every day for the last hundred years," she said, pleasantly and calmly. "I would be amiss if I didn't admit that I won't make all of our meetings. I won't always warn you and somedays I'll be here, but I'll be a raging bitch. My body hurts and my mode shifts. I have nights when I have tense dreams. Every day I feel weaker, but today I feel relatively great. So, it's a pleasure to meet you too, darling." Cordelia smiled weakly.

Autumn, having expected more rage, was so surprised that she didn't stutter. "I'll be honest. I was told you would be much meaner." She then let out an uncomfortable chuckle. "You're very sweet. Would you like to talk about anything specific? I'd like us to get to know each other, to be friends. How about we start with those dreams? How many times would you say you wake up each night? Do you generally feel like you don't get enough sleep?"

"Actually, I get great sleep, full through the evening, just not very restful. When I wake up still tired, it's one of my off days. My pain is worse after a good rest, ironically," said Cordelia. She then held her hand up to her head, Cordelia could feel a deep migraine behind her left eye. She pushed her flat palm into her eye, the pressure helping to distract from the pain, just a little. Suddenly, her demeanor changed—a tension throughout her body from the obvious pain.

"Are you sure you're, okay?" questioned Autumn lovingly.

"I'm fine, dear," muttered Cordelia in an annoyed tone. As she released the pressure from her hand, she held up a fake smile. The pain had changed her voice, now making her assume a less proper and less pleasant tone. A change Autumn had seen so many times before. Her heart sank, as she once again saw her parents. It was a behavior her father had done out of fear, and this woman, like her mother, out of pain.

"I was feeling well enough to come into the office today. You'll learn that means I'm feeling well enough for you not to worry," explained Cordelia.

"It says here you are on pain meds. Have you taken them today?" asked Autumn, beginning to split her page into sets of columns, ready to take notes about all of Cordelia's conditions. Her hand furiously wrote in concern and care.

Letting out a small sigh, a noise that helped her to push through the pain, Cordelia said, "My body feels fine, and I did take my medicine this morning, as I always do. My pain would otherwise stop me from even moving my body from my bed. You'll know those mornings; it will be one of my telehealth appointments. Again, I am sorry I cannot warn you in advance," Cordelia softly apologized.

Looking down at the patient file in her lap, Autumn could see that Cordelia was a very special case in today's society. "I am sorry I am not completely up to date with your treatments, Cordelia," apologized Autumn. "Could you please tell me about what you have done, specifically what isn't and is working?"

"Well, I have been undergoing pain management therapy, such as this, for many years now," Cordelia began to explain. "Seeing people again helps a bit, at least to distract myself. When the pain is the worst, I cannot get out of bed, and sleeping is my only respite. So, I have minimal time with others. I have weeks where I do nothing but sleep."

"Do you ever find yourself more energetic after a good nap? Is your pain attached to your mood? I know my father would have much worse pain in his arms when he was feeling down," questioned Autumn. "I guess it could be a chicken and egg scenario.... I'm sorry, I'm thinking out loud," she apologized. Suddenly she felt she had grown too familiar with her new patient—a mixture of over-enthusiasm and empathy.

"My naps are not energizing. Most days they work to pass time when I am too sick to do anything else," Cordelia continued. "My pain is not really in my body, though it seems to be getting worse by the day. I am not sure my Rejuverron is doing anything at all anymore. Or perhaps I am just noticing the changes in my face more."

Reaching her left arm over her head, she stretches and lets out a large yawn. "Sorry, dear, did not sleep well last night as well," continued Cordelia. "My pain is primarily in my head, a pressure behind the eyes. Some days it feels like a mask of tears attempting to push out of my eyes, a pressure with no ease."

Even on the mornings Cordelia felt strong enough to cry, the pressure would continue, as if she needed to know why she was crying to get it to leave. "It's all the physicality without any of the emotional release."

"That's terrible, Cordelia. I am so sorry you have to go through that. Is there anything you think we could do to help? Perhaps a stronger or different pain medicine? One specifically for headaches?"

"If you look at my file, you'll see one of the ones I am on is a very strong migraine medication."

"Oh, I am so sorry," said Autumn, embarrassed by her lack of preparation.

"No worries. It's one of a long list of things we have tried. It does help a bit, but it makes me tired and can take away my dreams; those are often the only good part of my day. I'd rather have a little more pain and at least remember something about my time on this earth."

As the two continued to speak, the pain seemed to pass, and Cordelia slowly returned to her joyful and sweet self. Autumn looked up and noticed the clock on the wall, a large digital monstrosity that had been placed there back when this wing of the hospital was dedicated exclusively for mental health visits. Large red block letters read 2:55, letting Autumn know there was only five minutes left in their session.

"Sorry-sorry, Cordelia," Autumn suddenly stuttered again, anxious about the question she needed to ask next. "We are running out of time on our first session, and I must say it—it's been a pleasure. I really look forwarrr-ddd to seeing you again. As we only have a few minutes left, I was wondering if you wanted to talk about our goals for your end-of-life therapy."

Contrary to what Autumn expected, Cordelia's smile grew larger as she made eye contact with her. "Don't worry, I've talked with many doctors before you. I am doing quite all right on that front. I know my days are numbered. It's something I hope you never have to feel. You can tell your body is failing, working less efficiently."

"I know what it's like to feel like you're drowning, and like your body is going nowhere," responded Autumn. "Many people do not have to deal with the reality of death anymore. They float through life without one of the worries that is so fundamental to the experience of being alive." Autumn looked down at her notes. "Not being alive. I don't truly understand what it means. I only watched my parents go and that seemed too heavy to deal with. I consider myself lucky. I hope I can help you and learn from your strength. Thank you for joining me. I hope I can find some way to help you in the future," ended Autumn. She saw this as a chance to learn about her own issues with Rejuverron, and a chance to retroactively help both her parents.

The clock ticked to 3 p.m. Their session was now over. Cordelia slowly got up and smiled at Autumn. "Thank you for the company, dear. Don't worry about helping me. I'm sure you'll do great," Cordelia said as she walked out of the room.

Cordelia stood in the doorway as Autumn asked, "Does that mean you'd like to continue to work with me? If not, we can find you another replacement doctor."

"You'll be fine. You're a sweet girl. We'll see how your patience holds up."

Autumn's heart was a flutter as she finally felt like she had truly accomplished something today. Her face was stuck in a large smile as she wished Cordelia a great rest of her week and made her way to the main desk. It was then that she was truly invigorated to start this new chapter in her life. Autumn's day ended with very little else of note. She exited the hospital and made her way to the corner opposite the one she had arrived on, waiting for the bus. Her legs were tired, but her mind still raced.

After getting onto the bus, she made her way to the back and took a seat against the window. Now calm and alone, she thought about her day. She thought about all that was new. She realized how much of her life had already changed, so much within a day. She attempted to think of the last major event that had happened in her life, that was not the loss of a loved one. When you live forever, life is a blur of time punctuated by intense experiences; by the pain you feel and the joy you cannot believe you feel. Those moments stand out and become your life, your history, and what you remember. So many thoughts and moments are lost by accident, in the darkest reaches of your mind; they only float to the top when they are gently tugged by the recall of another memory; then they disappear back into your unconsciousness, a cyclical pattern. The river of memory would flow back. Our lives are ultimately a feeling in our heart we have about a punctuation of memories. We always seem to lose track of the good ones, and the bad ones always seem to return with full force. Something about our minds always makes one so much more influential than the other.

Autumn, the woman who had been stagnant for so long, gazed out at the starry sky and wondered, *Does time truly heal all wounds? As we live forever, do we ever heal or are we merely collecting scars? Our memories are kind of like scar tissue. Scars that are not always bad but sometimes the only memories we have of things that helped heal you.* With infinite time, many people, religious or not, no longer thought about the afterlife but still people wanted to know their decisions were good, and that they made a difference. At the very least, people just wanted solace in that they were loved and mattered.

Through her father's work, Autumn realized that even those people who gave joy to millions in the world were too eventually forgotten by most. Their work only lived on in the minds of a handful of people, forever preserved by those it truly touched. Autumn had taken care of her small family and was ready to reach out to a larger group; perhaps she could be preserved in the patients she helped.

Dismounting the bus for the last time that day, Autumn silently walked home. Her return trip was much faster than her initial departure. As Autumn walked into her home, she quickly shut the door behind her, pressed it closed with her back, and dropped her backpack to the ground. Tears began to stream down her face as she slid down the door until she was sitting, her head now on her knees. She was finally home, and finally safe and comfortable. While it was an exciting and beautiful day, she was exhausted emotionally and physically. Those were tears of release. She was so happy, and so tired. She only wished she could have shared the success of her day with her father.

She used her sleeve to wipe the tears from her eyes and calmed herself by taking a few deep breaths. She then thrust her arms forward, using her momentum to stand up. She pulled on her clothes and adjusted her shirt, which had begun to bunch up, then picked up her backpack. Autumn meandered into the kitchen but first made sure to make a stop by her father's chair and place the backpack next to it. Autumn ran her hand across the top and her finger ran slowly across the imperfections—so numerous it almost appeared to be textured. As she moved past the chair, tears once again began to build in her eyes, and she began to scoop up the drawings that had been scattered over the dining room table.

Autumn slowly piled together each of the old bills, documents, photos, and drawings with a special stack of just her father's drawings. As she organized them, she delighted at looking at each one and enjoyed how different they all were. She tried deeply to remember something about each of the days the drawings were made. Most of them could be admired but not remembered, but a select few brought memories. The best of which were from his moments of recovery. The times he would come back. With each one she looked at it and felt him with her. Autumn finally felt the strength she needed to clean up. Not to move on, or to put him away, but to organize him back into her life. She would always have him in her heart, and his art on her walls. She was ready to face the future knowing that even time would not take away her memories of him, and this clutter was not necessary to preserve him. She would find something great to do with them.

She then randomly took one of her father's drawings and placed it above the fireplace. It was balanced against one of the framed pictures of him. She would keep it safe there, until she remembered to buy a picture frame.

Her father was still with her. If she lived forever, she could keep his memory alive forever. Autumn walked back over to the couch and picked up a small and comfy but generally decorative blanket. She walked back to the recliner and plopped down into its soft and warm body. As she cuddled into the chair her body melded into the indent of her father. Like when she was a child, she felt like he was holding her. Tonight, she would sleep in his chair, too tired to shower. She'd do that in the morning.

As she drifted off to sleep, she whispered to herself. She lay there telling her father about her day, knowing how happy he would be for her. She would fall asleep wondering what silly jokes he would make about her nightmare on the bus and the compliments he might bestow on her about her strength to talk to strangers. Autumn smiled because for the first time in a year, since her father had died, she was alive and happy. She was about to turn 147 but her life had just started.

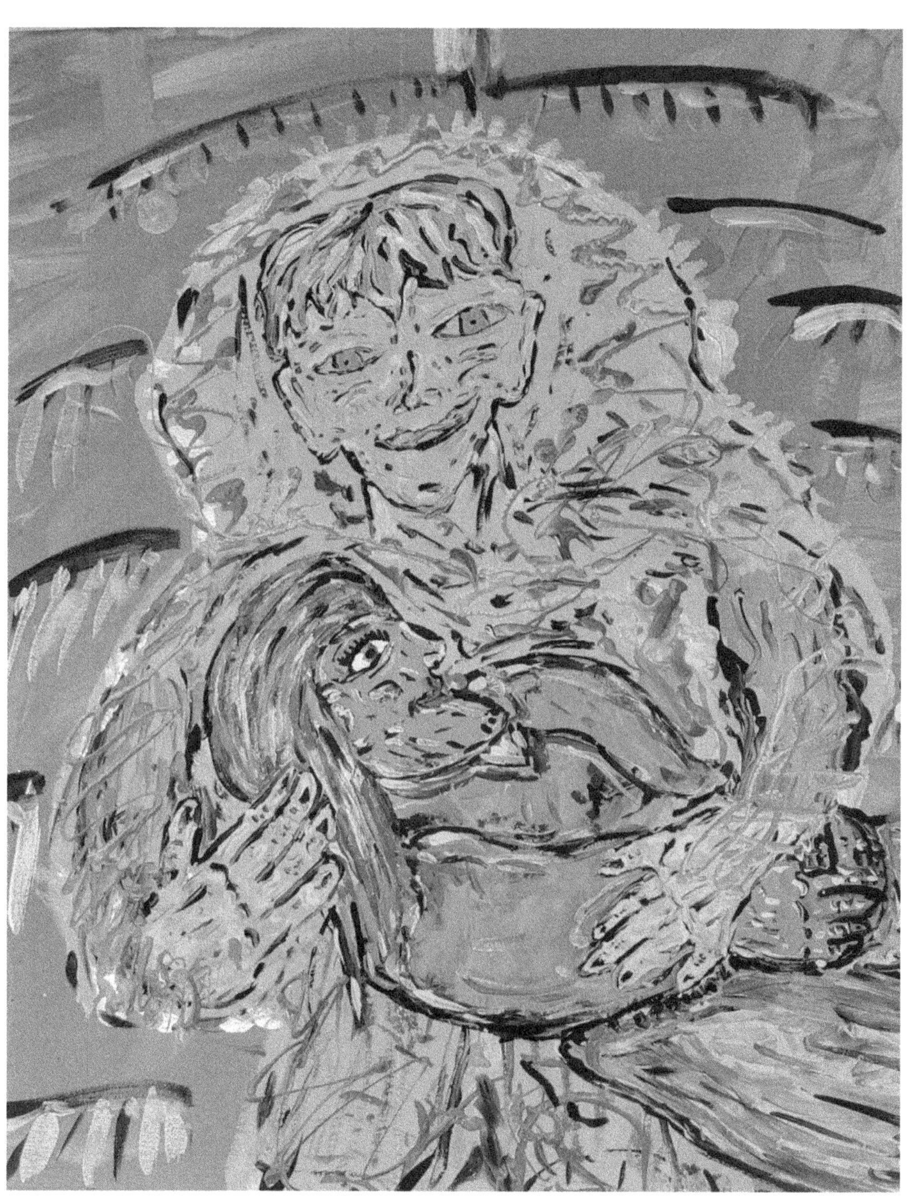

Waking From a Dream

Ligare, as he had come to call himself during his periods of consciousness, pointed his nose to the sky and took a deep breath. There was once again the delicious aroma he lived for while floated on the wind. As the scent traveled down the back of his throat and filled his lungs, he awoke from his hibernation. His body had just been moving aimlessly, his mind blank like the nap after a grand Thanksgiving feast.

He now stood still in the middle of a crowded city street. Masses of people swarmed past him in both directions, on both sides, like a stream diverted by a lone, stubborn rock. His long green and black mohawk pointed into the crowd, appearing more like the frill of a lizard basking in the sun than hair. The color of his t-shirt complemented the stripes of color in his hair. The leather jacket he wore was littered with patches—their symbols diverse but indistinctive. Each one called to your mind a faint memory that you were not able to fully recall. You were sure you saw that symbol…somewhere. His pants were stiff acid-washed jeans; their tears and rips appeared genuine and earned over time.

Ligare's long legs led down to large black boots. Their unnecessarily thick heels and soles made his already large stature even more looming. Though his presence was daunting, his large form brought not even a second look from those within the crowd. Even with his colors, he appeared to blend into the group, something about his presence making him almost invisible. When looking through a crowd, your eye would never really focus on him. His vibrance was lost in the diversity of life within the city.

Ligare had been called many things by many people throughout his eternity on earth. Each society and each person experienced him differently and named him differently. His name was often determined by the effect he had. In the past, religious people properly attributed the ailments he left to a dark and sinister force. As society progressed though, his life became easier.

As science took over, his symptoms were then attributed to disease or mental illness. He was free to live and feed, surrounded by meals that were unaware of his existence. The word *ligare* means "to bind." That was the word they used to describe the weight he placed upon one's chest—the symptom most universal of the experience of being fed on.

At one time he had been merely a shell of a being, an amalgamation of ideas, drawings, and the earliest stutterings of human imagination. Ligare's form was once insubstantial, almost gas-like, its atoms only able to reflect mild faces of beast, human, and light. From the beginning, his life was like the nomadic tribes, wandering. As they shifted, he followed his source of fuel and consciousness. If only they knew his intentions were not calculated. That he drifted through life mostly without purpose. His life was a series of meals, with brief spats of mindfulness in their wake. His body was shaped by the thoughts of his victims, their dreams, and their fears. His hopes and dreams only lived momentarily, his thoughts merely the thoughts of his prey echoing within him. Without them the signal of his mind would fade out, he would become a sleepwalking husk, and then silently wander the earth. As they evolved, so did he and his form became as complex as their minds.

An odor sat so thick in the air that as it entered his nose, Ligare could already begin to taste it. He breathed deeply and his lungs dragged the scent through the currents of the air, its trail guided him back toward its source. The scent quickly built up in his nose and dribbled down the back of his throat like a teaspoon of honey, soothing and appetizing. The warmth of the scent further awakened him from his coma. His chest was now filled with purpose and warmth that began to spread to his arms and legs. All the while, his hands simply dangled at his side, unnaturally. Like waking from a dream, his brain began, and he was suddenly aware that he hadn't had a good meal in quite some time. His last few meals had done their job but only kept him awake for a few days. They hadn't been a truly delicious meal, one filled with emotion and imagination. Pain, insecurity, love, lust and all the complexities of life that made it worth living were the spices that added taste and longevity.

A shiver ran down his spine and he stretched briefly, still obstructing the crowd around him. Cracking his neck and back, Ligare put his hands into his pockets, lowered his head, and began to walk. His motion seamlessly adapted to the current of the surging mob, he flowed like a raft on a river. As he walked in the direction of the smell, his breathing remained long, deep, and steady. His nose worked constantly to parse out the direction of the source, working to pinpoint the location of the smell among the millions of people who surrounded him.

What was once a city of merely a few miles now extended to hundreds of miles in diameter, the size of a small country. Each new district that was constructed consisted of circular streets radiating out of a central hub of community utilities and projects. The streets were made to overlap with neighboring hubs, creating beautiful, sprawling shared green space. At one time the city expanded daily, with new roads and buildings being added to house the influx of new people. The population boomed when Rejuverron was first developed but had since mostly stabilized. A few areas were added every few years, continuing the spread of humans—slowly radiating out toward the borders of the sea and mountains.

Sniff Sniff

Entering the large intersection between two sectors, he continued to walk through the city, his eyes anchored forward as if they hoped to magically spot what his nose so desperately searched for. Waiting at a crosswalk, the red light stopped the flow of traffic. Looking down for a brief moment, he now noticed his outfit. One that he had not chosen for himself. His form had been decided by whomever he had last fed on. On any given day, he could be the form generated by the thoughts of one strong person or a combination of the most striking features of a few weaker ones. His true monstrous form was often hidden by the safeguards of the human mind. His form almost always blended in as the strongest fears often revolved around other humans.

Ligare walked briskly for two miles before making a right turn. Then he continued to walk for another mile. It was then the smell finally began to get stronger. The source was close, relatively. With his hands still in his pockets, Ligare began to walk faster and faster. His pace then became skipping and bouncing. A bouncing motion between jogging bursts moved him past others in the crowd, his motion somehow never inhibited. His breaths were now sniffled but deeper; his chest slowly expanding. It grew larger and larger, as if it were ready to burst before quickly being exhaled, and the process began again.

Down a few more blocks, he walked through the stone arch that marked the 13th Street opening of the subway to reveal a busy city hub. Here each street that traveled toward the city center was roped off to traffic. The area bustled with people visiting the various stores, eating at the restaurants, and enjoying the parks and fountains. Among the various groups of crowds, he could see across the opposite corner a packed deli. The simple shop front was made of only two parts, a register and counter for ordering and a side table for order pickup. It's size was a relic of a once small village absorbed by the growing city. The line of the deli stretched far from the register, out a small entryway that clearly once housed a door. It then wrapped around the corner. Ligare scanned the line, slowly adjusted his head, and took periodic deep breaths.

Sniff Sniff

Though the smell was now stronger, it had begun to diffuse through the area. Small trails could be smelled going in all directions. Now, he would have to search for the right one. Walking to the front of the line, he hoped his meal would also be waiting for food. The size of the crowd prevented him from entering the small shop, so instead he peered over the waiting crowd to see if the smell came from within. Instead, he only saw signs for the incredibly popular American fusion restaurant meals. Signs for "Classic New York style pizza" and "Chicago style hot dogs" littered the room. Inside it was decorated with white and red checkered furniture and flooring, a delightfully loud color pallet.

Sniff Sniff

Nothing. Turning back around, he faced the line. The smell didn't seem to come from inside. It was now time to scan the queue. Ligare put his head down and began walking slowly down the line, his breaths now shallow and fast as he tried to smell only the immediate area. He could tell the source was near, somewhere. The anticipation and growing excitement began to blur his vision. Focusing on the ground helped to stabilize him against that.

Sniff Sniff

A quarter down the line. Nothing. The pressure built in his chest.

Sniff Sniff

Halfway down the line. Nothing. *WHERE WAS IT?* echoed in his mind. The pressure was building in his head and the blood vessels in his eyes bulged.

Sniff Sniff Sniff Sniff

He now pulled his left hand out of his pocket and put it up to his head and rubbed his fingers along the shaved portion of the side of his haircut. For a moment, he stopped sniffing as his head grew a bit dizzy. Like a tongue stinging from too much sugar, Ligare's body began to hurt. The source was close, but he hadn't found it. His lungs were now filled with their thoughts, the cloud, a thick combination of eagerness and glee. With his body shaking Ligare could already begin to feel his body change again. Their joy and excitement infected him, shortening his patience. He began to scream inside, as if the energy was stuck inside him, unsure of how to let it out.

Sniff...

Sniff...

Sniff...

Walking more slowly now, his head continued to spin. He walked a bit farther down the line. *Finally*, he thought.

Sniff...

Stronger. Still walking.

Sniff...

Stronger. Still walking.

Sniff...

Stronger. Still walking.

Sniff...

LESS!

He stopped suddenly and his heels dug into the ground. Turning around, he lifted his head and looked back at the line. He focused his vision, and he could finally see it—the air was sparkling. His eye followed the small glittering trail to find that it had settled on a short black-haired woman standing patiently in line. Her name was Jones and she stood in line waiting for an order for a party she was throwing. Her outfit, a deep emerald-green dress made of sequins, shimmered in the sun. Her smattering of freckles was the only indicator she was constantly exposed to the sun as her skin was otherwise perfectly porcelain.

She was not an innately expressive person, her face often blank in conversation as she listened intently. When she spoke, you could always tell her true emotions, though, her happiness marked as a long smile and excited tone. As a child she had learned to mask as she spoke, incorporating positive facial motions in her speech; it reminded her to show how she was feeling to others. Her natural coyness hid a deeply caring and observant person.

Upon seeing his target, Ligare grew calm. He proceeded to walk backward, seamlessly flowing to the back of the line. His eyes were locked and fixated on Jones. The creature that stood in the line was completely different from the one who had raced to this spot. Sitting downwind of her aura, Ligare stood patiently like a chef simmering soup. His spirit and his body were now content, calm, and stoic to the point of almost hibernation. From the back of the line, Ligare could see that there were fifteen people between him and Jones, and Jones was thirteen people away from the front of the line. Jones stood with her hands crossed in front of her, one holding her phone and the other supporting her dangling purse. Her eyes were fixed on the line in front of her, but her mind was elsewhere. She was hosting a party and inside her mind was racing, thinking about 10,000 different things.

Okay, I got dressed before the party… even though I'm hosting it… perhaps a little neurotic… but I think I'm going to call good job. Good job, Jones. Stellar work, she thought in a monotone voice. *So right now, I have plenty of time. I have this food I'm picking up, then at home I have the gluten-free options for Craig. Then I've got plenty of wine because it's been building up. Hmm… everything's got to be perfect. Hmm… we have decorations up already. What am I forgetting? Nothing…! You're golden, girl…. God, I haven't seen everyone in so long.*

Both Jones and Ligare moved forward in a robotic fashion, slowly shifting forward with each filled order. It was only once Jones had reached the front of the line did either of their behavior change. As if awoken, Jones began to smile, so excited to pick up her order.

"Hi, I am here to get an order for Jones," her tone not matching the excitement on her face.

"Pleasure to help. Let me look. Strange, I can't seem to find an order for a Jones. What would the first name on the order be?" responded the woman behind the counter, her blue denim apron matching her hat.

"That is the first name," retorted Jones, her tone seeming harsher than she meant it to.

"Oh, I'm sorry," responded the employee, now a little flustered. The change did not go unnoticed by Jones, who now felt bad. "Here we go, yes, Jones. Got it," continued the woman. "If you step over to the side someone will get your order to you in just a moment. Your pies are coming out of the oven right now."

"Thank you so much for your help!" shouted Jones as she walked away, her tone attempting to overcompensate for the previous misunderstanding. Once Jones stepped away from the counter, Ligare was activated, his posture ever so slightly changing. Though his face still pointed forward, his right eye shifted focus, turned toward Jones independent of the other; the cavity of his eye slid along his face, and his ear vanished under the focused pupil. Jones walked over and leaned on a small pillar near a second small doorway near the side of the restaurant. The thin flap of a door that covered it was mostly made of a large circular window. The window allowed the waiting patrons to view the activity in the kitchen. As always, behind it dozens of workers cooked and packed orders furiously.

Jones stood patiently, reciting her list and rechecking off everything—decorations, food options, music options, and then counting the number of wine glasses she would need to clean and dry. It was only a few minutes before another woman wearing a denim hat and apron emerged from the side door. In one arm she balanced several large pizzas, and in the other she held a large plastic bag containing several smaller paper bags. Jones placed her phone on top of the pizzas still balanced on the woman's arm and grabbed the plastic bag from her, letting it sit on the ground but dangle from her wrist with her purse. She then grabbed the pizza boxes with both hands. Jones threw her purse and bag onto her shoulder, lifting them with her leg before pinning the two with her elbow.

Jones thanked the woman, her tone this time controlled, poised, and practiced. She carried the boxes a short distance to a third counter, a long bar-like table covered in various condiments. The lot was split into two sections. The first was filled with vast jars of powders and peppers to sprinkle across your food. The other was where Jones posted to-go packets of all types neatly organized beside travel cutlery. Next to Jones stood another patron, a man gathering napkins and searching for hot sauce.

"Ha," Jones said out loud as the man's hand scanned the piles and stopped for a moment above the mustard. "They think they can fool us with that fake mustard," her finger pointed toward the packets. The man paused his search to look at her but said nothing. "Oh, because you know, the old mustard plants died out years ago? Noooowwww…everything has that fake mustard taste and it's just not as good. I luckily have an older jar that is still good. It's just so hard to find now. Right?" The man simply shrugged while he squeezed some of the synthetic mustard onto his food. He then placed his slice of pizza into his mouth and walked away.

Jones riffled through the sauces herself, throwing packets of ketchup, vegan mustard, and avocado ranch into her bag. Lifting her feast off the table, she rebalanced everything before heading west. When Jones' body passed the pillar, Ligare left his position in line, merely three away from the front. This was the first and only of his actions that drew attention to him. Those around him were perplexed he had abandoned his position for such delicious food—he was soooo close.

As he followed Jones, the two entered a substantially different neighborhood than the one Ligare had just come from. As they traveled uphill, they made their way to a section of the city, Garden Grove, that sat higher than the rest. This section was more residential, the buildings older, composed mostly of classic-style homes and two-story buildings with a smattering of mini skyscrapers. It was the summer, which meant the majority of the buildings were growing or in bloom. The sides of most buildings were modified to act as scaffolding for vines and trees. Their rooftops were altered flat to allow the planting of gardens and trees and for the placement of solar panels.

At the corner of 16th and 3rd Avenue, Jones approached her apartment building. Small compared to the skyscrapers, it was the largest building on this block at four stories. The front facade of the building was covered by rose vines and orchids bathing in the setting sun. The rest of the building was similar to the others in the area. Tangles of ivy and moss climbed to the top before being cut off by the placement of solar panels. Jones walked up to the front door and pressed her keys up to the control panel screen on the side, and all the while she struggled to balance her pizza boxes. The screen then prompted her to stare into the camera for facial recognition, her registered means of two-way verification.

The consul confirmed her name and displayed a small thumbnail of her registered photo before opening the automated door. Instead of entering, Jones placed her knee on the wall near the terminal, balanced her pizza on it, and placed her purse and bag on the floor. Using her off hand, she tapped the monitor to activate it once again. *Welcome, Jones Jessup. How can I help you?* appeared in bold yellow letters above a series of menus. She began to look through her phone for a list of her anticipated party guests. She selected option 4, *guest list*, and was then directed to a new menu for her listed events. She found the name *PARTY!!* already highlighted. Selecting it displayed a list of each person she had already remembered to register with the system, their name and photo listed just like hers was before.

Scrolling through the list of seven, she double-checked it against the names on her phone. Realizing each one was already accounted for, she thought, *Another win for me.* She then selected *activate, sign guestbook, announce arrival,* and *facial scan,* and ended with hitting *confirm.* Now back in the main menu, Jones selected *guest list* again but this time selected *permeant.* Under this listing was only her and her ex-husband, Arthur Jessup. Selecting his profile, she hovered her pointer finger over the delete button at the bottom right. When she selected *delete,* the screen then prompted her with an aggressive *"Are you sure?"* Jones hesitated before selecting the small *x* in the corner.

Across the street stood Ligare watching all of this from beneath a utility pole, it too covered in vines. His right eye, which had previously resided on the side of his face, had now traveled to his fingers and split into two, now residing in his pointer and middle fingers. He hid his body behind a shrub at the base of the pole that concealed a large utility box and stretched his fingers around to peep. When Jones entered, Ligare watched her ascend the building through the stairwell windows, knowing exactly which floor she was on.

3rd

Though he lost track of her, Ligare merely smiled while his eye returned to its proper place on his face. Stepping from behind the shrubbery, he casually made his way toward the entrance of the building. When he stepped up to the doorway, the camera failed to notice him entirely, and he ignored the terminal entirely. He pressed his hand into the lock of the door and his fingers began to crumble. His body began to collapse into sand; beginning with his hand, it traveled to his arm and spread to the rest of his body. The mass then spread apart and moved along the edges of the door before pressing itself through the tiniest of cracks. The sand made its way through the first set of doors. As the last few grains of sand dribbled their way through the keyhole, the pile grouped and began to return to its previous form. Ligare then easily opened the second door and stepped into the lobby of Jones' building.

The small, simple hallway was lined with antique mailboxes on the left, the names of each occupant engraved on their lines. All of the locks were rusted, preserved for posterity but never actually used. The floor in front of the boxes, however, was full of various brown and nondescript packages. Ligare walked past them and turned to see a staircase and a long hallway that led to all the apartments on the first floor. He took the stairs and walked up the chipped, black marble planks. It was complemented by cheaply painted, tan, sponge-patterned walls. He hastily made his way to the third floor.

The landing to the third floor was merely a lone door leading to the long hallway of apartments. Looking through the small porthole-sized window, Ligare watched for anyone currently in the hallway. The coast was clear. He silently stepped through the door, closed it behind himself, and took a deep breath. The tan sponge wall paint continued into this section, the pattern's waviness making the length of the corridor unsettling to the eye. The hallway was lined with doors on both sides, periodic and paired. Jones would be behind one of those doors.

Ligare began his short, fast breathing technique once again. As he made his way down the hallway, his movement was less walking and more dancing. His path wasn't straight; instead he glided from side to side, making sure to smell around the edges of both doors he passed. This time he was filled with anticipation, a side effect of Jones' mind. As he danced along the hallway, he gracefully searched for her source. Left, then right, then left, then right. Ligare moved and touched each door, raised his nose to the air, then placed his nose onto the door. He would sniff along the handle, and along the seams, rapidly searching for her scent. Then he dropped to the ground and smelled below the door before popping back up. As he continued to walk forward, he repeated the pattern, this flow, until he found Jones' apartment deeper in the hall.

When he got to her door he knew it in an instant. As he tracked his nose along the molding of the door, it pulsated; the wood of the frame creaked, and flakes of old paint fell to the ground. Ligare's excitement caused his body to apply pressure and force around it. Facing the door, Ligare once again crumbled into a pile on the ground, his face smiling as it fell into nothing. He then passed through her door and made his way into her home.

Unsure of where in the apartment she would be, Ligare remained a shapeless form of earth. Instead of moving in the open, his particles lined the molding of the walls, traveling along their grooves like water flowing through tubes. Some of him flowed on one side and some the other, each working independently to survey the parameter. They made their way through the small hallway into a large, open space, the four sections of the room split into a kitchen, living room, dining room, and another hallway.

He could see that the kitchen table and dining room table were fancily set. Both were covered in intricately designed platters, each one a fanciful plate of food with meticulously set combinations of colors and shapes. Together they formed a larger image, more of an art piece than the party buffet it was supposed to be. Jones always appreciated the handmade craftsmanship of platters, a level of tedious and creative. The dishes they sat on she had either bought during her travels or were gifted to her. The platters that were displayed were the ones that a) were good conversation starters, be it their style or beauty, and b) did not remind her deeply about Arthur.

Traveling deeper into the apartment, Ligare could hear music. At the end of the hallway, an open door revealed a light and its source. The sand made its way toward it, traveling along the floor edges and into the backroom, where Jones was gathering additional supplies. Jones sat on the floor, in the back of the room near her walk-in closet. In front of her were numerous boxes containing decorations from every party theme or holiday you could imagine; photos from throughout the years randomly fell out of them as she searched. Jones dug through the boxes looking for more streamers, more ribbon, more lights, more something.

Having located Jones, the sand made its way back into the hallway, where they formed back into his humanoid form. Ligare's right eye then fell back into his skull, and he spat it out of his mouth and let it drop to the floor. The base of the eye dissolved into sand, which carried the rest of it back into Jones' bedroom. While the eye watched Jones, Ligare would enjoy himself.

Ligare walked back down the hallway and he ran his hands along both walls, admiring the decorations he could see. So close to her, close to the things she was thinking about, the things that absorbed her life, Ligare could once again see sparkles. This time they floated around the room and drew his attention toward particular items. When he looked upon them, each object brought jolts of joy and flashes of her memories to his mind; each object triggered things inside of him…he might have even been here before.

Within the space many items caught his eye, but the first he approached was a memorial poster sitting at the intersection of the dining room and living room. The poster sat on a large wooden easel next to a small table ornamented with a vase of fake flowers and a few framed photos. Scanning the photos, Ligare saw none with Jones in them. The collage of photos showed a heterosexual couple in different locations. Their faces and smiles never changed—only their outfits. The bottom of the poster read, "Happy Anniversary." Ligare ran his finger up and down the board as he scanned the photos once again before realizing this was not the source of the sparkles.

His attention was now drawn to the side table beside the poster, and he reached his hand out to pick up the photo on the table. An old silver frame held a photo of Jones from thirty years before, when she had just graduated from college, where she sat under a tree. The age of the photo was only given away by its low resolution. The item had a glow, but it brought to mind no memories. Placing the photo back on the stand, he noticed there was space for several more. The table was surprisingly clear considering the concentration of knickknacks throughout the rest of the apartment.

Ligare was drawn to investigate further and attempted to open the drawer on the front of the table. He found it to be a false handle; he could open nothing and merely shook the structure.

As it jiggled, he could hear something rattling from within. Reaching around the side, he found a latch and he immediately turned it. The side was released, which opened flat and transformed into a small work desk. The internal compartment was filled with several more photos, these in frames that were much more expensive and beautiful. Ligare pulled each one out and assumed the photos he held were once on the table. He found two frames whose pictures pulsated and intensely shimmered. Like we see different colors, Ligare could see unique rays that bounced off the photos and danced through the room leading back to Jones. The exterior of the frames was flawless and polished, signs of being well cared for recently; their edges were bands of gold, hand engraved with intricate floral patterns, making each piece unique.

When he held up the first photo, Ligare saw Jones in her wedding dress, her ex-husband proudly holding her in his arms. The rays of the photo showed a brilliant swirling pattern, the deepest coming from the window, where a nook with a seat existed. A book was propped up against the window decoratively, but a bookmark was clearly in it. The image brought flashes of intimacy; a series of cuddles, hugs, laughs, and deep conversations flew through his mind in an instant.

He then changed his attention to the second photo, where he could see a slower-flowing zigzag of rays almost exclusively bouncing throughout the kitchen. The photo itself was clearly taken in the kitchen, Jones and Arthur in aprons, several friends surrounding them. He could easily recognize that two were the couple present on the poster. The image brought flashes of security—the community they cultivated, the family they planned to create, and the security they felt in each other. A reel of past dinner parties flew through his head; how they always hosted and cooked together. The joining of their friends occurred almost weekly—parties that hadn't happened in a while. Ligare would feel all of Jones' emotions within the walls of this apartment.

It was a box containing all of her hopes and fears. They floated in the air and sat on his tongue. This was going to be fantastic.

In the backroom Jones jumped to her feet and carried a handful of banners and photos. The eye scurried back to Ligare to warn him and joined him as they both turned back into sand. The photos he was holding crashed to the ground. Jones skipped out of her room and into the living space with her supplies, but changed to a jog when she heard the noise. She instantly identified the sight of shattered glass and her grandmother's antique frames. Jones' nose began to tighten as she tried to choke back a small pool of tears. She would NOT ruin her makeup. Jones threw what she had in her hands onto the couch and ran into the kitchen to grab a broom, pan, and garbage can. First, she picked up the frames and held them over the garbage can. She used the top of the broom to break the remaining glass and allowed the photos to fall into the trash. She then opened the back of each and used her dress to clean out any small shards in the corners. Jones examined the open drawer but then placed the now empty frames into it and returned to sweeping.

The amorphous Ligare appreciated the welcome distraction as it allowed him to easily dart his way along the walls and toward her front door. He charged straight toward it, passed through the seams in the door, and vacated her apartment, for now. He flowed back down the hallway, making his way down the stairs and toward the entrance. Once he exited the building, Ligare re-formed and walked back across the street to retake his position under the utility pole. Then he waited and watched the arrival of many people from behind the shrubbery. He tried to recognize some of the faces from the photos he had seen, but he was never sure which were the inhabitants and which were visitors to the party. He would clearly need to wait a long time to be safe.

It wouldn't be until around 2 a.m. that the first people he recognized would leave. It wouldn't be until 3 a.m. before the couple he recognized from the banner, the guests of honor, showed themselves. He watched as a female carried a much larger man, his face adorned with a large smile. He attempted to kiss her as she struggled under his weight; the two of them chuckled and she pecked him on the cheek. The pair traveled to the curb and waited for a taxi, which quickly arrived. The party might be over, but to be safe Ligare would still need to wait. At 4 a.m. he finally made his way back into the building, his sand technique working as swiftly and effectively as always.

As he entered her apartment again, he could hear that Jones was not yet asleep. The pile of sand watched from the dark corners of the hallway as Jones tended to a friend, Craig, still located on the couch. The androgynous individual already had their eyes closed and their head tucked into one of Jones' many decorative throw pillows, the rest of which were strewn about the floor. Jones drunkenly stumbled her way to the hall closet and grabbed a large quilt. She then made her way toward her sleeping friend, the blanket unfolding in the process and dragging on the ground by the time she reached the couch. Jones fully covered her indifferent friend by haphazardly throwing the quilt into the air. She then adjusted the quilt with attention and diligence and tucked them in with care. Picking up another pillow off the floor, she lifted Craig's head and placed it under. Jones then gently kissed them on the forehead.

A beautiful evening with beautiful friends, she thought. Jones was happy to have people over again. It was wonderful to hear her food was not terrible without Arthur. To have someone stay over and share her space. To feel like she wasn't alone anymore. Jones dimmed the lights and blew out some candles as she made her way around the room for one final sweep before bed. She picked up some trash, including a paper plate full of leftover gluten-free pizza crust, and threw it in a trash can. Then she reached under the sink and pulled out a small bucket. She once again approached Craig and put the bucket on the floor near their face, just in case. Jones then made her way into her bathroom to get ready for sleep.

Now that she was alone, she immediately disrobed, pulling her arms through her dress and letting it drop to the floor. Stepping out of it with one foot proved easy, but it remained firmly attached to her other. She kicked her foot three times before the dress went sliding across the floor and collided with the tub. Jones leaned on the sink with stiff elbows. She began to exam herself in the mirror before noticing a message written in soap from her friends. *Love you, JoJo.* She chuckled to herself and smiled as she picked up a washcloth, turned on the water, and used the now-dampened cloth to clean off the message.

Jones scanned herself in the mirror as she put up her hair into a messy bun. She began to brush her teeth. When the toothbrush hit her tongue, she began to feel a shock of nausea. She dropped her toothbrush in the sink, ran over to the toilet, and began to gag. Gagging became dry-heaving, but nothing but a faint groan emerged as she fought it. "Should I just pull the trigger?" she queried. "No…no…I'm fine. You're fine." Jones breathed slowly and deeply as she tried to control her nausea. After a few more coughs, she settled her stomach. She finally was able to finish brushing her teeth. She made a bowl with both hands and leaned in and sucked in some water, now afraid to put anything else into it. Jones walked directly toward her bed by crawling over to the front of the frame. She flopped onto it and took the shape of a starfish as she snuggled into her many pillows. She was soon fast asleep—drunk, happy, and content.

The lights were low and the inhabitants were asleep. Ligare was free. He reformed in front of Jones' door and placed his palm on it. He turned his body like he was trying to hear better and focused on the energy coming from the room. Through his hand he could feel the rhymes of Jones' mind echoing in her room. There are many stages in the human sleep cycle, and Ligare had learned when they were most vulnerable and the most delicious. He had not always been a careful feeder. In the past he had ravished small towns on a whim; the fear his feeding generated infected their minds and those around them. As he spread his lust among the community, he would drive them all into madness. Jones was not yet in a sound sleep, so he placed his back against the door and slid down to the ground. Ligare then removed his left hand and placed it against the door, behind his left shoulder. This allowed him to maintain tabs on Jones' mind within.

Jones looked peaceful in bed, but alcohol creates uneasy and unstable rest. That is why Ligare hated it; it always delayed a good meal. It increased the chance his prey would wake up. A good REM cycle could take hours to properly establish' it wasn't worth it to feed prior to that. There he waited, his eye on Craig and his ear on Jones. With his remaining arm, Ligare reached into a pocket on the inside of his jacket and retrieved a golden lighter. The shiny lighter was engraved with an image of several beasts basking in the sunlight of a larger divine creature, shown only as lights in the sky. The eyes of each beast were replaced by pairs of tiny, precious stones. Ligare began to play with the lighter by passing it between his fingers—rolling it back and forth, back and forth. After a couple of passes he gripped the top and began to snap it open and closed. He then added that to his pattern of rolling it between his fingers, now sometimes doing it by the cap and sometimes by the base. Every now and then a snap open or a click shut echoed in the small apartment.

Then it happened, he smelled it. The smell of imaginative deep sleep. Ligare had finally waited long enough. Doing a back summersault, he turned into sand and rolled through the edges and under the door. His body reformed through the bedroom door with a flip as if the door was not there. Ligare popped up to his feet and turned to see Jones asleep in bed, a pillow between her legs and one cradled in each arm. She was peacefully resting, in the most uncomfortable-looking position.

Ligare took a deep breath and once again pulled out his lighter. He held it at his side and sparked the lighter. From it an unnatural and toxic green flame formed, the top of the flame flickering with baby blue embers. The inexplicable fire began to unspool from the lighter and travel, as his coils of sand did, along the seams of the room to the edges and along the corners. As the rope of fire hit the first edge, it split into new trails, one to follow each new path until the entire room was filled—a cube of flame. The one small flame began to build up with a phantasmic glow. Through the window, what was once an alley of flowers slowly faded into darkness, dimming a little more each time the flame grew brighter. Outside, the light of the moon could no longer be seen. The room seemed to no longer exist within the apartment and was now part of a completely different dimension.

A final new rope of flame reached out from the lighter. This time it swirled through the air toward Jones. Ligare began to approach as the flames gently flowed over Jones. By the time he reached her side, the flames rolled about her but then disappeared into her. A faint hew was given off by her skin as it began to glow with the faint lime green of magic. Ligare took one last deep inhale and filled his lungs with the energy of the woman within the room. He exhaled heavily and smiled. He was so hungry, and finally it was time to eat.

The sun was now shining, and rays of light bounced off the warm rocks of the cobblestone path Jones found herself walking on. Though she had never seen any of it before, she found something familiar and comforting in her landscape. It was as if the unfamiliar scenery she saw in front of her bore the soul of a best friend. The path took her through the woods, where she arrived upon a large stone wall covered in moss. The only path forward was a darkened tunnel with only a speck of light visible. Without hesitation, Jones continued into the darkness with her eyes pointed toward the light. Despite its grand distance, the trip through the tunnel happened in a flash.

As she exited on the other side, Jones found herself walking into the courtyard of an old castle. The unfamiliar had now truly become familiar. She now walked on a more properly paved stone path. On either side, she could see scattered willow trees along half-dead grass that ended in more stone walls. Glancing up, she could see the walls turned to towers and all the structures connected into a giant hedge. She stood in the old courtyard of a once grand castle, now turned into an apartment. Jones immediately recognized her surroundings. She had stumbled back into the apartment complex from her childhood. There was something about the simple layout of trees against the old, worn red and brown bricks that reminded her of a simpler time. As she made her way down the path, the sun began to shine brighter and brighter. *The clouds in the sky must have parted*, she thought. The sun shone on her head, and the warmth sent bright shivers down her spine. Jones was happy.

Her walk became almost a skip. Something inside her was billowing with excitement. Upon reaching the center of the courtyard, she could now see all four entrances, each an archway like the one she had come through. Just left of the western entrance she could see an antique mailbox, a relic that wasn't ever used even during her childhood. The tall bronze body once housed parcels for all the inhabitants of the castle. The mailbox gave way to bushes that lined small patches of mostly dead grass—small, symmetrical, decorative foliage. She remembered how she and her friends had continued to ruin that grass as children, every day. Each season the maintenance team would plant seeds, then she and her friends tried to sprint and jump over the bushes like hurdles and wrecked it. In the rain, this was especially sloppy when they challenged each other to see who could leap over as many bushes in a single wet sprint.

A slight tingle appeared in her thigh as her memory continued. Jones on one particularly rainy night was the last one to jump the bushes. She was in heavy competition, not sure how many times they had leapt. The rain began to come down harder and harder. In an attempt for one last jump, for the win, Jones sprinted and leapt over the first bush. Her foot hit the ground and mud splashed up into her face. Luckily, her sweater was brown so it would be the least of the reasons she got in trouble. Continuing to sprint, she felt her legs get heavy as the mud got deeper and stickier. She cleared the second bush with relative ease, and she saw her goal in front of her.

As Jones stomped her right foot into the mud and extended her leg for the last ballerina-like leap, she felt the ground below her give way. Her body began to fall forward, and though she tried to stomp her foot in the mud, it only seemed to make it worse. She began a slide, human hydroplaning. She crashed into the bush and her body flipped over it; her momentum was too high. The contact of her thigh into the bush snapped a branch and lodged it into Jones' pantleg and her thigh muscle. She continued to fly through the air and ultimately landed on her now bruised ass. Jones laid back in the rain, letting it wash over her, as she caught her breath. When she lifted her head to look at the branch, she had to immediately look away—try to pretend it wasn't there.

Her friends ran over to check on her. They gasped at the sight of blood, and then their eyes migrated to her face. Though Jones was sitting and bleeding, there could not have been a larger smile on her face. As they helped her up, she looked at them and said, "I win."

"What!" they all exclaimed, surprised she was worried about claiming victory and simultaneously bleeding out.

"I made it—I made it over. It counts. I win." Little Jones continued to smile but her face grew paler as the adrenaline wore off. Adult Jones woke herself from the happy memory and turned around to find she had been so happily skipping toward one of three massive willow trees. The grand old trees stood before the creation of this castle, their power and beauty contained by its walls. Between all the owners of the castle and all its inhabitants, the changes with time and seasons, those trees stood mighty and eternal. They stretched five stories tall, and their tops reached as high as the castle walls around them.

Jones removed the black flats she was wearing and held them with one hand. She stepped through the mostly dead grass, which was cold but the dirt was dry. Not the most comfortable sensation but one that once again reminded her of her childhood. It was wonderful how some things never changed. Jones made her way to the base of her favorite tree that stood directly between her and her best friend's apartments, their usual meeting spot. On many days throughout their childhood, the two would sit in that tree, doing nothing; they were children and that was their job. Fun was everything in their lives. The base of the tree was not a single straight trunk but was actually a group of four smaller trees that had grown together. The group of trunks each curved outward before returning and becoming one. Their series of entangled branches were perfect for the shape of a human to lay on.

Jones began to climb the left side of the tree, always her favorite spot. The branches had since grown denser, making climbing to the second layer of the tree a bit more difficult than she remembered in her childhood. She was also perhaps a bit bigger now. She was able to squeeze through the branches and she found her way to a break in the leaves, a teardrop-shaped opening.

As a child it was a perfect spot for stargazing. They had called it "the eye." Once Jones had reached her desired branch, she began to squeeze her butt into the old warm spot within the tangled branches. She then leaned back and basked in the small spot of sunlight.

From her position, Jones could see clouds rolling through the sky, the roof of the castle barely visible. As a child she would watch a stray cat, The Boss, who lived on the roof and was often spotted lying along the edge. It was always amazing when she would spot him carrying a bird or a mouse, being a dynamic and solid hunter. It must have been nearly fifty years ago, but it felt like yesterday. It was amazing how in addition to living longer, many people taking Rejuverron felt their memories sharper and for longer. A beautiful side effect for some. Perhaps a nightmare for others.

Jones began to drift off in the sun and leaned her head back. Her branch then began to give, and the sudden drop of her body startled her. Shifting quickly, and staring up at the sky, she thought she could see a flash of a cat running across the roof. She rubbed her eyes and looked again. *What on earth?* she thought. A fat orange cat trotted along the wall with a pigeon in its mouth before it jumped down to hide. *Could it be The Boss had children?* wondered Jones. *I wonder if I can find it.* Jones started to climb back down the tree and questioned if there was an entire family of cats at this point. Perhaps she could meet the great-great-great-grandchildren of The Boss.

She lowered herself onto the group, climbed out of the tree, and then tiptoed across the grass to the stone path before putting her shoes back on. Jones remembered that each apartment unit had an entrance to the roof. She would go to her old one as she remembered it the best. Her path took her west, where she made a stop by the old mailbox once again. She couldn't help but touch it. She slid her hand across it as she walked toward her old apartment building entrance.

The metal of the box was warmed by the sun, almost too hot to handle. The front door that led to the stairwell of apartments was open, its ancient lock purely decorative. There seemed to be no terminal installed to monitor this building. *Strange*, Jones thought. Her building had been the last to get this bit of tech.

Jones made her way up the staircase of the building; the red and brown bricks were significantly darker without the sun. The stairwell was tight, only a person's width. She had once lived on the fourth floor, with no elevator, and had to walk up and down the flights each morning and each evening. The stairs were much harder to go up now that she was older. As a child she would challenge others to a race down the stairs. She would easily win by climbing down the banisters between the floors. This acrobatic terrified her parents, annoyed her friends, and won her every race. She was by far the fastest and most reckless person in her family. Now the doors of each apartment all looked the same; worn red and brown brick surrounded a brown door. Nearly all the apartment letters were still there. Too busy remembering her childhood, Jones failed to notice that with each floor she passed the sky outside grew darker. By the time she had passed the final floor of apartments, the sun had set. At the top Jones came up to the rusted double doors. Jones pushed them open, excited to get back into the sunlight.

Jones triumphantly flung open both doors at the same time and stepped into nothing. The large doors swung open with ease but revealed not a dark roof but a world absent of light. Jones began to fall through the air, tumbling, her body weightless. She became nauseous and confused. She closed her eyes and tried to settle her stomach. *How did I get here?* She thought she might be falling but she had no frame of reference; the darkness gave her no hints.

It was then Jones woke up, not entirely but from her *own* dream. She found herself instead, like many, in one of Ligare's memories. Her mind was now in the interwoven connection between her dreams and the fragments he carried of others' dreams (though she, like nearly

everyone else, had no way of knowing that). By feeding on her, he created a connection, drew on

her imagination, and fed on her life and memories. Sometimes events were stained into his soul

by the minds he affected. Jones' thoughts and memories of lost love echoed throughout her

apartment and mind. Those thoughts resonated and merged with the memories of Ligare's. They

were the memories of a woman he had fed on, a woman wronged by his actions and a

community that paid the price.

Ligare's feeding had not always been as controlled and methodical as it was now. His

feeding strategy was also not always so kind. When he was younger his hunger was never

satisfied, no matter how ferociously he would feed. There were periods in history when he would

cause mayhem for humans, his loss of a feeding ground his only punishment. Because of these

actions, throughout time some religions had both revered and feared him. With age he learned to

control himself and that came as a way to guarantee food and freedom, something that made his

life easier. It was an instinct bred into him by trial and error. By reading our imaginations and our

minds, he learned the habits of humans, when and how best to feed, and those things were

implanted in his soul and very nature.

Jones quickly sat up, finally able to feel her body. When she looked at her clothes, she

realized she was wearing a long, white, flowing gown. Her body was covered from her hands to

her toes. She looked around to see that she was not in her bed and the room she was in was not

her bedroom. The room was small but loosely furnished, a row of dressers lined her walls, and

her bed was large but uncomfortable. She threw off the covers and jumped out of bed. Her bare

feet felt the chill of the raw wooden floor.

Perhaps she rose to her feet too quickly, but Jones became dizzy. A halo appeared surrounding the edges of her vision, shifting as she moved her head. Jones felt her head wondering if she had hit it in her fall. Running her fingers across her scalp, she failed to find anything. There didn't appear to be anything wrong with her. Jones attempted to walk it off, and moved across the room toward a small sink with a window above it. As she walked, she used the small, old, and askew furniture to stabilize herself. Luckily, she found that the more time she spent there the less the halo bothered her—like getting your sea legs she became used to the motion. Jones stood over the sink and waited for a moment, stabilizing herself until she was no longer inhibited by the glow.

She looked across the room and attempted to search for a clue as to where she was. It was then she noticed the small hand mirror on the counter, and the reflection of light caught her eye. In fact, she saw her eye in the mirror and it was not hers. She lifted the mirror and examined herself. Jones looked over the face and failed to see any of herself in the reflection. Her nose was flatter and stouter, her hair similarly shorter and rounder. Jones was shocked and her heart raced as she noticed the wrinkles on her face. Her body was significantly older, and her face showed the long life of the woman she possessed. She was ashamed of how much fear came from never having thought of herself as old, being lucky enough to never have to worry about it. Little of her shock came from not being herself.

Through the window Jones peered through the blinds to see old New England streets. She scanned the houses looking for an indication of where she was, for someone or something she might recognize. From the window she could see nothing, and no one. The streetlights were lit by flames. Their thin black bodies only dimly illuminated the street below them. The streets were well paved outside, but only a few blocks away the road became rough and rugged. Through the window she could see rows of similar houses, large but not lavish. The area was a village, not even a town, filled with less than two thousand individuals. It was late, the witching hour, and everyone stayed off the streets, as was the proper and God-fearing thing to do.

It was then her eye was drawn to the south, down a road labeled Oak Street. There she saw something moving, a figure, perhaps a man. His shadow hovered around the entrance to a house. At first, he stood in front, analyzing the door. *Perhaps he is admiring the architecture*, she thought. *Inconclusive*. Jones gently opened her window and hung her head out to get a better look. The figure began to circle the building, entering the yard and passing through the garden. He crushed flowers underfoot. That was her cue. Jones ran from the sink and scurried toward the door, where she grabbed shoes from in front of it. She donned a large, furry coat that was hanging there as well and walked out of the house.

The air was thick, and her every breath formed a large, frozen cloud in front of her face. She gripped her coat closer and shuffled her way toward the house where she had seen the figure. Her shoes were slightly too big, and her feet were unsteady on the cobblestones. All the while, she felt drawn to check on the shadow. When she reached the front of the house, Jones searched for any indication that someone was still there. To the right, she saw proof—footsteps within the garden continued around the back. Following the footsteps, Jones quietly crept, not sure what she was looking for. Then the footsteps suddenly disappeared. She turned back but then noticed a break in the blinds of the house. Then she saw it.

Through the back window, Jones saw the monster more clearly than she had before. The figure walked through the small one-room home. It stood no taller than the average person, thin and covered in a cheap cloth robe. Jones's and its robes were not too different—cheap, homemade, and hand-woven cotton. This was a young Ligare, searching for a meal. His skin was scaled and his face lizard-like, his nose wide and long. The top of his head was raised, a small bump where a fin would one day grow. Ligare ventured to a girl sleeping in a bed on the far side of the room. Jones did not know how or why, but she knew her name was Mercy Lewis.

Jones watched as Ligare drew from his sleeve a fist of fire, the flames chaotic and pulsating. The flames whipped around like snakes attempting to escape a bag and traveled throughout the room. His hands were locked around the swirling ball of light. Jones gasped as suddenly she could see nothing within the building, a blackness obscuring any view inside. Jones gripped her coat tightly once again and started to run to the front of the building. *I have to find a way in*, Jones thought, hoping to help the girl.

She walked up the two small steps to the front door and attempted to jiggle the handle. She found it impossible to move, as if it were not real at all but a decorative stone. Jones stepped away from the house and examined the façade for any way to enter—another door or window perhaps.

"Who's there?" shouted a woman's voice. Jones turned to see a group of people, at least fifteen, standing to her side. The leader of the group, a tall, thin woman, stood in front. Shocked by their sudden appearance, Jones stood silent for a moment. She searched her mind for a way to explain what she had just seen. She then perked up upon realizing she now had someone, now many people, to help. She stepped forward and began to explain herself.

"Be weary," Jones began. "There is a monster with the shifting face of a beast. I have seen him. You must help me. I have see—." She was cut off.

"Oh, don't worry!" The leader shouted, ignoring everything Jones had said. "We know all about what you were doing, Bridget. We've finally caught you red-handed, Mrs. Bishop. You claim there is a monster but why are you out so late yourself? If not for mischief?" Jones did not know what the woman meant but the crowd behind her began to grumble.

Jones began again, "There is a beast, a beast within this house. The young girl, Mercy, must be saved. I saw him upon her. Please help."

"We have been up and down these streets my dear and we have seen nothing but you. How convenient the monster is here, at the same house you outside of. You failed to answer before: What are you doing here? You know this girl has already accused you of haunting her dreams. Yet, you come here still?" The woman began to pace. "That's why we are here, to protect her from the unholy. Here, we find you. How curious. God has clearly led us to the truth."

Jones knew not how to argue with this, but she shouted, "Check the house, go inside, there is dark magic over its walls. There you'll find the monster—please believe me."

"I believe we have already found our monster. Seize her," commanded the woman, pointing at Jones. Two men then grabbed Jones' arms. As she struggled, a pitchfork was held up to her throat by a third man. "Your victims have claimed you have a witches mark, signifying your coupling with the devil," she continued. "Check her."

The men began to pull at her clothes, pulling her dress to her waist with her arms still locked in her sleeves. They ripped her blouse to expose her breasts and stomach and spun her. "AH HA," the woman screamed. The men held Jones still, but they looked up confused. The brash woman stepped over to Jones and pointed over her back, right above her butt, a small skin tag. "This is of the most unnatural perversions. Who amongst us can say they have seen this on a woman?"

The men grabbed her even tighter but try as she might, Jones was only able to minimally cover herself with her ripped robes before she was lifted off her feet. A crowd gathered with their weapons and torches and followed the group to an open field, just beyond the houses. Jones was carried over to an area already set up, a large stake sticking out of the ground. The men placed her down next to the stake; one still held onto her and the other unraveled a rope. They bound her hands and then tied her body to the stake.

"Mrs. Bishop," the increasingly aggressive woman began again. "You stand accused of witchcraft. How do you plead?"

"Not guilty," Jones responded, monotone but frustrated. She was not sure what else she could say that she had not already.

"We've watched you for a long time. We have a group of ten who have many claims to your treachery, including those who have now seen you stalking around at night." The men who once held her now stood with torches; others began to stack hay and wood beneath her feet. The leader approached Jones and took the torch out of the hand of an idling man. "May God have mercy on your soul," she shouted as she raised the torch high into the air. She wished to bring it slamming down onto the kindling in righteous glory.

"Stop!" shouted a voice from among the crowd. It was an old, portly gentleman wearing much nicer clothes than anyone else in the crowd. His robes and wig signified he was someone of power and status. "As the head judge, I decree you cannot do this. If we murder this woman, we are no better than the witch herself. We must have a proper trial… Tomorrow." The leader looked at him, angry but defeated for the time being. Her arm still held the torch high in the air.

Jones had tears in her eyes as she was untied from the stake. But she was not free yet. She was immediately thrown over the shoulder of one of the men, with her arms still bound. "The witch will sleep in the jail, tonight," decreed the judge to the crowd as he motioned with his hands for the crowd to disperse. As they carried away Jones from the mob, she could see Mercy's house in the distance. As if made of water, Ligare emerged from the door, flowing through every imperfection in the wood. She watched as his reptilian scales smoothed and were replaced by human skin. His face and form were now transformed into a bastardized model of Mercy's. Then she watched as Ligare hunched over onto all fours and trotted down the street.

Only a few houses down, he rose and used his now smaller stature to leap through an open window and disappeared. Still atop the man's shoulders, Jones began to scream and thrash. She attempted to warn them. She attempted to plead for her life. She begged for them to just look. Displeased with her screaming and struggling, the man beside her untied a sack from off his belt and threw it over Jones' head. Then everything went black.

When the sack was lifted, the sun had already risen and Jones stood on the witness stand. The court was filled to the brim, overly stuffed to a degree not physically possible, the entire village there and seemingly more. Her hands were still tied as Jones stood isolated in the center of the room. When the bag was removed it was as if she had removed earplugs; the sound of the court inhabitants was a large and consistent roar. The judge from the night before sat up front and attempted to gather everyone's attention.

"Let the trial begin," bellowed the judge. The courtroom was now silent. As the judge talked, his body grew larger with each sentence, as if he was filling with air. "This will be a proper trail, under the eyes of God. If the witch is found guilty, she will hang by the neck until dead. In the case of the village of *Salem vs. Bridget Bishop*, how do you plead?"

This time Jones felt like a passenger within her body. She watched as it responded, faster than she could think, as if her words were being guided by something. That thing was the memories of Bishop. "Not guilty," she pleaded, stone-faced and proud.

"Fair enough, then. We will have the prosecution provide their evidence. Then you defend yourself, if you can. The jury will then decide your fate. FIRST CHARGES," shouted the judge.

The leader of the mob was the first to take the stand, her seat suddenly raised on a stage as she spoke to the crowd. "Last night and for many nights, for that matter, we have watched Mrs. Bishop wandering the streets and peering through windows. Just last night we caught her doing that very thing. When questioned she had no excuse nor wished to defend herself. We have also found the mark of the beast on her.

"I do believe she is not a woman of God. Her three husbands have all mysteriously died! God would not punish a pure woman with such tragedy. She must have done it for gain. She could have told us anything about them before she got here. Is there one within the audience she has confided in? Showed sadness or remorse? She cannot be trusted. God does not bring so much misfortune on just one soul for no reason. I think perhaps she killed them herself. We know her and her husband Oliver were abusive—they both were jailed for such things. She has always had the devil in her." The woman ended her testimony by lowering her head and signed a little prayer.

"My husband's deaths were not mysteries. They were sick and unfortunate. Your failure to show pity of my misfortune shows how close and truly far from God you have come, madame. I have not done anything but use my husband's wealth to help others feel joy," Jones responded in a calm and collected voice. The crowd let out a blaring sound of disapproval. Their noise was broken up by the thundering crash of the judge's gavel.

"I do believe we have someone else from the neighborhood watch up to report," said the judge. "Please tell your stories, you brave, brave man."

A man Jones had never seen before appeared on the elevated stand, a hat held in his hands, and his eyes locked down and forlorn. "I have known Mrs. Bishop for a long time. Before her name had changed, even for the second time. I have always known her as an unfit mother, losing her first infant. She has also been previously accused of witchcraft. You are not the first people to notice her evil spirit. Furthermore, I have reports from ten neighbors within the village who hold accounts of her mischief and have the strength to testified against her." With his words, two new stands rose from the ground. "Among her accusers are these girls," said the man. As he spoke a group of young women appeared on one of the stands. "They are afraid to speak now but they have all attested that Bridget has tried to pressure them into signing the Devil's book. We are only lucky their spirits are so pure, and they fought off her evil advances."

"I have seen her crafting dolls for spells. She comes into my shop to buy her lace," shouted a woman from the back of the courtroom. "She muttered something about counter-magic. I think there are more witches!"

"Her specter has visited me in my dreams. Her face haunts me morning and night," a man shouted from another part of the courtroom.

"How many men have felt the presence of Mrs. Bishop's specter?" queried the judge. The crowd started to growl and roll. Hands of men shot up throughout the room. "I see, she has taken to trying to steal the purity of our men as well. Mrs. Bishop, you have been busy. For our last witness, the village of Salem calls Ms. Mercy Lewis."

On the tall and center stage appeared Mercy, her hair disgruntled and her eyes bloodshot and crazy. Like the others she stared at the ground; her eyes were barely visible behind her hair. She wore what she'd worn to bed the night before. As she stood, her body shook, and it spontaneously contorted. As she spoke, she groaned. "She did this to me! Coming into my house at night. I have seen Bishop stalking my house and into the house of our neighbors. She comes and goes, flying in the dark of night. Sometimes she comes as a bat, and I've seen her turn into a beast and flee." Mercy pointed a crooked and sickly hand at Jones as she continued, "She visited me just last night. I awoke while she fed. I couldn't move or breathe, feeling her weight binding my chest. I saw her face, her evil face. Look at her arms, look for the scars of me fighting for my soul."

On the smaller stands behind Mercy appeared groups of several men and women. "Your honor, these people corroborate my story. They too have borne witness to Mrs. Bishop transforming into a black pig, as well as an imp. They have seen her flying as a bat into her attic and landing on the ground like a bird after surveying her orchards from the sky."

"What do you have to say to these most direct and unarguable accusations?" questioned the judge as he played with his gavel.

"I too have seen the beast you mention. It is not me. I have seen it take the face of others in our village. I have not seen it turn into a pig or bat, but I saw it enter the home of Mercy last night. I tried to help but was taken away," Jones explained.

"So, you agree there is a presence of a monster, but you deny having any connection. Many in the town have seen you for certain, but you say that we have a monster that looks like you but isn't you. How convenient. Then tell us who else has made a pact with the devil. Who shares their face with the monster? Who else is an agent for the devil? You expect us reasonable people to assume that a monster is pretending to be you. Always you to these girls," shouted the judge.

Jones attempted to speak once again but nothing came out. As the courtroom stared at her, she searched the crowd for the friendly face. Instead in the distance a board dislodged from the wall. As it fell to the ground, the crowd shifted. The loud crash echoed in the hall, causing a brief moment of silence. Then the silence was broken.

"GUILTY," roared the courtroom. The echo of their voices shook the foundation of the building. The railing around her disappeared and the crowd in the courtroom began to approach. Her head began to spin, and she found herself now standing on the gallows. Inexplicably, a noose now hung around her neck. The crowd now in the distance was still shouting.

"Do you have anything else to say?" echoed the judge's voice, rolling over the crowd. "You failed to confess. So may the Lord pardon your soul. Any last words?

Something took over Jones once again and she spoke in her strong monotone voice. "I will not lie. I will spit in the face of God and claim I am a monster. That I am a witch. I am nothing more than a strong woman who has faced a life of misfortune and adversity. Even so, I have done great things for many, with and without a man. I believe that makes so many of you uncomfortable. I am a woman who has had the misfortune of not losing one love but three within my lifetime. To have lost children, I have lost love, and now I suppose I will lose my own life. You all only know the shallowest parts of my misery. I have nothing to gain by lying to you and I will not tarnish my soul. If I say I am a witch, you will punish me just as much. I will lose my freedom and thus my life. I will not trade in the truth of God for the foolishness of man. I pray that God may forgive you all. I pray you may never make this mistake again."

The judge then gave the signal by swinging down his right hand. To her left Jones saw rows of women similarly handcuffed. She now knew she was wrong, and she was only the first. Those who stood in the distance were the next to be tried, eighteen others. The trials would continue. Jones' mind became flooded with flashes of memories, not Bridget's, but of Ligare's. The images would bring tears to her eyes. She saw how the rest of the village would go mad, how Ligare would go on to cause the deaths of so many more women. As he fed and fed, he sent each person into madness, enveloping the village into chaos. These memories flashed before her eyes as the floor below her gave way. It felt like a millennium, but her weight finally took over and she began to fall—the noose quickly tightened. The rope cracked as it caught her weight, and a large snap echoed in her ears and across the open field.

As her neck snapped, Jones could feel a searing pain engulf her body and the dream became only a nightmare. Jones' extreme distress spread throughout her body, tainted the flavor of the dream with her pain. Ligare could feel the shift as he fed. Ligare learned that once this toxic and negative taste began to spread, the dream, the meal, was ruined. He began to loosen his grip and separated his mind from hers. The green flames began to pull from Jones' body and entered his own body. That is when Jones woke up, for real this time, lying in her own bed. The panic of her nightmare thrust her into the real world. Standing above her, she saw the monster that had existed in her dream. She saw that what stood before her wore the makeup of a man, but she could still see the monster that he was.

Jones struggled. She attempted to strike out at the beast in front of her using any arm or leg she could; she would never be a bystander. Try as she might, none of her limbs moved; nothing responded to her commands. Jones struggled and attempted to wabble, to bounce, but she was unable to do anything. She then attempted to scream, to wake up Craig from the couch, but a weight sat on her rib cage. Her chest was heavy and so her breath was short. She felt only pressure and pain and as she tried to scream; only faint whispers poured out. It was then her eyes started to tear out of frustration.

Ligare paid no attention to the struggles of Jones below. His flames had rendered her body paralyzed. Her mind was actually still asleep, almost completely empty. Though she could see him now and remembered what horrors he had done, she most likely would not remember it in a few hours. He simply began to walk away from her, his lighter still open. The flames moved their way backward across the corners of the room and returned to their golden home. Once all the flames had moved into the lighter the flame extinguished itself. Ligare then snapped the lighter shut and turned toward Jones. Before Jones' eyes, Ligare began to change, his face and his body morphing closer to what she saw in her dreams. He shrank, his skin becoming less of a man's and more of a scaled beast's. His clothes were replaced by robes. Ligare smiled and looked Jones in the eye as he turned into sand. His body then rushed from the room and then the apartment.

Jones continued to struggle in bed for only a few more moments; her body and her mind were both shocked and exhausted. As she failed to move her limbs her head became heavy, and her mind unresponsive. She swiftly fell back asleep. It was already sunrise and Jones would not wake up for many more hours. Craig would let themselves in in the morning, leaving a note on the counter. In the morning Jones woke up with a burst of adrenaline. In a rush, she sat up and searched her room for the monster from her dream. Her eyes darted around the room and then her hangover began to take over, her head began to pound. Jones held her head in her hands, eyes closed, and caught her breath. When she opened her eyes again, she frantically searched the room but couldn't remember what she was looking for. Then she tried to remember what she had dreamed of altogether.

She remembered that something stood above her and the fear she felt when unable to move, but she could not recall what had led to that point or where the fear had come from. All Jones knew now was that her body was weak, and she was incredibly nauseous. It was only a few minutes before Ligare was forgotten by Jones altogether. Then her illness took hold of her body, Ligare's effects making her hangover even worse. At first, she tried to get comfortable and adjust her position in bed, but ultimately, she had to throw the sheets off the bed and run into the bathroom, straight for the toilet. That's when she finally threw up. Figments of the dreams would return throughout her life, as small déjà vu. Her dreams were forever tainted with an indescribable eeriness.

Then Ligare exited the apartment and turned down a random street. He looked at his arms and touched his face. He was aware that his appearance was strange. The human side made him a little self-conscious about it. He covered his head with excess fabric on his robe and hid his scaly skin under them like a poncho. With these slight adjustments and his innate ability to fade from memory, his monstrous form was now hidden from the public. Now that he was conscious, his soul was being guided by Jones' mind; the small fragments of Jones' life bounced within him. He would walk through the city for the next few days and evenings. Though Jones had been monotone in her personality, her spirit was happy and joyful. That spirit filled Ligare as he wandered through the town. Day and night he breathed it all in. The small things that sparked joy in Jones did the same for Ligare, the grand architecture and the beauty of the wildflowers. This was the short time that he felt alive. Like a drug, a short high gave way to his low blankness. As the energy in his mind began to fade, so did any memories of Jones. The joy too would fade and Ligare would forget her, just as she did him. His personality would melt away into nothing, until he once again became a hungry trolling predator; his nose would turn on and the cycle would begin again.

On the Run

On the Run

For the first time in a long time, Percy was sound asleep. Though his shirt collar had smatterings of vomit on it, a messy mixture of liquid and chunk, his face was adorned with a half-smile. Looking at him through the rearview mirror, Mary breathed a sigh of relief—and unknown to her, a tear ran down her cheek. A small release of tension. She was driving but staring caringly at her son in the back. Their small dog, a teacup yorkie, Wilder, was asleep in a small bed in the passenger seat. Mary lowered the music, a local radio station playing contemporary favorites, and basked in the calming silence that was the roar of her car's old engine.

It was now deep into the night and Mary had been on edge since earlier that day. She had a fair complexion with dark hair and eyes. Her makeup consisted of a simple layer of blush on her cheeks. Percy had another one of his fits, his stomach uneasy and his body weak and flush. She was happy the small and sickly boy could finally find a moment of peaceful sleep. No one believed her when she told them he was ten years old. Percy seemed at best the size of a small eight-year-old; his hair was bright blond, and his eyes were a bright blue. His skin was pale from his illness, though their lifestyle allowed him the pleasure of sitting in the sun most days. Any natural color he may have had was always flushed away from his face, as he lay weak and sick.

No doctors, so far, had been able to pinpoint what ailed Percy; his abnormal stature, lack of color, disorientation, and nauseousness were a mystery. On increasingly common occurrences Percy would have seizures; Mary was forced to hold his body as he spasmed uncontrollably. Determined, she had spent the last several years traveling with him, taking him from doctor to doctor for an answer. The doctors were rarely around for his episodes, but to each Mary would attest they often occurred in the morning and/or after dinner. Then would come a slew of medical procedures that would turn up nothing. Mary was always insistent that they run additional tests. She could see her child was in pain and she demanded to know why. Those failings were partially why Mary didn't trust doctors. The other part was because she didn't trust anyone, at least not when it came to her son.

Mary had always known she wanted to be a mother. Even as a toddler, she was the child following around the others, attempting to care for them and loudly exclaiming, "Baby." When Rejuverron was announced it promised a life of youth and an infinite timeline for children, family, and fun. Though the original batch was limited to the wealthiest and most prestigious of individuals, it was only a few years before the first off-brand pill was developed for mass distribution. The poorly made knockoff had a common but serious side effect, sterility. Mary, like an entire generation of youth, had been accidentally neutered. She was lucky enough to have been able to save a few eggs, and by a miracle of science she had Percy, her last chance for a child of her own.

Mary used her right hand to squeeze the rearview mirror and quickly moved it off of Percy to look at the road behind her. She scanned the pitch-black scene and examined it for any evidence they were being followed—the gleam of light off an undercover car or the small, quick lights of a surveillance drone. After the quick search, she was again satisfied with their safety and turned the mirror back toward her son. As she watched him, her eyes barely glanced at the road ahead of her, which gave her car a small drift; the vehicle would sometimes come uncomfortably close to the wooden guard rail.

They were driving on dark, countryside roads, the gentle hills helping to calm Percy's aching stomach. Mary was not driving anywhere in specific; they were simply moving on, as they always did. Mary no longer stayed anywhere for more than two weeks at a time. This was often enough time for the local doctors to run tests and fail to find anything conclusive. She would then pack up their car, check out of their hotel, and move on. When she first fled or "set out on her own," Mary attempted to establish a life for Percy. She sent him to school and even bought a house. It was the incompetence of his doctors and the threat of his father that sent them on the road. It became safer to never stay still for too long.

It was almost 2 a.m. and Mary was starting to get tired. Her cup of coffee was mostly empty. There was only a small dribble of cold leftovers at the bottom. Mary gazed at their dog, now snoring, and wished she could be doing the same. Mary, now tired and still staring at her son, neglected her speed and continued to swerve. As she came to the bottom of the hill, Mary noticed the gleam of a car hidden within the foliage; the bright lights of a police vehicle flickered on. In front of her Mary noticed the speed limit had dropped from 45 to 25 kilometers per hour in an instant. Mary's heart raced as she saw she was now being followed.

Her every instinct told her to speed away, to lose the police officer on the long, vacant roads. "These local hicks probably know every backroad," she muttered angrily, trying to convince herself otherwise. The profession she trusted the least were cops. Her ex-husband had been one, and it continued to sour her perception of them. The cop car turned on its siren and Mary begrudgingly slowed her car and pulled it off to the side, deciding on the path of least resistance. She preemptively rolled down her window, surprised by the cold autumn air that flowed in. Its fresh scent began to replenish the stagnant, vomit-filled air that Mary had grown nose blind to. The small chill alerted her to the presence of the tear on her face; she then wiped it off. She quickly grew tense as the police officer exited her car and made her way to her window.

"Hi, ma'am, I'm sorry to pull you over, but you were speeding and swerving. Is everything okay?" asked the officer politely. She was short and skinny, but her large vest made her look barrel chested. She had light brown hair that sat in a bun under her hat. She used her flashlight to scan the car, then pointed it in Mary's face.

"Would you please not shine that at my son, please! He just fell asleep," Mary barked through her teeth as she attempted to keep her voice at a whisper.

"I'm so sorry," responded the officer, her voice now also a whisper. She turned off her flashlight and continued to scan Mary's face, checking to see if she appeared inebriated. "Once again, sorry to pull you over, ma'am, but you were serving something fierce. Could I please see your license and registration? Also, your little dog is adorable."

Mary reached over to the floor of the passenger side of the car where her purse sat, her movements awaking the dog. She fumbled through the purse's contents; she struggled through a rattling mess of medications and snacks while she looked for her smaller card clutch. Wilder was now awake and noticed the officer's presence, then he began to bark. "SHHHHH," Mary screamed in a whisper. She was trying her best to remain calm and to keep Percy asleep. She used her right hand to pinch Wilder's mouth shut as she grabbed her ID and handed it to the officer.

"It's a pleasure to meet you, Mrs. Nesbit. May I ask what you are doing out so late? You don't seem to be from around here—pretty far from home, eh?" the officer said as she scanned the driver's license. Mary's home address was listed as several states away.

"We are on a trip to visit family. My poor boy is sick, and the car helps him to fall asleep. Well usually, except for when we hit the terribly windy roads around here." All the while her voice grew increasingly more anxious with each word. She attempted to play it off with a smile and began to use her fingers to drum on the steering wheel. Now that his mouth was free, Wilder murmured small protest growls.

"Your registration? Also, if you don't mind me asking, what's wrong with him? I have a child of my…," the officer said, genuinely concerned, as Mary cut off the rest of their statement.

"It's a chronic condition that I do not feel obligated to talk to you about. Now please let me take my son home," she snapped. Mary pointed her face forward, stern, her eyes on the horizon. She made it clear she no longer was interested in the officer.

"Registration?" she beckoned once again.

"I don't keep important documents like that in my car, in case they get stolen. I was just taking my son out for a drive. Now please check my ID so we can be on our way home."

"I'll run your ID now."

Mary failed to respond. The officer's jovial face melted away to a serious slouch. "Why of course, ma'am. Just one moment," muttered the officer as she walked back to her car, spinning Mary's ID between her fingers.

Mary returned to adjusting her mirror, watching the police officer enter her car. For five minutes they sat in wait as the ID was run through the system. For the first time all evening, Mary was staring at something that was not her son. The police officer exited her car and made her way back. Mary assumed her stern position again; face forward, arms at two and ten on the wheel.

"Well, everything seems to be in order, Sarah. Sorry for the delay. We have a lot of drunk drivers and wild kids who like to be crazy on these roads. I'll let you go with a warning, but you need to have that paperwork IN THE CAR. As a sleepy mother to another, I hope your child feels better," she said while handing Mary her license. Without a word, Mary began to drive away, the officer still where her window once was. Mary then rolled up her window, heart pounding, as she attempted to put her ID back into her purse. Wilder sensed her distress and jumped into her lap, with his tiny paws on her chest. As he pawed at her chest, she smiled and let out another sigh.

Mary never knew who knew her ex-husband or how many agencies he may have been in contact with—any officer could be on his side. Their first attempt at starting a new life had been demolished in a flash as her husband was able to locate her through local law enforcement. Even the threat of a ticket could put their lives in danger. That's why she insisted on using fake IDs; up to five were in her purse at any point. That is also why she didn't show her registration; it was not going to match. She had meant to grab an ID closer to where she was currently driving. *Elizabeth*, she thought. *She might be from around here.* Mary had instead accidentally grabbed her mother's old ID, Sarah Nesbit. Though they had distinct noses, their eyes were both a deep dark blue, which often discouraged further analysis.

It took about ten miles before Mary could convince herself that the cop was not secretly following her. It was then she readjusted her mirror and returned to watching her son. She knew she was beginning to get too tired to keep driving; her anxiety was increasing, and her coordination was decreasing. She then realized she would only have a few hours at most to sleep before Percy would wake up and needed to be taken care of. She needed some sleep. The trio traveled another few miles before the country sideroads brought them to a larger intersection and a ramp for a highway.

"Route 23…seems as fine as any place to sleep," Mary yawned, rhetorically talking to her son. Wilder now stood up in her lap, placed its paws on the steering wheel, and attempted to peer over the proportionally gigantic controls. Across the highway overpass, she saw a large white sign. *Superb Suites.* It was a well-taken-care-of sign and even looked recently painted. The baby blue trim of the letters was surrounded by small, hand-painted red flowers. It was an aesthetic Mary appreciated. As she made her way slowly through the parking lot, she circled the building, once to find the entrance and once to find the exits. As she pulled her car under the awning, she made it a point to park directly outside the front door.

"I'm going to have to leave you in here, Wilder. Protect Percy…BUT don't wake him up. I'll be able to see you." Mary placed Wilder into his bed and began to unbuckle her seatbelt. As her eyes raised above the steering wheel, they were met by the clerk behind the desk—a young girl, in a sharply fit but cheap suit, dark hair and eyes. Her face turned from stern to a smile upon noticing Mary. She placed her pen onto the table and stood up from her desk and began to walk toward the front door.

Something within her smile struck a chord with Mary. Her tiredness was overtaken by a cold sweat and panic and her hands began to shake. Her hands fumbled as she attempted to secure the seatbelt back into place. "I do not feel safe here. Nope. Nope. Something strange," she muttered as she failed to hear the click that meant she was secure. The clerk leaned out the door to ask Mary if she needed any help, but was met with the squealing of tires. Mary had given up putting on her seatbelt and now drove with the buckle tucked under her right thigh.

She took the nearest ramp onto the interstate. *North.* On the highway she drove for another twenty-five minutes before another exit arrived. She had chosen the wrong direction if she had meant to head for civilization. Instead, they traveled deeper into the countryside. As they approached Exit 26B, a large blue sign alerted Mary that the next exit was forty-six miles away.

A smaller, more crudely made sign hung below that one. It was clearly handmade; the letters were sculpted with vigor and enthusiasm but were also lopsided.

Home-away-from-Home. Motel and Car Service.

They took that exit, their only choice. Mary turned off to a surprisingly industrial road, two large lanes sandwiched by warehouses and lined with steel fences. Behind the chain links sat rows of trucks that protected empty parking lots. Down the road a stretch, beyond the warehouses, sat a flat and open piece of land. In the center sat the motel, a single-floor establishment, fake dark-brown wood panels lining its exterior. Chipped paint fell from the neon sign as they pulled into the mostly empty parking lot. Two rows of single-story rooms stretched to the north. To the south was a small building separated from the rest. Car services ran across the top of the building in faint red lettering. A few old and broken cars sat parked out front, and two gas pumps sat out beside them illuminated by a dim fluorescent bulb.

"The isolation…the openness…seems like a perfect place to hide. How's that sound, Babyboy?"

"Of course, Mama," responded Percy, half asleep.

Mary drove around the building, doing her survey. At the end of the building, she saw the room she wanted, 210, the farthest and most isolated room. She circled back to the main office, and Mary once again parked in view of the lobby. She left her car on but locked it from inside and took a spare set of keys with her. Wilder began to bark as she exited, which was met with a "Hush." When she walked into the lobby, she saw an older black gentleman in a deep-blue shirt and black suspenders sitting at a desk. His pants were not visible below the counter, but Mary could tell he was sitting on a stool. At first he failed to notice her, his face buried in a small computer that sat on the table in front of him.

"Ahem, excuse me," Mary said, wondering how he'd failed to notice her during her small walk to the counter. The gentleman's small afro was black, faded to one side, and peppered with faint pink and blue polka dots. His long beard was similarly colored. Finally aware of Mary's presence, the man's face brightened in an instant. "Oh, hi! Welcome to Home-Away-From-Home. Sorry, I didn't see you there. We usually don't get any visitors so late. Just one room for you then?" His voice was soft and deep.

"Yes, one room. A room for me and my son. If possible, can we please have room 210?" Mary changed her voice to match his tone, much gentler than she had been with the police officer. She had learned, with many, it was often easiest to take on that tone of voice.

"Well, we don't usually let people choose their rooms. Is there a particular reason? Usually we fill from front to back. Would 115 be okay?"

"I really would prefer the other room." Her smile never faded but her tone grew noticeably raspier. She did not have the energy for this.

"Well of course not—it's just this is a simple place. The ice machine is right around the corner here and you're going to get all of the morning sunlight soon through that room. I just think you'll be more comfortable…"

"Thank you for your concern," Mary interrupted. "I appreciate it, but I assure you I love the morning sun." She then adjusted her top and straightened her coat. "I can see the key to the room on your wall, so I know no one is in it, and we are so tired. I can sleep through anything, really. So, can I please have the room for my son's sake? He really appreciates his privacy. I truly find it so charming you still use analog keys." She then let out a fake little laugh.

The man was simultaneously unfazed and concerned by her tone, his eyes clearly questioning her intentions. "Of course, we aim to be accommodating." His tone was slower but smoother. "Could I please see your ID and a credit card for incidentals?"

Mary went into her purse and once again found her small clutch and removed her credit card and one of her many IDs. After handing them to the gentleman, he examined them as he typed her information into the computer. As he began to enter the credit card, he noticed the names on the two cards were not the same—*Sarah Nesbit and Sarah Carrey.*

Do you have another card? The names on these don't match. I need an ID that matches the name on the credit card. "

The ID is in my maiden name! Please just use my card." She now sounded a tad defeated and began digging through her purse again. Mary quickly located another ID card, this one from a grocery store that confirmed the name of *Sarah Carrey.*

The man shrugged his shoulders and handed her a metal key that acted as a key ring for a blank white card. "The metal key is just for show. We phased those out a long time ago. Just hold this part up to the door to release the mechanism."

Mary made a polite smile, disappointed by the keycard. *What is to stop them from turning off my card?* she worried to herself. *I have to find some way to secure the room to prevent that.* Mary made her way back toward her car and entered. She grabbed Wilder in one hand and placed him on the passenger seat floor. She hoped to hide him from the clerk, who was still watching her through the door.

Mary moved her car and parked a few spaces from room 210. The few minutes it could take for someone to check room 207 could be all that they needed to escape. She exited the car and made her way to the back seat. "Come on little Pea," she whispered to Percy, gently nudging him. "We need to go inside. Don't wake up—just climb into Mommy's arms." Without saying a word, he rolled his body into hers. His sickly frame made him effortless for her to lift. When she closed the door, Wilder stood on the center consul barking at her to bring him too.

She balanced Percy with one arm and used her other hand to lift the card key to the door. She could hear a mechanical click as the lock opened. The room was dark but luckily the light was easily within reach, and she switched the lights on. The motel room was rather modest, as suggested by both its price and location. It had a rustic theme, in stark contrast to the industrial park around them. Though poorly done, Mary appreciated their attempts to mimic what she assumed was "majestic wine country." At the back of the room sat one large king bed, the sheets green and gold to match the carpeting on the floor. Mary made her way to the bed and maneuvered the covers with one hand before she placed Percy under the sheets. She made her way into the bathroom and turned on the light before making her way back to the front door. She turned off the main light before exiting the room.

Mary made her way back to the car and headed for the trunk. She proceeded to shift around its contents before eventually removing a duffle bag. Then at the front she grabbed Wilder with her off hand and locked the vehicle. Instead of heading directly inside, she walked past their door and made her way around the corner, where she scanned the tops of the building for cameras. Once she was convinced they were alone, she placed Wilder onto a small patch of grass growing out of the shattered sidewalk concrete.

"Go potty," she pleaded, beginning to loosen her coat and stretching her neck side to side. Wilder took his sweet time finding the perfect spot among the square foot of grass. The two then made their way into the room. She placed Wilder onto the bed, and he joined Percy under the covers.

Mary adjusted the blinds until all the light was gone except for the faint illumination that came from the bathroom. She removed her coat and placed it neatly in a pile on the floor by the front door. She then grabbed her duffle bag and placed it onto a small chair against the wall. She unzipped it to reveal several dresses and shirts neatly folded. She shifted the clothes to the side to reveal a series of assorted tools; some medical, some hardware, gloves, glues, and other unrecognizable contraptions.

She pulled out some vials of medicine and put several pills into the pocket of her dress. She donned white latex gloves, then began to dig further into the bag, eventually pulling out a contraption with a small screen. When turned on, it displayed an antique screen with a weakly lit axis. A small value for mV randomly fluctuated in the corner. Mary walked around the room, scanning each object and each inch of the room using the two antennae that protruded from its top. As she ran over the electronics, small signals appeared but quickly went away. The nifty machine would pick up on electrical signals, detecting any bugs trying to transmit a signal. It was the type of tool they simply didn't make anymore. Mary had purchased it in a thrift store during their travels.

She scanned the room, finding nothing. She then placed Pea's medication onto the table and jotted a little note. Her last task was to seal the front door, and she did so by placing a chair under the handle, so it was incapable of being turned. It was followed by a moment of calm and respite. Without removing her clothes, Mary took her shoes off and lay in bed next to her son. As he nuzzled into her chest, she used her finger to clean off his collar. She pulled him in tight and the two fell asleep together. Throughout the night Percy's occasional coughing would stir Mary's hand to tussling his hair and kiss his forehead.

There was a strong discrepancy between the body that Percy inhabited in his dreams and that of the real world. In his mind, Percy imagined he was a much older, taller, and healthier man. One at this point, he could only hope to be. As he slept within his mother's arms, Percy was free of the muscular and mental limitations his poor health allocated him. In his dreams his hair lost its youthful blond glow and instead took on a lighter brown tone; a smattering of highlights were the only remains of his childhood color. Despite the grogginess from his medication and his persistent illness, Percy was not a slow boy. His head was just always fogged with an unknown tension within his brain. On especially bad days he could feel a similar tension in his muscles, as if they were locked. His body felt stifled, like a crab trying to grow within its shell. It was as if his skin was pressing back on his bones and trying to hold his body back. This resulted in a pain that he felt over most of his body, a pain that then often translated to nausea. In his sleep, Percy felt none of this and was free.

On this particular night, Percy found himself bathing in the sun, a large straw hat shielding his face. Below the hat a smile ran across his face as his body absorbed the soothing warmth. He was laying stretched out over the seats of a long canoe and could feel the smallest drift. He knew they were barely flowing downstream. Below him he could hear Wilder snoring. It was a much louder noise than he was used to. In this dream Wilder took the form of a medium-sized blue pit bull, white smattering on his paws and ears. Percy sat up and removed the hat from his face and let out a small, content yawn.

Percy turned his head sharply as he could now hear music. He gazed forward to find the source of the gentle tug on the boat. In front of the canoe was a young man in a baseball cap, a metal band T-shirt (the sleeves were inexplicably ripped off) smoking a cigarette. He was trudging through the stream pulling the canoe forward by a rope and singing a song whose lyrics Percy could not quite make out. Percy then looked to the helm and saw the source of the music. There sat a tall and lanky gentleman. His hair was strawberry blond so faint it bordered on white. His eyes and skin were the fairest Percy had ever seen, and he was smattered with light freckles. He was a distinct man painted in only faint colors and outlines. He sat playing a ukulele, which he accompanied with loud and boisterous singing. Percy now realized the man pulling the canoe was providing commentary and backup vocals. He stared at the bard for a moment; a name came to mind, Pasty. It was then the words of the two performers came into focus. Percy sat and watched the show in front of him.

What the two men lacked in professional training, they made up for with vigor and banter. As Pasty sang, he strummed chords on his ukelele.

"Ohhhhhh, we're floating downstream!" began Pasty. "A twenty-minute ride turned into three hours of blissful floating. Ohhhhhh, I messed up the calculations. In my young life, I've learned a few things."

"What did you learn?" responded George.

"You know what it was?"

"I'm asking!"

In a much slower and more dramatic tone, "Never get a Chinese major to do your math." Then he continued, once again upbeat, "Ohhhhhh, 'cause we're floating downstream. Let's hope it don't dry up. My boy George keeping us going. Party in the back and music in the front. Ohhhhh, we're floating downstream! Dry pants and a party, on land. Our dream only three hours away. HOOOPEFULLY!"

"Now, for a haiku!" Pasty proclaimed. He stopped strumming his ukulele. His face provided evidence that what was to come had not been rehearsed.

On a snail's journey.

Nowhere to go but together.

We sail for the fun.

"Isn't a haiku supposed to be 5-7-5?" George sang back, reaching his arm blindly behind him. Pasty pulled out a cigarette and lighter and handed it to George, who proceeded to spark up once again.

Still singing, Pasty retorted, "American English wasn't made with haikus in mind. We can bend the format a bit." Then he proceeded to recite another seemingly off-the-cuff Haiku, this time adding his ukulele strums between each line.

We've been running all day.

Our bones ache more than they should.

No, we're not that old.

Their words then became silent, and as they faded out Percy now looked behind himself for the first time and saw he was not alone. The back of his canoe was roped to a giant plastic inflatable. Within it sat six men making joyous and loud conversation. The raft and their hands were decorated with a variety of beer cans and liquor bottles. In their excitement they failed to notice Percy's movements. He continued to look around himself and finally appreciated that they were in a beautiful valley with alternating trees and grasslands. It gave the landscape a depth and look of bountifulness, as if it could go on forever. As he watched the distance, he lost time.

Percy then found himself in a hotel bed, tightly wrapped in blankets, the swaddle covering him up to his neck. Mary was nowhere to be seen. Instead he was nuzzled on all sides by large, comfortable pillows. Only the small beams of light that came through the blinds illuminated the dark room. Strange shadows that reached throughout the room seemed to be cast out of nowhere. Percy attempted to turn onto his side but found himself unable to move. His body felt glued to the sheets. As he fought to rock back and forth his chest grew heavier. He was beginning to panic. The sheets now felt like his personal straight jacket. He stopped paying attention to himself when he heard something strange. Percy listened as the room around him began to creak, the fake wood straining under some unknown force. The sound of the bending wood echoed in his head.

The door of the hotel room flung open and revealed an unnaturally bright light. The light was quickly blocked by the movement of two shadowed figures that now stood in the doorway. Percy squeezed his eyes shut and attempted to calm his pulse, the pain in his mind building. As he struggled, the two figures glided into the room. The light behind them faded as the door slammed behind them. He could still hear the wood of the room buckling. The two figures moved their way to the foot of his bed, their faces and outfits now visible under the banded light.

To his left stood Mary, her face in an exaggerated smile, her muscles uncomfortably high against her cheekbones. Her outfit was strange. A very proper pink suit and skirt graced her body, much more flamboyant than her typical wardrobe of blacks and browns. Next to her stood a masked man, who though disguised, Percy recognized as his father. Percy had very few memories of his father and the ones he had always seemed to get lost in his mind. The broad, tall man was dressed in a police uniform, but his face was covered by a sheet of metal acting as a mask; only a small section of his eyes was visible through two small slits. The mask was joined to his skin by a series of staples, small bits of blood dripping out of them and down his face.

For a moment, the two watched over him, moving their heads from side to side as they analyzed him. Percy continued to struggle within the bed, but the blankets became tighter against his body. They were beginning to shrink and constrict his breathing even more. He breathed deeper and deeper as he gasped for air. His parents moved closer, than further, to the left and to the right. Their faces all the while tilted left and right, like the pendulum on a clock. Mary was always smiling. It was then that his parents were upon him, the two now at this side. As they peered down at him, they appeared to stretch higher and higher. They began to loom, casting a dark shadow over him, towering over his body. They seemed so high over him that it felt like they would fall into him.

Mary reached down to Percy and effortlessly picked him up. Percy felt weightless in her arms, suddenly no longer within the blankets of the bed but now trapped within a smaller swaddle. Mary began to rock him within her arms, staring down at him and beaming with pride. Percy was no longer his adult form but now a baby within Mary's arms. Percy could still not move, his body paralyzed, and his view fogged. It appeared as if he was falling back into his mind, his eyes acting like windows he was slowly backing away from.

Percy was now watching himself and his parents from deep within a hole. Mary began to fuss with the blanket around his body. As she did so, no pressure was lifted off of Percy's chest. She unwrapped the swaddle around his lower body by flicking it off one side. She looked up at her ex-husband and he moved his head against hers sweetly before he put his hand up to baby Percy—he pinched his cheek and rubbed the top of his head. It was then that Percy felt as if he was floating out of his body and rising out of the dark hole. He was now watching himself from above, still unable to move. Mary then removed the second side of the blanket to reveal nothing at all; from above, Percy could see he was nothing but a head.

Finally, Percy woke up for real, this time cradled within his mother's arms. A weight was still on his chest. Afraid to look around the room, he closed his eyes and buried his head into her. It was then he heard a small crunch and noticed something under his shoulder—something he had squished into his mother's torso. As he rolled slightly away from her, he saw the note she had written the night before.

Good morning, Darling. I'm sorry but I didn't fall sleep till very late last night. I have set an alarm and will be up shortly. Please take your medicine and have some breakfast. I left some instant oatmeal on the counter. Just add water.

Love, Mom

Before he could get out of bed, Percy held the blanket up to his face and scanned the room for anything that might have escaped his dream. Looking left, then right, then left again, he gained confidence that nothing was there. Percy then proceeded to get out of bed, as gently as he could, as he didn't want to disturb his mother. Wilder immediately noticed the lack of Percy's warmth and awoke. He stretched below the sheets before emerging.

Percy made his way across the room using the bed and walls like makeshift canes to support his body. He was weak and tired, both his mind and his body. On the table he found the oatmeal and medicine that his mother had promised. He popped his pills out of the container, the one labeled *Th*, and grabbed the package of oatmeal in one hand. He worked his way to the bathroom sink using his off hand to support himself. As he moved across the room, he tried to remember his dream and his nightmare. Images flickered in his mind but quickly faded from his memory. All he was left with were the feelings they had provoked in him, dread and misfortune.

Upon reaching the sink, Percy threw his pills into his mouth and turned on the water. He placed the bowl of instant oatmeal on the counter as he hoisted himself forward, placing his mouth under the flowing water. He took a big drink and downed his pills went. Percy then turned off the cold water and turned on the hot. He leaned on the counter while he waited for it to heat up. After a minute he placed his hand under the water. It was warm but not nearly as hot as he'd hoped. He could already start to feel the pain that his medicine placed on his stomach; he needed to eat soon.

Percy opened his oatmeal and filled it with water, stirring the warm mass. After he gave it a few swirls, he grew impatient and started to spoon it into his mouth. At first, Percy gagged, but once he had gotten a few spoonfuls down he started to feel better. The flavor of his meal was "original" natural, nothing added. The blandness of the meal meant he could eat it no matter how terrible he felt. Sometimes he felt it was a nifty trick and other times a burden he had to bear.

By the time Percy had finished using the bathroom, the food had hit his stomach and he started to feel better for the time being. He walked back into the main room, where he sat at the lone table and continued to eat his oatmeal. Between bites, he muttered aloud to himself. He found that with the fog in his head he could keep a better train of thought if he spoke.

"I've never even been on a boat. Who was that weird guy? His voice was so odd. I don't even remember my father's face but that was him, right? I can't remember if I've ever met him, but I know that was him. I wonder what happened to his face. I just…I was so scared. And small." While talking to himself with his hands, Percy accidentally dropped his spoon. The clanging of the metal against the table stirred Mary.

"Darling, is that you? You're not making a mess, are you?" After a brief pause, she continued her autopilot questioning. "Did you take your medicine? Did you eat?"

Percy's voice came out dry and forced, his emotions from the night before finally catching up with him. He found that speaking was much harder than he anticipated. His thoughts and his mouth were out of sync. "Yes…I ate. I also took my medicine. I just didn't sleep well. I had…umm…a bad dream." When Percy attempted to explain his dream to this mother, he found he had lost more and more of it with each word he uttered. "I was on a boat but then I was with you and Dad. I was really scared." He could no longer remember what had scared him and so he fell into silence, tears falling down his face.

"I know Daddy is scary, but he can't hurt you anymore. You probably don't even remember much about him, but he isn't an evil man. He'll never take you away from me. Don't worry." She then stretched, her eyes still closed. "You're always safe with me. How are we feeling today? Are you excited?" Mary yawned.

Mary rolled out of bed and made her way to the windows, then she peered through a slit in the blinds. She stood there for a few moments and scanned the parking lot for new arrivals. No new cars had appeared so far, but several trucks were now parked deep in the lot. Mary began removing her clothes for their day from her bag. A small, red, blinking light then caught her eye; it was coming from her electronic scanner. She rushed toward it and turned it on. There was a notification that something had triggered it.

"Percy, darling. Did you touch Mom's tool?"

"No, of course not. I didn't even know it was there."

Mary looked over the device once again; the notification had documented a prolonged electrical event within the room. "What if something transmitted? What if I missed something?"

She briskly walked over to Percy, who was now sitting on the edge of the bed. She got down on her knees to meet his eye line. Grabbing his face, she repeated, "Darling, look at me. Did…you…touch Mom's tool?" Percy continued to deny he'd touched it by shaking his head. "It's okay if you did. You won't get in trouble. Mommy just needs to make sure she sees what she sees. Are you sure you didn't touch it?"

With another shake of his head, Mary released Percy's face. Her mind raced with possibilities and planning. Her face was now a blank stare over to the other side of the room and she continued to mutter to herself. "What could I have missed? What would have triggered it? Maybe it's set to relay only during certain hours. Maybe one of these switches turned it on. No matter what, it's pretty clear. The room *must* be bugged. We…huh…yeah…we have to get out of here."

Percy watched as Mary stared off into space, making hand movements as she planned. After a few minutes, she finally whispered, "All right, darling, come with me for a moment." She led Percy outside the front door and continued. "Just in case someone is listening in there, we're going to speak out here. Just shake your head if you understand. We're going to be leaving here this morning, but I don't want anyone to know. We'll head to the pharmacy so we can get some snacks and medicine for the road. If we can find something to help us find the bug, we'll come back. If not, we'll hit the road and try to find something fun to do today while you're feeling full of energy. Wouldn't that be nice?"

Percy nodded in agreement and then the two made their way back into the room. Quickly, Mary picked out clothes for Percy to wear. He donned his outfit for the day—a green, striped, long-sleeved turtleneck, dark-brown jeans, and a heavier coat than was normally necessary for the season because he so easily got cold. As he dressed, Mary began to pack up their supplies. She quickly moved in and out of the room as she packed things into the car. She then led Percy into the car and buckled him in the passenger seat. Last but not least, she picked up Wilder and brought him out. Only once they were all packed in the car did Mary speak again. "We'll just pay the nice guy at the desk a visit and see if there is a pharmacy anywhere close to here, then we'll be on our way."

Mary drove them to the lobby, where she left Percy sitting in the front seat. Wilder was happily in his arms. She made her way inside and to the counter, where she found the same gentleman working the desk as the night before.

"I see you didn't get to go home. Are you here all the time?" Mary joked.

"Good afternoon, Sarah. Well to be honest, I live here so you're kind of right. Anything I can do you for?"

"Oh, well that must be nice. It is a lovely property, but yes, thank you. You could help me. You clearly know the area. We were wondering if you could direct us to the nearest pharmacy. Need to pick up some supplies."

"Why of course. If you make your way north and go past the warehouses, you'll first hit some wooded area, but after a few miles you should find the town. Kathrine's Market is the place you're looking for. It's a good family business."

"That sounds wonderful. Well, thank you for everything. We'll be seeing you." Though she was leaving for good, Mary did not ask for her card back. It was an old one she wasn't even sure would soon work. She figured it would give them some more time, perhaps a day or two if they were lucky. As they drove away from the hotel, Mary did not intend on ever coming back.

When Mary's car was clearly in the distance, the hotel manager picked up the phone on his desk. "Hi, Trisha. Yes, it's Phil down at the Home-away-from-Home. Yes, I was wondering if you could do me a little favor. I sent a woman to you with her child. She said she needed to pick up supplies for her sick kid. Something about the situation makes me feel strange. Could you just keep an eye out for anything suspicious?"

"Sure, Phil. We'll keep a lookout. It's the slow season, eh?" the voice on the other end laughed.

Mary and Percy followed the directions Phil provided and made their way toward town, following the signs that said "X Miles to Harborton." They made their way past nondescript brick buildings that were occasionally broken up by small homes and their yards. Among it all, they easily found the pharmacy, a small edition attached to an old home. A sign read "Small Family Practice."

"Okay, Percy, so we'll go inside and we'll get some snacks. You can pick out anything you want. Mommy will be at the pharmacy trying get an advance on our medicine."

They entered what was a converted garage. Mary scanned the room and saw the pharmacy counter in the back, hidden among six small rows of shelves. Mary walked straight off toward the counter while Percy wandered off into the farthest aisle. As he stumbled down the aisle, he held his hand out at his side, sliding it across the shelf, touching everything. He found something oddly satisfying about the *thud thud thud* his hand made as it contacted each subsequent package of pens.

"Isn't it a little warm in here for that coat, buddy?" he heard a man ask him. Percy looked up to see a tall black man in a doctor's coat hanging up some items. He didn't respond. "I'm just kidding, son. Can I help you find anything?"

"No, I'm actually very cold. It's been a rather drafty day we've been having. But anyway, I like my coat—it's comfy. But uhm yeah anyway, I'm just looking for a snack. Something to hold me over. If you could help, that would be much appreciated."

"Wow, well what a proper and well-spoken boy you are. I think I know exactly what you are looking for. If you look over on the other side of that shelf, you'll find some chips and other candies." The man then looked over the shelves and noticed that Mary was the only other customer in the shop. Shouting across the room he asked, "Is this your boy? He really is a charming little fella."

"Why yes, thank you," Mary responded, still patiently waiting at the counter to be helped. After a few moments, a woman, Trisha, appeared from the back, seemingly having been on her break. She bore a striking resemblance to the man who had spoken to Percy. They had the same small nose and big eyes. Her hair was long and blonde, and sat curled backwards into a large a ponytail.

"Oh, I'm sorry to keep you waiting. How can I help you?" she asked while rushing toward the desk, her hands now placed on a keyboard in front of her.

"Hi. I am simply trying to refill some prescriptions for my son and me. We're new to town and so we haven't had time to find a primary care doctor. We were hoping we could get the refills left on my account?"

"Sure. We may look old-fashioned but we're connected to the health care system server. We'll just have to look up your social security number and you should be all set to go." That news was disheartening to Mary as she hoped to use the falsified prescriptions in her purse. She would have to use one of her fake accounts.

Mary opened her purse and began to look through her ID cards for verification, settling on Victoria Vargas, a name she had not used in quite a long time. She read off her information to Trisha, who effortlessly entered it.

"All right, Victoria. Pleasure to meet you, by the way. It seems we'll have to call in to renew some of these prescriptions. A few are rather out of date if you still want a refill on those. Perhaps the recent ones are under your son's name?"

"No, I'm sure there must be some mix-up between my husband's and my prescriptions. I get his…he gets mine…he gets the kids. I'm sure you know how it is. We'll just check back later."

"Well either way it seems like it should be fine to refill your Rejuverron. In that case, are you just looking for a refill on the one medication?"

"Yes, if that's all on the file. Unless you have a doctor, who could refill/prescribe some of the others."

"We're actually both doctors. Between my brother and I, we have a hundred and seventy years of experience. This is both a pharmacy and a family practice. It's a little late in the day so we can't fit you in right now, but if give us access to your son's medical records we might be able to help get you some of the previous medicines. We'll need to do a physical and checkup and maybe some bloodwork. Shouldn't be too bad. You can think about it while I get your medicine. It'll take me about ten minutes to fill your order."

Mary waited in silence, debating the offer but knowing they did not have the luxury of waiting that long. Percy then came up to her, his arms filled with as many chip bags as his arms could carry. There was also a candy bar dangling from his mouth, giving him a slight lisp as he talked.

"I couldn't decide what I wanted to eat so I figured I'd bring all the options and you could help me choose."

"Well, I don't know—how about I pick this one?" she said, selecting the only purple package. "And you can pick whatever one looks good to you, and we'll have snacks for the road?"

"How about I pick two more?"

"Fine."

Trisha returned with a large bottle, a full year's supply of Rejuverron. "Here you go. Now did you want to come back tomorrow for that appointment?"

"Yes, of course. That sounds wonderful. Thank you for fitting us in on such short notice."

"We'll just need his name. How does 2 p.m. sound?"

"Michael, and yes, 2 p.m. sounds lovely. We'll see you then." Mary then turned to Percy. "Now let's pay for those snacks and be on our way."

Trisha leaned over the counter, looking at Percy. "It's a pleasure to meet you, Mike. You're a handsome young man. How are you?"

"That's not my name," he responded, confused by everything the pharmacist had just said to him.

"Oh sorry," Trish responded, thinking she confused him by shortening his name. "I just gave you a little nickname. Sorry if you didn't like it."

"Oh okay, no, I like nicknames. That one is nice. You just confused me. I do love chips, though, so can we please buy these?" He reached up, handing some money. Mary opened her purse and added some more to the table. The pair then left.

Once they had exited the store, the pharmacist picked up the phone and made a call to the motel. "Hi, Phil. I think I just saw that woman you mentioned. Yeah, she was in here with her kid. A real poor-looking child like you described. Her card didn't go through immediately and it took us a moment to find her prescription, but the woman seemed fine. She and her son were very sweet. A very smart little boy. He was definitely sick and a little sweaty, but he seemed happy. She actually said she would bring him by tomorrow for a physical. So, I can keep you updated then."

"Okay. Well, I guess I must just be overreacting. Thank you for helping to calm an old man's mind."

"No worries, Phil. You have a good heart. Victoria seems like a sweet woman. Take care now." As Phil hung up the phone, he became confused by what he had just heard. He looked down at the guest list and failed to see a Victoria. He searched the listing for her room and remembered her name was Sarah. He then picked up the phone again, this time to call the police.

"Hi. Sorry to bother you, sheriff, but I think something strange is going on. A woman has rented a room and has been using multiple aliases and cards. I honestly wouldn't pry too much into it—sketchy people who have lived various lives come through all the time—but she has a child with her. The poor boy seems very sick, and I'm really just worried about him…. Yes…. Yes, I understand…. For reference, if it means anything to anyone, the grocery store said she was Victoria Vargas but here she checked in as Sarah Nesbit and/or Sarah Carrey. Yes…. I understand…. I'll wait for y'all here." Phil hung up the phone, hoping he had done something good; not just ruined some woman's life. He was a sucker for kids.

It took four hours before the police, including Percy Sr., arrived at the hotel. His frame and body were much smaller than he had appeared in Percy's dreams. It had been quite a long time since he last saw him. His face resembled Percy Jr.'s but with a grizzle of seventy-five years of police stress mixed with sleepless nights since his son was taken. Phil then led them to Mary's room. They knocked a few times, but after receiving no answer they kicked in the door to find nothing. Mary, Percy, and all their belongings were gone. They searched the room and only found the note she had written tossed in the trash can.

"We found something," called one of the officers to the pack. Percy Sr., the leader, turned on his radio to call in the update.

"They were here, but they have left the premises. Last seen four hours ago at the pharmacy and headed west on Glenn Brook Road. We have intel on her car. Send out an Amber Alert to the counties in the surrounding two hundred miles to be on a lookout for a single woman and child. Put up checkpoints in all directions. This is the closest we've been to locating them in years. I will not lose them."

After Mary left the pharmacy, the three of them drove west for an hour. They finally stopped at Exit 128 when Percy noticed a sign for the annual street fair.

"Mommy, there's a street fair! Do you think they'll have elephant ears?"

"Elephant ears? You think you could eat all that fried dough right now?"

"Yes, I'm starving," Percy pleaded, pretending to faint with a smile on his face.

"Don't do that. You know I don't like that game," she scolded, beaming serious eyes to Percy through the rearview mirror. "Well, I need gas…so… I don't see why we can't get ourselves a little dinner. Maybe they'll have some games?"

"Yes, yes, yes," cheered Percy as the car pulled off the exit.

While it was true that Mary needed gas, she also knew this would be a great chance to lose the police. Even if anyone saw them enter the small town, they would never see them leave. The exit took them through some trees, to a small village of houses. They drove along the small, quaint streets; nearly every house had a white picket fence. There was no difference in structure from the shops to the homes. Doctors, mechanics, and lawyers worked seemingly out of their houses. It didn't take Mary long to find the small traffic jam of three cars as they approached the single closed street that contained the fair. As they drove by the many tents, Percy grew more excited, and his stomach began to audibly rumble.

"Oh wow, my hungry boy. You weren't kidding. Let's find somewhere to park, huh?" Mary found a parking spot on the street only a few blocks away from the fair. She grabbed a purse from the back seat of the car and placed Wilder inside it; his little nose poked out through a small break in the protective mesh. As they walked away from their car the streetlights began to turn on.

The fair was very small, only taking up two blocks. Much to Percy's delight, the fair had several stands offering various types of fried foods and one of them had elephant ears. The other booths were all dedicated to games, except for one dedicated to the local church, which was hosting the event.

"I am excited to see this," said Mary as she and Percy sat at a small picnic table set out on the street. She placed two large elephant ears in front of Percy, with a big smile. "So, you have your pizza sauce and cheese ear and your powdered sugar ear. Which are you going to eat first?"

"I'm going to eat them at the same time, or they'll get cold."

"You're going to eat all of that, right now?"

"Try me," Percy smiled as he began to rip off the edge of the ear with sauce, dipping it in the pool that had collected in the center.

"You know Mommy loves you very much—right, darling?"

"Of course. I love you too." Percy failed to look up from his food, continuing to rip off pieces and dip them in their respective condiment. Mary reached her hand out and grabbed hold of one of his. She used her other hand to grip his chin and move his eyes to meet hers.

"Okay, well I need you to know. I'm telling you this because I know you're such a smart and strong boy. I have a feeling Daddy might be close to findings us. I'm not sure why but I have a feeling. If anything happens, remember we have to fight to be together. Remember, I love you."

Percy nodded, not exactly sure how to reassure his mother that he loved and appreciated her. "One day, I'll be bigger and stronger, and no one will be able to take me away from you. Don't worry, Mom. I love you. Here, I love you so much, you can have some of my ear. I'd prefer if you ate the sugar one, but I love you enough to share either."

A tear began to build up in Mary's eye, but she chuckled to stop herself from beginning to cry. She let go of Percy's hand, took a small piece of his sugar ear, and began to eat with her son. After they finished eating, the pair made their way through the booths again, looking at the few carnival games that were available. Much to Mary's joy, Percy failed to toss a ball into a fishbowl, which kept her away from the burden of another pet on the road.

"Well, we should be hitting the road, Pea. I'd like to get a few hours driving before we find our next hotel." They made it back to their car but instead of driving back to the highway, Mary found her way to a small parking lot in a nearby park.

"Percy, how are you feeling? Are you feeling sick or strong? Mommy would like your help on something if you can." Percy put his hand over his stomach and felt for a moment. He then nodded his head in agreeance.

Mary was accustomed to and prepared for the threat of needing to flee. From her trunk she pulled out a small wrench and handed it to Percy. "Can you please use this to take off the bolts on the license plate?" She went farther into the trunk and removed a new set of license plates that were wrapped in an old t-shirt. Working with Percy, the two changed them. Then Mary removed a large roll of blue metallic colored tape. "Grab this end for Mommy and stick it to the side of the car, please." Mary then handed Percy the sticky end of the roll as she slowly backed away from him. The two then placed the tape along the side of the car, creating a long racing stripe. They did the same to the other side.

"You've always wanted to ride in a race car, right? Well now we have one. No way they'll be looking for a car with a racing stripe. Great job, Pea." The two then shared a small high-five. Now that the car was disguised, Mary and Percy made their way back through town and onto the highway. This time they would head south.

Mary's fear was realized an hour later, after they made the transition off the highway and returned to traveling on backroads. Mary wanted to avoid any tolls that might have cameras. As they traveled across the state they moved through small, quiet villages. In one such nondescript town, near its Main Street, they found themselves stuck in traffic. Late-night construction was forcing cars to funnel past a large service truck. To Mary's chagrin, two police officers were stationed at the intersection directing traffic. Though it was getting late and there were not many cars on the road, the traffic managed to pin Mary into going forward, unable to turn around.

Percy was napping in the back seat when she noticed they were stuck. Gentling shaking him awake, she spoke in whispered urgency. "Pea…Pea… darling, you need to wake up. Don't panic but your father's friends are here. I'm going to need you to hide, just like I taught you, okay?"

Percy's eyes opened, as if he had been waiting for this moment, and he nodded his head. He turned his back to his mom and found a small seam in the lining of the seat and peeled it back. As he pulled on the cushioning it revealed a small hole leading to the trunk. With tears in his eyes, he crawled into a secret compartment. Once his foot was clear of the hole, Mary leaned back and did her best to replace the flap.

As they got closer to the construction, Mary noticed that the police were not just directing traffic but stopping each car that passed. The traffic was more caused by them than the construction on the road. Her heart began to race as she prepared herself to lie. She searched the glove compartment and removed a large, black, plastic folder. Then she removed a set of papers, vehicle registrations— she searched and found the one that matched her falsified plates. The papers identified the ID she needed to locate to match her registration, *Ingrid Curry*.

She had to ease her car into the blocked intersection where she was flagged to stop by the two officers, two young men, one with a mustache. "Sorry to bother you, ma'am, but we're going to need your license and registration," said the clean-shaven one as he made his way to her driver's side window. "We're checking all out-of-town cars on account of a recent Amber Alert. You wouldn't have seen any suspicious women with a sick child, have you?"

"No, of course not. I would report something like that immediately. Children are the most precious things on earth, but what right do you have to pull me over like this? I am simply trying to get home."

"Sorry, ma'am, but it's a full alert. We've actually never had one this large before. Somebody in power must really have an investment in this. I can't give you full details but to be honest, your vehicle matches the make and model in question. So can we please see your documents?"

Mary pulled out the two documents that she had tucked away in her pocket and handed them to the officer. "My make and model? But surely it couldn't have had such a design? I'm sorry for my demeanor—I am just very tired," she muttered, faking a yawn.

"Well, ma'am, we honestly don't always take witness descriptions at their exact word. Witnesses often forget or create specifics in their mind. So, really, we are still checking everyone. I'll be back in just a moment." The clean-shaven officer returned to his car to begin to run her license.

The mustached officer circled her car, shining a light into the back seat as he scanned the perimeter. The officer's light fell on Wilder, which stirred him to action and he began to bark.

"My god, that dog is adorable!" he said out loud to himself, smiling. "What kind is it? Oh, you are just adorable," he continued to ask rhetorically, making his way to Mary's window. The two sat in silence as Mary ignored the cop's enthusiasm. It only took a minute before the clean-shaven cop made his way back.

"Well, everything seems to be in order," he proclaimed. "But your registration is technically a few months overdue. You should renew it before the grace period is over or you'll get a ticket next time."

"Thank you for the warning officer," Mary said, shifting her car back into drive.

"And it was so nice meeting you?" the mustached officer said, gesturing toward the dog.

"Wilder," Mary responded as she began to roll away.

"Wilder! What a cute name. Strange at first, I thought I saw at a distance someone else with you, but it must have been this adorable little guy."

"Must have been. Well, good night, officers. Tell them bye, Wilder."

As they slowly rolled away, the clean-shaven officer grabbed the rear door handle. Mary stopped and leaned her head out the still-open window.

"Sorry, hold up one moment. It was something you just said that struck my interest. Ma'am, are you sure there is no one else in the car with you?"

"No, of course not," she said as she stretched her neck and used her peripherals to look behind. She noticed that during this time, a number of cars had built up behind her.

"Well, it's just that you have a rather strangely sized coat sitting in your back seat."

"I don't know what else to say, but I don't think you should be commenting on my style choices, sir."

"Sorry, it's just strange that it looks far too small to be for an adult, such as yourself, but also far too big for your adorable little dog. I just find it interesting."

"I'm happy for your interest but you're holding up traffic for the poor people behind me."

"You're right, ma'am. Could you please pull over to the side? We need to continue our conversation." The two cops stepped back and directed Mary over to a set of parking spots. As she was forced into the trap, she moved her car at a snail's pace and scanned the horizon for an exit. Once she had pulled off to the side, right past the construction truck, she waited for the cops to make their way back to her. For the time being, they had moved the roadblock, allowing the traffic to flow forward, which also blocked her path. Instead of putting her car into park, she sat idle with her foot firmly pressed on the brakes.

As the cops approached her car, she sat in anticipation. The mustached officer was the first to reach the car. He placed his hand on the rear light as he continued to walk toward Mary's window. When he had reached the rear door, Mary let go of the brakes and slammed on the gas. Her tires squealed as she attempted to merge into the small bike lane. The passenger side of her car lifted up onto the curb. She managed to bypass a crowd of cars on her left but as she made her way through the first intersection, her car was blocked by another making a turn.

She slammed on her brakes but couldn't manage to stop in time. Mary skidded into the turning car, a larger trunk that bounced her car back. Mary was now surrounded on all sides. The driver of the other car had gotten out to check on her. Close behind, the cops followed on foot. They had notified their superiors to Mary's attempt to flee, and backup was on the way. The collision left Mary a bit woozy, and as she sat in the front seat of the car, she was both catching her breath and thinking.

"Percy," she yelled, unable to gauge her volume with the loud ringing in her ears. "They are going to take Mommy, but hopefully they won't find you. When you can, escape. I promise I'll find you." The officers then reached the car. Mary, still sitting in the driver's seat, waited for her punishment. She sat silent, the echoing in her ears drowning out the words of the officers. She thought about how she would get back to Percy—when it could happen.

"Ma'am, we have suspicion that you may have a kidnapped child with you. Where is he?"

She didn't respond and instead offered no resistance as she was taken out of the car and put into handcuffs. Mary sat on the cold floor as the cops searched her car. She saw as her massive collection of documents, tools, and clothes were revealed and scattered onto the ground. Amongst it all, the police failed to find Percy, who was still silently hiding in the compartment in the back. As Mary was taken away, the mustached officer took Wilder and left the clean-shaven officer with the car to continue to direct traffic.

Down at the station, Mary sat in a blank interrogation room, the mustached officer and a new detective across from her. In front of her sat a cup of water they had given her. In front of them sat a folder of Mary's past her ex-husband had given them.

"Where is Percy?" questioned the detective, his voice tired and pleading. They had been sitting here for more than an hour, Mary only repeating the same line.

"I want my lawyer."

"Please, we are just trying to help you. A lawyer is on the way but your child. This is time sensitive. To help Percy, we need to know where he is. We checked your car; he is nowhere to be found. We know he was with you at the fair. Where did he go? We have officers circling the town so we will find him. So please, you can make it easier on yourself if you help us. I'm sure your ex-husband would appreciate your cooperation."

"You don't want to help him. You're hurting him. You're taking him away from the only person he's ever loved. The only one who has ever truly loved him. I will never tell you anything. I haven't done anything so don't you dare bring Percy into this. I've done…nothing…wrong. I love my son and I WISH I knew where he was! You're helping my husband to take him away, just like he tried to take away our other son. You're monsters just like him. Took away my one last chance at being a mother. All I ever wanted, taken away from me. And I was a damn good mother. Wherever Percy may be he would never betray me. He's a smart boy and I'm sure he's doing great."

"We found your IDs, your tools, your false addresses, and documents. We have grounds to charge you on many different crimes. You can make it easier on yourself if you turn yourself in and help us find Percy. It's getting cold and we need to find him. From what we've heard he's very sick. Make this easier on yourself, Mary."

Inside the car, Percy was still hiding, and the chill of the night was beginning to take him over. Since he forgot his coat, his thin, fatless frame was exposed to the elements. Percy's body began to shiver, at first slowly but it grew increasingly more violent as his body fought to maintain heat. Outside he could hear the murmur of the officer directing traffic and the buzz of the streetlight nearby. The sounds outside were still too loud; he knew he wouldn't be able to escape. He could also hear the shuffling of things within the car; the sound of an officer just a few inches away, who was looking through Percy's coat and the back seat for some sign of him. The cop then turned on the light of the cabin and returned to the trunk. As the clumsy officer searched through the trunk, he accidentally hit his head on the light above the trunk bed, breaking it. Now against the darkened trunk, he could see a small faint light coming through a small hole in the back.

"Sir, I think I may have found something, a secret compartment in the car. I'll update you shortly." The officer stuck his finger into the small hole and he began to peel away at the fake wall made of corrugated cardboard and carpeting. As he peeled the layers back, the officer allowed more and more light from the streets to shine in. Eventually he revealed Percy.

Inside, Percy shivered, his eyes closed as he attempted to ignore time and keep himself warm. A gentle touch of the officer on his shoulder alerted him that he was found. He pushed away from the officer and tried to compact himself—to dig deeper into the trunk. When the officer reached his hand deeper to follow, Percy began to use the last of his strength to fight, throwing punches and kicks to the best of his ability. He hoped if he could push the officer back, he might have enough time to climb back through the hole in the back seat.

"He's here—I've found him. He's still in the car. He doesn't look good. He's pale and looks as if he's been vomiting. He's also freezing. We're gonna need an ambulance," the officer called in, using his radio. He held out his palm to Percy as a sign of good faith; he no longer attempted to get close enough to touch him. Then he remembered the coat. The officer ran to the back seat to grab it and quickly returned to the trunk with it. Percy wanted to escape but knew he was far too weak and slow to get fully out of the trunk before the officer could return.

"Please put this on," he pleaded as he offered the coat to Percy. "I'm only trying to help you. You look freezing." Percy saw that the officer blocked his exit, and he had no way to go but past him. Percy crawled over the many boxes still in the trunk. He slowly made his way toward the officer, who stood peacefully and offered a sleeve of the coat. Percy stepped out of the trunk and onto the ground. He then begrudgingly started to put his arm into the coat. Then suddenly, he turned away from the officer and attempted to dash away. Unfortunately, he slammed his hip into the bumper, which knocked him to the ground. The officer attempted to catch Percy and lunged for his arm. Percy began to scream and twist. He tried to break the officer's hold unsuccessfully. Instead, his cold, frail arm snapped. His body began to go into shock from the pain. Percy then blacked out.

The next thing he knew, Percy awoke in a hospital. His hair was long and wild in front of his face. Under his left arm lay a handmaid doll, a crocheted armadillo. His arms were filled with various needles leading to all matters of machine, fluid bags, and tubing. The most intrusive thing he felt was the oxygen mask that sat on his face. When he lifted his right arm to remove it, he realized it was in a cast. His hand was barely able to move. He instead used his other hand to remove the mask and then began to look around the room. Though he was still groggy, the sterile smell and blindingly bright lights alerted him to where he was. Someplace he had been many times before.

Percy began to sit up by sliding his body slightly back and accidentally triggered an alarm. His body was too tired and atrophied to panic at the sudden noise. A doctor, Autumn, who was standing in the hallway, made her way into the room.

"Percy, are yo-yo-you there? Are you okay?" she asked while holding up a penlight to his eyes to check for their responsiveness. "We were waiting for you to wak-ak-ake up. We weren't sure how long you'd be out. How are you feeling?"

Through a raspy and sore throat, Percy responded without thinking, "Where is my mother?" He was taken aback by how much deeper his voice sounded.

"She's not here. I don't think it's my place to tell you the specifics, but you'll be happy to know your father is here. I'm sure he can explain everything to you."

At the thought of his father, Percy began to hyperventilate. Autumn quickly responded by grabbing hold of Percy's good hand and rubbing his chest. "If it hurts too much, don't try to talk. It's possible your lungs have not caught up to the rest of your body and you might make yourself pass out if you get too excited. We're hon-on-onestly not sure—no one has ever seen a case this severe."

Percy began to calm down. He quickly learned to take long, deep breaths. He had to actively try to expand his lungs. Autumn continued, "What I can say is that you're in the hospital. Specifically, the wing to deal with disorders with Rejuverron. I hate to tell you, but you have been overdosing on it for a long time. I guess your mother's plan was to keep you young forever."

"What? Is that why my body hurts so much?" Now awake, Percy could feel his whole body again. This pain was new, though. His body no longer felt trapped. Now it felt over-stretched, like a rubber band pulled too tight.

"You've be-ee-ee-en asleep for a few weeks now. To be safe, we had to put you into a coma for your pain. Growing back bones isn't as easy as one would hope."

Still unable to grasp what had happened to him, Percy could only utter a staggered "What?"

"I know this is a lot, but extended exposure to Rejuverron reverted you in age, making you younger but sicker. If possible, we'd love to learn from your experience, if you remember anything about being a child. With Rejuverron, it doesn't hurt to go back in time a little, but for the severity of your case, we're amazed you have been able to stay alive this long. To be safe, we'll have to let you age forward to your appropriate self before we put you back on Rejuverron."

Autumn checked her watch, then continued. "Your father should be in any moment. I think he fell asleep in the waiting ro-oo-oom trying to make himself eat some food. He's been here every day since we recovered yo-o-oou."

As Percy's father entered the room, Percy's heart began to race. The man was short and stout, his face was gentle with wrinkles craved into a fair but leather like skin. His presence was gentle and sincere. The machine monitoring Percy's heart rate began beating faster and faster, eventually setting off another alarm. "No, please, calm down. I'm sorry. I don't know what your mother has told you or what you remember, but please know I am just happy to have found you."

"Percy, if you want I caaa-caaan have him leave until you're ready." With no response, except for the slowing of the heart rate monitor, Autumn began to walk out of the room, her voice low as she assumed she was being ignored. "I'll gi-gi-gi-ve you two a minute. You probably want some water for your throat. I be-be-bet it's so dry from the O_2."

Unable to look his father in the face, Percy looked at the ground as he asked, "How long was I dosed for?"

"Thirteen years. You've been on the run with your mother for almost thirteen years. After you came home from school and decided to move away, your mother drugged you. I tried to stop her but by the time I realized you were not simply on a trip with friends, she had fled with you. I've been trying to find you ever since. I promise I never gave up looking for you. I just worry what all that time has done to your brain. I hope you remember how amazing of a man you were; such a future was ahead of you. It'll be great to have you around again. Oh, and I have a surprise for you. Now I know he's not the original Wilder but look at this."

His father pulled out his phone to reveal photos of a blue pit bull with white spots and patterning. Percy's head began to hurt as his dreams returned to him. Dreams he realized now were really memories. "Poor old Wilder held out waiting for you as long as he could, but I'm sure his grandson will be ecstatic to meet you."

"Dad, this is all a bit fast. Can you start by just answering me one question?"

"I'm sorry. I'm just so excited to have you back, son. Sure, anything, of course."

"How old am I really?"

"You're thirty-five."

The Matriarch

The Matriarch

Sometimes Ligare's feeding appeared more like wandering than hunting. As he traveled across uninhabited land, his nose pulled him weakly in a direction. Like an itch, a tingle in his nose drew him—aching to find its source. Oftentimes he'd take small meals along this kind of journey, his nose still more interested in something elsewhere. These meals were filling but not satisfying. This time as he wandered through a valley, the color of the trees had changed in response to an increasingly cold world. Their beautiful colors—oranges, reds, yellows, and browns—were ornaments of hibernation. Their bodies, vessels of hope for the future. Each one believed they could wake up again one day and things would be better.

On occasion there were minds the demon would feed on that would draw this love of beauty in the world out of him, their minds providing intense inspiration that awakened a dormant part of his soul. The sudden rush of feelings, a painful flooding. As humans evolved, the demon itself evolved. As long as he fed, he was able to feel an ounce of empathy, inspiration, and excitement, though the energy slowly burned off. Sometimes the feelings were so intense, they brought tears to his eyes, but the emotions always ended when his hunger began to cloud his mind again. This time was the latter.

Ligare looked emaciated, his mask-like face sunken in. His eyes bulged from their sockets, and his cheeks were sharp enough to cut wood. His body matched his face, deflated. Though his form was distorted, his pace persisted steadily forward. He moved toward a particularly enticing scent. Imagination and inspiration clouded the air, like a small fog that he steadily followed. Like someone fasting before a big meal, this time Ligare did not eat, hoping to save room. As he grew hungrier, he also grew more feral. As he made his way through the woods, the predators and him avoided each other, the monster oblivious and the predators fearful.

The isolated region he traveled through were woods he might remember if only he had been able to pay attention. His journeys to it were far and few between, but sometimes this local jail would secrete an interesting smell. The trouble with jails was that their sole purpose was to break the human spirit, stifling the inspiration and passion the demon fed on. On rare occasions such as this, the call of an inmate could be sensed miles away. Many times, though, the smell would dissipate before he was able to arrive. The trail steadily thinned as the inmate died or their spark that was so alluring was lost. In some places, a steady spark could draw the demon to the same person over and over again. As of now, none of those places had ever been prisons.

This time the scent lasted for days, which allowed plenty of time for the demon to briskly make his way to the stone walls. He arrived at the prison during a bright evening, when the moon shined high in the sky. The sight of the full moon elicited a primal response and made the demon's mouth water; a single trail of saliva flowed down his defined bones and off his chin. He had been trained over the generations that the moon's presence increased the minds of man. Imaginations and dreams tasted far sweeter when filled with passion, whether joy or mania.

Normally, Ligare would approach with caution, worried about being spotted, but with his growing appetite, it failed to hesitate. A chain link fence stood as the first layer of defense, but the monster simply walked through its large, gaping holes. His body phased through the chains, their presence turning the monster's body to sand around it; Ligare's form otherwise remained sturdy and determined. Then as the monster approached the front doors of the jail, its form began to take on a less defined shape. The monster maintained its pace as it approached the door, but its legs began to shave away into sand. Like a slug leaving a trail of snot, behind it a trail of sand was left. The monster's body was now more like a colony of ants, each particle of sand working together and moving as one mass. The pile slipped its way easily through the front jail doors. When it entered the building, the sand began to flow along the lines of the walls; their motion was predatory and swift.

As he traveled through the jail, Ligare could feel the intense pull of slumber. All around him brains lay in various states of sleep. The aura of the few who rested peacefully was clouded by the sensory overload that was the fear, pain, and sorrow that surrounded him—those were the tastes that made dreams disgusting and unpalatable. His nose sifted through the fog of despair to find his meal. Like a dog raising his nose to the air, he smelled for the direction of the taste. Within these walls he could feel her passion. *Which inmate was she? What was this taste?* the demon thought, as the scent grew denser and stronger. As he grew closer, the smell began to overwhelm him. It became intoxicating to his starving form. The particles of sand of his body now vibrated with anticipation.

The prison wing he found himself in was of an older section, an ex-asylum, once run by the church. Its white walls led to high ceilings with large, flying blunderbusses—complementary to the attached cathedral. It was jointly agreed on by the wardens that the structure and history provided a good moral compass for the inmates. The large halls were once an activity area for rehabilitation, but as the jail grew overcrowded, the comforting wooden rooms were filled with concrete and separated into much smaller spaces. Only a few had access to windows, and those that did were mere slits. Now this wing only housed the most heinous of criminals, those who society had judged as irredeemable.

Ligare made his way past all of the unworthy minds, and finally saw his destination at the end of the long corridor. He could see her passion billowing out of the room like a thick, purple-hewed smoke. Ligare easily slid his way through the bars, every atom in his body shaking more and more violently as he drew closer. As he stood over her body, he breathed in the smoke that emanated from her mind. Without hesitation, he pulled out his lighter from his jacket pocket. He then flicked the wheel and released the green fire. It shot to the corners of the room, but even their bright light was lost in the purple cloud. The demon reached out and entered her mind. He began to feed.

As Mary rested, her mind raced with the memories of losing her sons. Winter was always her favorite as she celebrated Christmas and the holiday season with her children. This time of year made their absence from her life even harder, which drove the inspiration that drew the demon to her this evening. As she slept, she worried about all the terrible things that could be happening to her youngest, Percy. She worried about the trouble he could get himself into, and the trouble others would force on him. She worried about all of the terrible people in the world and all those temptations that could drive him away from being her perfect baby boy. The boy that she always knew he could be. The boy his father had taken away from her. A son who never came to visit.

As Ligare made his way through her dream, he slowly devoured everything around him. He felt her mind throbbing with one thought in particular. It was a deep pain buried behind the false joy that was her dream: When would she see Percy again? Her dream resembled the evening that they were having, a bright moon overlaying a snowy landscape. As the monster wandered through the woods of her mind, the trees melted away and became part of the cold fog that rolled in on the town below. Elsewhere in the dream, Mary was no longer staring through jail bars, but was once again in a car. This time both of her sons were in the back seat sleeping.

When her mind registered the beautiful sight of Percy's pure blond hair and Michael's dirty blond mop, her heart raced. She began to stir in her sleep and a pain shot through her body, a broken heart. She not only thrashed because she missed her sons but because they never got to meet. As her heart continued to break, the throbbing sent rays of misery throughout her mind. Each pulse momentarily tainted the demon's meal, making it taste thick and gritty. Among it, though, he tasted her love, pure, the flavor he yearned for. This is what he had been looking for, what made his long walk to the prison worthwhile. He made his way toward the source of the pulses while he continued to feed. Ligare's presence began to split Mary's mind into two, half of her soul with her memories of Percy and half with Michael.

In one world, Mary looked into her rearview mirror, focusing on the back seat of the car, not paying attention to where she was driving. Her eyes were fixated on Percy, who was fast asleep in the back. Michael was no longer present. Her heart rate calmed as she was back in her favorite time; she was able to take him from place to place under the peaceful and silent moon. The road they drove on was lightly covered in snow; her headlights bounced between the small flurry of snow that fell. Their icy bodies disintegrated as they hit the salted pavement.

Mary smiled as she noticed Percy stir. His thin arms instinctually reached out to her, calling to be held. She took her right arm off the steering wheel and reached back to grab her baby. Percy placed his head on her shoulder as she pulled his small frame across her body. His sickly structure, mostly bones in her arms, applied no pressure. Now that they sat at a red light, she let go of the steering wheel and adjusted her seat to create space for her son to hang over her like a small sloth. His weight was so low that she could not even feel him dangling off of her.

As she nuzzled his hair under her chin, Mary was happy, and a single tear dripped down her face onto his scalp. In response to the water, he nuzzled deeper into her body, once again fast asleep. Mary's pounding heart intensified the beacon sent to Ligare. She closed her eyes as she nuzzled back, her car now idled at a green light. Ligare was still making his way through the woods, walking toward the car. He could see her pulsating in the valley below.

In her other world, Mary was no longer in her car but now at the edge of a white porcelain tub. The walls of the bathroom that surrounded them were a pristine light green with gold and white trim, the interior expensive and lavish. The floor of the bathroom was covered in small ceramic tiles—repetitive black and white hexagons. Her arms were elbow deep in warm water, and her hands were on her son, Michael. He was simply sitting in the tub, splashing the water around him. He sat there giggling, as his hair bounced in unison with his arms. The water was filled with bubbles that bounced through the air and into Mary's face.

Michael was four years old. His dirty blond hair fell in a bowl cut just past his eyes. Mary took her hand and dipped it into the suds. Then she placed them onto Michael's head and used his long hair to form it into the shape of a small crown. She gave him a bubble beard to match. The bathroom door was open and through it they could hear music; a vinyl record crackled in the distance. Mary recognized the song, a holiday favorite, and began singing it to Michael. As she sang, he giggled; as she tickled, he splashed.

"Come they told me. Pa rum pum pum pum. A newborn king to see. Pa rum pum pum pum. Our finest gifts we bring. Pa rum pum pum pum. To lay before the king. Pa rum pum pum pum."

Back at the car, Mary sat holding Percy, peace once again flowing through her soul. The harmony was broken by the sound of a honking car, headlights now beaming behind her. The flashing lights on top of the car alerted her to the presence of the police. The officer signaled for her to pull over. He adjusted his position to be closer to the curb. He got out of her car and approached her driver's side window. As she looked up into the sky, Mary could see the moon beginning to dim, its light dissipating, growing duller by the moment.

Ligare and the cop both approached her car, one near and one far. Her heart began to race; she was now reliving the worst night of her life. Like last time, she hit the gas and attempted to peel out from the street—she was not going to fail again. Her back tires wavered on some snow that suddenly appeared on the road. Her tires spewed snow at the police officer and eventually caught enough traction to take off. The officer rushed to the police car and, though Mary was far away, she could clearly hear the sound of the police radio.

"Calling all units. We have her. Swarm." When the message ended, the static crackled and echoed throughout the car. Mary realized it was coming out of her own radio. She reached for the knob and attempted to lower it. The sound only grew louder; the voices became screams and the static deafening.

"CALLING ALL UNITS. WE HAVE HER. SWARM.

"We HAVE HER SWARM!

"WEhAVEhERsWARM!"

Though she was driving as fast as she could, the landscape around her failed to change. The horizon was dark, the light of the city was faint behind her, and trees blanketed her sides. She was now stranded in time, and the demon she could not see was still approaching. Her love for her son pulsated through the air. Suddenly, there were lights in front of her and police cars circling around them. The road below her disappeared, and her efforts to turn the wheel instead led them into an uncontrollable spin. Having lost control of the car, Mary grabbed hold of the motionless Percy, pulled him in tightly, and closed her eyes.

Her stomach turned as they spun, then a cold splash of water hit her face, causing her to open her eyes. She was then sitting at the edge of the bathtub, her hands washing Michael's hair. As she scrubbed his scalp, his giggles quickly gave way to screams as he began to cry. She then remembered how defiant of a child he could be; how he would so willfully ignore her directions. As he pulled away from her, her nails dug deep into his flesh. Michael began to thrash, and splash water, once again getting it into Mary's face and onto her clothes. "STOP!" she screamed, but instead he splashed more and more intensely. The water now began to sprinkle onto the floor. Each water droplet warped the floor, creating waves that flowed out to the bathroom door.

The waves rocked the room, and soon became too much. Mary was knocked to the ground. Once she had released him, Michael's arms became covered in faint black bruises, the shape of fingers. Mary fought to stand up but the continued shaking of the ground knocked her back several times. She finally settled on a crawl and wrestled her way over the wood waves toward her child. From behind her she could hear her husband's voice echoing from somewhere beyond the door. His faint "Is everything okay?" was lost in the sound of the violently warping wood.

Battered, Mary made her way back to the tub, gripped the edge, and pulled herself up. She could finally see Michael again. As she looked down at her child, the once faint bruises grew deeper and darker. The blackness spread like tendrils all over Michael's body. The sight caused Mary's heart to race faster and faster, the wooden distortion now fluctuating with her heartbeat. The bathroom door cracked, busted open, and blackness bled in. It swallowed the room.

Mary was back in the front seat of her car, Percy strapped to her chest. Her seatbelt was being removed by a cop. She held tightly onto her child as the cop pulled her from her car. She attempted to stabilize herself, but the icy road below made it impossible. As they fought for Percy, the two fell to the floor, Mary struggling to pull against the cop's endless strength. Her fingers started to slip off her child. Her grip remained tight on his right arm, but Percy's left arm had broken free and was solely in the officer's clutches.

It was then that Ligare came over the crest of the hill and was finally able to see Mary. That was when the demon's movement slowed for the first time. In the struggle, the blasts that emanated from Mary grew stronger and thicker. He was now forced to push through them. Though he was now within a hundred feet of her, she had still not noticed him; her eyes were transfixed on the officer. Around them all, the snow started to fall heavier, the flurries becoming a blizzard. The snow began to blind Mary; the crystals built on her face and covered her eyelashes. In the blinding white, the image of her son disappeared.

She continued to pull on Percy with all of her might; her rage grew as she struggled, pulling harder and harder. They had tried to take her baby, not once but twice. She lost Percy once before because she was not strong enough to keep them from taking him. At least in her dreams they would not take her son from her again. As the officer pulled on Percy, Mary yanked even harder. She reached out for his other hand and pulled but instead grabbed his head. She continued pulling him into her chest; she squeezed as hard as her muscles would let her. There was a sudden crack, and she could hear the sound of his bones snapping within her arms. The crack of his bones boomed throughout the valley, their vast space echoing like the smallest and most claustrophobic cave imaginable. The world around her began to shake, and the city around her fell apart. The once crisp lines on the horizon began to blur. As if she was trapped in an earthquake, her eyes could not focus on anything in particular and she could feel her hand still gripped to her child's leg. Their struggle made marks in the snow; a trail of bright red blood covered the landscape as the child began to bleed.

In the haze of the snow, the officer was gone and now only Ligare stood above her. Though he loomed over her, his body was frozen in time, his icy transparent claw reaching out to her. Afraid to move, her vision was pulled past Ligare and toward something parting the storm. The faint outline of a woman emerged, her clothing a gown made of beautiful black lace. The woman approached Mary, her face a blank slate and her long hair wildly swaying with the wind. The woman bent down, extended her arms, and gestured to the motionless child. Mary instead pulled his body toward herself with even more aggression. Especially in death, they would never take her son from her.

The woman stood up and Mary was once again in her bathroom. From beyond the now broken door, long, pale fingers crept in from the darkness; it then turned palm side up, expecting an offering.

"You won't take my baby!" she screamed at the figure. Michael thrashed within her arms. Her grip grew tighter as she watched the woman reemerge from the door; first came her hand, then a skinny skeletal body covered in dead skin. Mary turned toward Michael to find him struggling below the water's surface. Though Mary tried to pull him from the aquatic prison, her hands were trapped in the transparent cement. She watched as his lungs filled with water. His cries were at first muffled but as the bubbles reached the surface his screams released one by one. She looked down at him. The dark bruises now encompassed his body, his skin becoming black and necrotic. Mary's eyes glazed over as she looked at what she had done. Her ex-husband rushed into the bathroom; the mystery woman was nowhere to be found. Percy Sr. jumped onto

Mary and pulled Michael out of the water. Crying, he held onto their lifeless child as Mary stared into the distance.

Mary awoke in her cell. Her nightmare was finally over, and again she saw Ligare standing above her, his arm extended out, one long finger dangled above her face. The purple smoke that had once filled the room was now gone. She lay in her bed, paralyzed, and forced to stare up at him. All her fear lay in her balled-up fists. Their rigor mortis-like grip attached to her comforter, unable to let go. As she stared at the monster above, she could feel tears streaming down her face. As she tried to move her limbs, they only seemed to get tighter.

Ligare's rigid form began to shake, and suddenly his hand recoiled. Then his entire body was propelled and pushed back. The demon grabbed his head. A good meal could make him light-headed, but this was not that. Something was wrong. As he turned from her, he began to throw up. A black ooze dripped from his mouth, not so dissimilar to his own birth. Unable to stabilize himself, he instead fell to the ground. He was now forced to prop himself against the back wall of her cell. Sitting with his back against the wall, Ligare could see that Mary's face no longer matched that of the one in her dreams.

Eternal youth left the majority of people frozen in time. This allowed their minds to never have to adjust to change; their photographs were dateless. It had been a long time since he had fed on someone who had aged. Mary was on death row, and in these times, they no longer executed anyone. The action was considered inhumane, and society had deemed itself better than that. Instead, Mary was suffering their more sadistic punishment; they confiscated her Rejuverron. Those on death row were not killed but instead forced to die a natural, relatively short life. Nature was the cruelest executioner.

Mary had not been able to take her Rejuverron for the last thirty years. Her body had now changed. Like her, the other inmates on death row were the saddest and angriest of society's souls. Besides their meals, they were forgotten by society. The decay of aging devised its own unique punishment for each person. Each of their minds and bodies would slowly shut down in its own biological way. They had to watch their youth leave them, knowing no one else had to. They watched as their bodies changed, their faces drooped, and felt their mind slipping as they lost memories. The inmates whose minds went first were considered the lucky ones, living out the remainder of their isolation carefree. It was far better than the idea of being trapped in an unmovable body, your mind unable to do what it wanted, amplifying the isolation.

Every day Mary waited for a letter from her son that never came. The last time she saw him was the day he was taken from her. He was not at her trial, still in the hospital, a fact that was used against her. She knew he wasn't getting his medicine, and often wept for how he must have changed, not being taken care of. She was painted as a monster at her trial. Her son was kept from her. She was never able to explain. Her sentence could have been lighter, but she was merciless in her conviction that she had done nothing wrong.

Every day Mary watched as her life was drained by time, her increased aching and shaking hands were a stark reminder of its passage. Her hands were now thin and delicate, paper white. Her cell had only a single window, small and rectangular near the ceiling. It provided no sight and barely any sunlight. She often sat underneath it in the morning. She hoped to hear the sound of some animal or other sign of life outside. Those were her only friends. Sometimes she would tell these imaginary visitors about her sons. Her tone was joyful and sweet as she discussed their laughs and their smiles. All this time aging was time lost with them; her wrinkles were hours and minutes without Percy.

The once thin and inert black fluid on the floor began to bubble. Its surface behaved more molten than liquid, a thickening goo. Ligare and Mary both sat unmoving; the feeding had overwhelmed them both. The blob began to rise. Its particles spun like clay on a stand, and took the shape of a human. As it grew taller, it moved into Mary's peripherals and her eyes were drawn toward the mass. As she did her tears began to be torn from her face. They flowed off her cheeks and floated as if weightless—pulled by some magical force. The tears floated toward the blob, now tall and thin. The form slowly inflated and deflated, as if breathing.

Over a few moments it took its final shape, the figure becoming one she recognized. It was the woman in the black dress. The figure stared down at her, its face still a blank slate. Mary's tears continued to be pulled from her face, now a steady stream being dragged from somewhere deep inside her. The figure's face became obscured by the liquid, and under it a new face began to form. A mirror image of Mary, had she still been thirty younger, took shape. The only thing that distinguished the two were its eyes; it had yellow irises, which were bloodshot with purple veins. This new creature was the Matriarch. It stared down at Mary and could still feel the memories they shared. It remembered their son.

A force billowed from deep in its chest, like a long, slow sigh. The Matriarch searched over Mary one last time. It could no longer feel the rage and anxiety that had fueled its birth. With her departure, Mary lost that part of her soul. As the monster with her face walked away, Mary's mind was once again flooded with images of her son. She began to cry dry tears, but no longer about his freedom but instead for what she did to him. She finally saw the pain she had caused him, and her heart filled with feelings of guilt. Gone were the delusions of her perfect motherhood.

Ligare, who was still sitting pressed against the wall across from Mary's bed, finally felt strong enough to stand up, but unsure of what the Matriarch was, he hesitated. Though the room was tiny, she paid no attention to him, as if he were invisible. After walking away from Mary, she made her way to the back wall and stood below the tiny window. She raised her head to look at the tiny strip of moonlight that was entering the room. Out of her mouth drifted a light pink dust that danced in the air. It floated up and out the window. The trail was like a leash attached to her, showing her where to go. She pressed herself into the wall and reached her hands out in a large hug. For a moment she pressed against it, and then all of a sudden she fell through it. On the other side of the wall, the Matriarch stood in the air, steam rolling off her shoulders in the cool autumn breeze. Her pink leash floated ten feet in front of her. It was headed down, and it was growing by the moment. She followed it as if walking downstairs, taking a long route from the prison cell to the floor.

With her gone, Ligare began to rise. He looked down at Mary, who was now unconscious. Her mind was now too tarnished, too saturated in sadness to eat. No longer was there any of the passion he had come here for. Now that his stomach was full, his mind was active; this new creature had piqued his interest. Ligare returned to his sand form and moved up the floor and out the window at the top. His sand spread like ashes on the wind and floated haphazardly to the ground. As he reformed on the ground, the excess sand was pulled out of the air to join him. Luckily for him the Matriarch was not moving particularly fast, and he could still see her.

They had both landed in a grassy area surrounded on all sides by large concrete buildings. Through the center ran several paths lined in fences and barbed wire and illuminated by oppressive floodlights. As the Matriarch approached the fence, the lights grew brighter and brighter; a large hum echoed off the buildings. As she made her way toward the sheriff's station that guarded the entrance, the first security camera attempted to scan her. The electronics were unable to keep focus on the raging molecules that made up the Matriarch. Once she approached the building she made her way through each door in the building with ease, uninhibited by the thin metal.

From within the security desk, the guard saw the camera feed begin to flicker. He watched as her image flashed in and out, blinking chaotically. In the foreground, he could see a long, thin man following at a gentleman's distance behind, fiddling with his lighter. He watched as the image of the woman traveled from camera to camera, as the Matriarch made her way past each checkpoint and through the building. He realized she was getting closer to his station. He stared at the door across the hall from him and he placed his hand on his waist and unclicked his gun from its holster. His hands shook with nerves as he looked quickly back and forth between the door and the security feed. She was about to come through the door. Her black dress was the first to pass through the threshold of the metal door; it billowed forward from her momentum. The lights began to flicker and the security feed went dead. The guard stared at her, unable to believe what he was seeing. He froze as he tried to decide if his gun would be enough to engage her.

Only once she had made her way past him did he coax up enough courage to attempt to issue a command. He began to yell out to her. "Sta-sta-stop." His voice tremored with uncertainty. She turned toward him, but her eyes fixated through him, as if she was talking from a stage.

"Sssssssooooonnnn?" she exhaled, long and dry; her lungs were still new. The pink dust wrapped itself around her for the moment, no longer leading.

"Wha-wah what? I am going to have to ask you to—" He hesitated for a moment, thinking of what to say. "I'm going to have to ask you what you're doing here. Please come…please come with me." She continued to look past him, but the blood in her eyes became a darker purple, deep and violet. The electricity then flickered one last time and the computer began to short out—the screens became static, and smoke rose from behind them. Starting with the ones in front of her, each lightbulb started to shatter, traveling like a wave through each hallway in the building. Even those not on grew exceedingly bright before bursting.

On the front consul of the computer glowed a bright red button labeled *power failure*. The red emergency lights turned on as a sound began in the distance; the emergency sirens could be heard. The loud crash of the automatic sliding doors of the jail cells could be heard opening. The Matriarch then walked out of the building. The guard then ran out of his booth and picked up his walkie-talkie.

Taking a deep gulp, he said, "Help! We need backup! Call for medical support! We have an energy failure." The guard's voice was steady and monotone. He did not mention the woman or what he saw. He didn't think anyone would believe him because he did not even believe his own eyes. Once she exited the building, the pink cloud began to move again. It shifted side to side and wiggled in the air, acting like the nose of a dog.

"Where is my son?" the Matriarch said rhetorically. Her voice was now full and raspier than Mary's had been. The cloud thickened in response to her voice, glowing brighter pink. Their route was into the woods and toward the city. They ignored the roads, her guide leading her into the gloomy trees. Though Ligare had been following closely behind as sand, the woods were where he lost her. When they reached the forest's edge the Matriarch made her way through the woods that surrounded the prison, a distance of miles, within an instant.

On the other side she stepped out and could now see the city. Its distant lights brought more memories flooding back, images of her driving with Percy. She remembered the final time she saw her son, his body being ripped from their arms. Mary had been too weak to stop them. By the time she had reached civilization and her form was illuminated by the evening streetlights, the clock tower above the small city hall read 2:53 a.m. The three-story building presided over a slew of one-story shops. Currently the shops were all empty, but their holiday decorations and the small frost on their windows painted the picture of a lively town. The streets were empty except for the Matriarch, who followed the pink cloud down Main Street and back up a small hill to where a small hospital sat.

The majority of the hospital sat in darkness, the front entrance a dark collection of windows. Like the clock tower, it stood as the largest structure in town, three stories. The first floor consisted of specialty offices, the other two used for overnight patient care. The Matriarch walked toward the only light visible within the hospital, a dim bulb that came from the emergency room entrance. When she approached the building, the automatic doors failed to sense her presence. From within, a clerk hit a button and released them.

"Welcome to New Horizons Medical Center. What seems to be your emergency?" Her was tone cheerful and boisterous. Her voice, though gentle, was amplified by the quietness of the room. She was a nurse wearing light blue scrubs. There sat in the many multicolored chairs in the lobby only one other person, a gentleman in a cabbie hat and a large mustache who was working on a small computer in the corner of the room—his face was deeply focused on the screen in front of him.

The Matriarch gazed around the room, taking a deep and heavy breath as her cloud sniffed the air around them. As she scanned the room, she noticed several doors, all leading to other wings of the hospital. Her eyes began to shake as she contemplated the many choices. It was then that the aid noticed the piercing yellow of the Matriarch's eyes. She let out a concerned sigh as she got up from her chair.

"It's really late. Are you okay? Do you know where you are? You…appear…jaundiced…? Are you okay?" Her sweet voice was concerned. She now moved from behind the counter and toward the Matriarch.

"Michael…Percy," responded the Matriarch. The nurse could now hear the Matriarch's heart audibly pounding in her chest. Its sound was deep and long like a conga drum. Hearing the sound echo in the room, the nurse tilted her head, her once sweet concern quickly transforming into confusion and fear.

"Are you here to see a patient? Is that one person or two?" The nurse stopped her approach and started to slowly back away.

The Matriarch placed her hands on her chest and her breaths began to grow increasingly slow and deep. With each breath she bent farther backward, arching her back. As her head finally reached the ground behind her, her body emitted a large and deep crack, like the release of air from a thousand knuckles. The crack echoed through the hospital and then she heard it; she heard a cry. Through the northeast doorway, the Matriarch could hear a child. Her cloud pulled her toward it. She could hear her baby. "Percy," she whispered. Her body was still held in an arch. She let go of her chest; her arms dangled by her ears, and her fingers lay against the ground. Her back then snapped forward like a rubber band, its unnatural speed creating a mild wind in front of her.

The nurse now stood frozen, tears streaming down her face, as she uttered muffled cries. She no longer worried if the woman was okay; she knew she wasn't. The Matriarch stepped forward, her feet shuffling in the direction of the child's voice. She pushed through the automatic door. The hallway led her to a new part of the hospital, clean white walls with light brown paneling. In the other room, the now unfrozen nurse ran to her desk and picked up a walkie-talkie. The nurse attempted to speak but muffled cries were the only thing she could muster into its receiver. Whenever she tried to speak, her body began to hyperventilate but her throat opened slowly with each attempt. The man on his computer finally looked up and noticed the face of the nurse. He then raced to her side.

Through the walkie-talkie, they could hear the voice of the lone security guard on duty, currently making his rounds within the pediatric unit. Unfortunately for him, he was in the path of the Matriarch. "What's wrong?" he asked. "You seem to be cutting out. I'll be on my way in a moment." The gentleman picked up the phone and placed his arm on the shoulder of the nurse.

"I'm not sure," he answered. "She seems really upset—she can't speak. Is there another nurse or doctor on staff?!"

"The few doctors who are still here are with a patient," he informed them. "But I'll see what I can do."

The nurse, still panicked, finally grabbed the walkie-talkie from the man. "Ruuunnn," she squeaked. Her voice quivered and her breath was short. "There is some woman coming toward you and something is wrong with her. She's headed to the Pediatric wing."

"Wait, that's where my sister is," said the gentleman. His voice finally sounded concerned. He attempted to move toward the wing, but the nurse grabbed the sleeve of his shirt.

As the Matriarch walked down the hallway, her hand glided across the clean walls. Her movement was more joyful now; a skip in her step guided her down the hallway. Her face, in stark contrast to her body language, held a stern look. The Pediatric wing lay two hallways down. The one in between was a small four-room maternity ward. The Matriarch entered the maternity ward at the same time as the security guard who came from the other side. "Ma'am, are you okay? Are you the one who needs help?" shouted the guard from across the room. His flashlight was pointed toward her. The Matriarch walked toward him. Her youthful face was at first disarming to the officer. He turned off his flashlight and he walked toward her. He paid no attention to the muffled sounds that came out of the radio in his pocket.

In between the two was the one currently occupied room. A light shone out of the open door where the noises of frantic doctors and shuffling nurses poured into the hallway. The Matriarch walked toward the sound, all the while ignoring the guard who stood in front of her.

"Hey, hey, hey, don't go in there," he barked at her, now concerned. Ignoring him, she placed her hand on the doorway and glided into the room. Her motion barely stopped as she moved through the doorway toward the action. In the room sat a single patient, a young and vibrant blond woman who was in the process of giving birth. In the room were also four doctors and nurses still working by her side. The labor lasted twenty-five hours.

"Darling, we need you to push again," one of them said.

"I'm trying to," she cried, exasperated. She continued to push but her muscles were damaged, too weak now; nothing was happening. With another large push something went wrong.

"She's starting to bleed out," called a different nurse. A doctor ran to grab towels.

The machinery in the room began to go crazy as the patient's vitals flatlined, a long and ominous tone. They slide the bed back from the wall and laid down the woman. Her body grew grayer and colder with every moment. The Matriarch watched as the group worked to save both the mother and the baby.

"She's been in labor for over twenty-four hours. She's exhausted. I think the baby is not inverting. If we do nothing, she is going to die. We have one choice. We have to attempt an emergency c-section."

Half of the staff worked to bring her back to life, applying pressure to the bleed, pumping oxygen, and readying zap paddles. As soon as they were able to stabilize her, the doctors cut into her body. A doctor pulled the baby from her stomach and handed it to a nurse, who worked to clean it off. The infant made no noise, though. While a doctor worked to seal up the patient a nurse instantly noticed the baby had failed to yell. Though they were able to stabilize the mother, they were too late. As they cut the umbilical cord, a nurse lifted the stillborn in her arms.

The group now noticed the Matriarch in the room. The security guard silently stood behind her. "Ma'am. I'm sorry, I need you to leave," said the security guard as he reached out to her, his fingers gracing her shoulder. The Matriarch's neck bent straight back to meet the gaze of the security guard. He gasped and pulled his hand back. "Don't touch me," she whispered. Her quiet voice somehow shook the room. The LED lights above them burst.

The security guard backed off and covered his head as sparks fell from the ceiling. "Call the police—we need backup!" yelled the security guard into his radio. He hoped someone was still on the other end. The nurses and doctors in the room dropped to the ground, except for the one who still held the baby. The Matriarch walked toward that nurse and reached out arms for the lifeless child.

When she was within arm's reach she stopped. The pink dust pulled away from her, and back out into the hallway. She turned her head toward it as if she heard something no one else could. A faint cry in the distance caught her attention. Bending her neck back up, the Matriarch walked past the security guard and back out of the room. She made her way out of the maternity wing and into the pediatric unit.

Back in the bed, the mother awoke with shallow breath; a bit of color returned to her face. The nurses and doctors rushed to the now conscious woman's side. "Where is my baby?" asked the weak and weary woman.

As the Matriarch exited the room, the security guard raced to the door. He did not wait for backup and instead raced out of the room, closed the door behind him, and attempted to follow the Matriarch. He stepped through the automatic doors, and he could see the lights in this hallway were blown out as well. He lifted his flashlight and wandered down it. He scanned each doorway as he passed, looking for the Matriarch, unsure of what he would do when he found her. He finally remembered his service revolver. In his fifty years on the force, he'd never had to use it. He pulled it out and assumed an assault formation; he placed his flashlight over his weapon and marched forward.

He entered the pediatric unit and could once again hear the flatline of a machine coming from somewhere. He rushed down the hallway and tried his hardest to move as fast as possible while still making as little noise as possible. Though his body was still young, he was not as agile as he hoped he would be in an emergency. He made his way down the hallway and turned a corner. Somehow the lights in this section were still on and he turned off his flashlight. He carefully looked around the room and wondered if he had missed her. He followed the sound of the flatline by pressing his shoulder against one wall and moved slowly.

The hallway he made his way to was made entirely of windows on one side. The glass allowed for a clear view into the infant room. There sat a row of five beds. Only two were filled with newborn babies who slept peacefully. The hospital was so small that the one room also doubled as the neonatal office. A few small chambers for premature babies sat against the far wall. There he located the sound of the flatline, a premature baby, within the unit. The security guard noticed the Matriarch standing above the child. He sprinted into the room as she moved her hand across the surface of the sterilized chamber. "Son," she whispered, as she kissed the container. The pink cloud floated into the pen and surrounded both her and the baby.

The Matriarch then reached into the unit and picked up the child, somehow ignoring the plastic; a breathing tube was attached to his mouth when she placed his head onto her shoulder. She pressed her head into his and gently nuzzled him. The security guard raised his gun and his voice stammered. "Put-put down the baby! Ma'am! I mean it." The security guard picked up his radio once again. "Please, we need help. This woman has a child—I can't shoot her."

As she held onto the lifeless child, something started to happen. The pink cloud that surrounded them became thick and opaque, and from under it, a light began to glow. The dust began to storm, and the light grew brighter until it exploded. The force threw the guard back and onto the floor, which knocked him unconscious. The babies in the room seemed completely unharmed. The dust then floated back to the Matriarch, whose clothes had now changed. Instead of her black dress she was now wearing a long veil, a habit, and a loose robe-like dress. Her clothing shimmered iridescently in purple, yellow, and silver.

She then placed the baby back down into its plastic shell. She caressed the side of the baby's face, then gently yanked the breathing tube out of the cold, blue baby's mouth. With the release of the tube, the baby began to cry. She then picked him up again, except this time his body did not move. Instead, she placed onto her chest the spirit of the baby. Within her arms, the child calmed down and nuzzled into her. Within a moment the baby had fallen asleep on her shoulder. The Matriarch walked past the other children, who were still sleeping, and paid them no mind. She merely nuzzled the baby in her arms. While she did so, she hummed a sweet and joyful tune. The dust around her fluctuated with its beat. She started to walk her way back out of the hospital.

When she passed by the maternity ward, the doctors were still hiding within the room. Some were standing in the painful silence as they figured out how to escape, while others attempted to clean up the room to make it safer. In the middle of this action, the now awake woman was holding and mourning her child. The sound of the mother's cries traveled into the hallway, drawing the Matriarch. The staff unplugged everything from the walls and prepared to try to escape with the grieving mother. Before they could leave, though, the Matriarch came through the door and blocked their path. She gazed down at the woman who had laid in the bed and spotted the other lifeless child in her hands. The Matriarch's eyes began to twitch and shift between the baby she held in her arms and the baby within the bed.

"Stay away from her," commanded one of the doctors, suddenly brave. He drew the Matriarch's attention for only as long as it took for her to raise her arm to him, then he was suddenly shoved across the room by a blast of pink dust.

Then there was silence. Both mothers clutched their babies to their heads, their eyes locked. The Matriarch then stepped forward and approached the side of the woman's bed. The doctors and nurses stood back in fear. The Matriarch stood above the patient and stared with her yellow eyes, peering into her soul. Then she gave a small smile before she leaned down toward her. She brought her face within an inch of the woman's, who was frozen. Then she brought her head down farther and gently kissed the head of the cold, stillborn baby. The crowd looked on in shock as the Matriarch used one of her hands to adjust the blanket around it.

Lastly, the Matriarch turned her attention back to the mother, whose face was now filled with tears of every emotion, all of which streamed down her face. "You're going to be a great mother," the Matriarch whispered as she straightened up and returned attention to the child in her arms. As she made her way out of the room, life returned to the once stillborn child. Within its mother's arms it filled with color and its body grew warm. Its arms began to stir, and it let out a single cry that echoed through the silent hospital.

The Matriarch made her way out, back through the now empty emergency room. She stepped out into the crisp, morning air. "Let's go find Percy," she whispered as she adjusted the bonnet on the baby, who then turned into a blue mist and began to rotate around her. The entire time it gleefully giggled. The Matriarch and her new son set off back through the woods, in search of another lost child's soul, led by the pink mist. It was then that she became a reaper of souls for the lost, the unfortunate, and the unloved.

Markov's Home for Guidance Toward Joy

Markov's Home for Guidance Toward Joy

Buster let out a deep and exhausted sigh as he sat on a bench immediately beyond the walls of Markov's Home for Guidance Toward Joy. He had not been back to this place, his once home, in over fifty years. The top of his large nose was crooked, from a childhood accident, and it led down to a broad and flat snout. As he sat with his hands in his pockets, the beautiful fall weather was interrupted momentarily by a stiff breeze, which chafed his uncared-for and cracking skin. Though his complexion was dark, his hands and face were ashy—not that he could tell. He had not looked in a mirror in a long time. He leaned forward with this back and his shoulders hunched. His mangled position was not because he was cold or sick; no, instead he attempted to hide his face from any pedestrians who might be wandering in or out of the compound.

With long, deep breaths, he attempted to steady his heartbeat, but every time he contemplated standing up, his heart raced again, and he would become a tad lightheaded. Buster sat on the bench, overwhelmed by the decision he had only half made a few days ago. He wanted to do it, he fully supported it, but he didn't know if he could. His body was aching, his stomach was on fire, and his hands were shaky. He was only a few days sober, and the alcohol was still sweating from his pores.

Worse than his physical pain was having to readjust to the harshness of reality the sun, the sounds, the people, everything. He attempted to enjoy the beauty of the changing leaves that surrounded the hill the compound stood on, but the pain of his withdrawal created a fog in his vision. Every time he almost stood up, he was equally as sure he was going to go in as he was that he was going to go back to the bar. He was confident in his decision to return and to get clean, but as always, he was filled with self-doubt. He was hesitant that he had the courage to go through with it at all.

Buster did not remember much of his life during his time away from home, as he had quickly started drinking once he went beyond the large stone walls. He was frustrated with his ex, heartbroken over his mother, and afraid of himself. Alcoholism to his degree was no longer common in the world. With the ability to live forever, people drank more conservatively as they needed to make sure their livers and bodies stood the test of time. Most were concerned the tiniest mistake would cut their infinite life short, though it was amazing how one's body was able to recover due to the youth provided by Rejuverron. Try as he might to destroy himself, Buster was one of the lucky people whose body never seemed to fail him.

Buster's fifty-year drunken stupor was put to an end when he sat on the bus three days earlier. After closing the bar, he stammered down the street barely about to hold himself up. The sunrise was about to begin in a few hours, and he needed to get some sleep while he could. He made his way toward a back alley; he was exceptionally comfortable using trash and debris as a makeshift cot. He somehow failed to notice the buildup of clouds above him, and as the sudden storm raged, he instead searched for cover. His first instinct was to run under the light and awning of the nearby bus stop.

He sat there for a moment contemplating if he could fall asleep under the harsh LED lights and let out a hiccup. He used his left hand to tug at his beard, which was long, scraggly, and like his afro, matted. His other hand reached into his pocket and pulled out his favorite brand of cigarettes, Nails. Like his alcoholism, he was in the minority of people who still smoked real tobacco. It was just another way he was trying to expedite his death—too afraid of the unknown to actively hurt himself and too scared of aging to stop taking his medicine.

Buster smoked for the burning sensation and found that the warmth helped to satisfy his hunger for a moment. At this point, his diet of liquid dinners made eating most real food a painful chore. As he smoked, he stood up and paced, but after a few moments grew lightheaded. He then leaned against the support beams and slid his back down the pole. His single cigarette became a chain. He then, as he often did, lost time. He wasn't sure if he had been sleeping or not paying attention, but when the bus arrived, he was no longer alone. A number of other people had lined up under the awning and patiently waited.

He ignored the bus as it pulled up, content to wait out the rain there alone. He had nowhere to go. It was then a soft and friendly voice beckoned to him. A woman, Autumn, getting on the bus, called out to him, "We-eer-re you waiting for the bus?" Apart from bartenders, Buster had not been noticed by anyone else in a long time. If they had, he had been too drunk to tell. He looked up in disbelief, surprised at the question.

"Uhh, no thank you," he responded awkwardly. The woman continued to stand in the doorway of the bus; everyone else had already gotten on. Behind her, the bus driver gave her an exasperated face as he waited for her to clear the doorway. She looked Buster up and down and frowned at his tattered clothes. The wind began to pick up, and Buster now noticed he was cold and pulled his clothes tighter around him.

"I'm sorry to insinuate, si-i-ir, but you look a little co-oo-ld. Do you have somewhere to stay? If you take the bus, I know of a lov-vvv-vvvely shelter. I'm sure they could offer you a nice warm bed."

"A nice bed." Buster pondered as he slowly stood up. He had not slept anywhere *comfortable* in a long time. As he stared at the sky for a moment, he failed to see any sign that the weather was going to get any better. He stood up and pulled up his baggy hammy-down pants and adjusted his coat. To the glee of the driver, the two made their way onto the bus. Buster walked to the back of the bus, and Autumn used her phone to pay for his ticket.

After he sat down, Autumn made her way to the back as well and sat in the seats directly in front of him. Buster looked at the mostly filled bus and noticed the diversity of the patrons. Their outfits ranged from the mundane, suits and dresses, to the extreme, gothic lace and brightly colored kimonos. As soon as she sat down, Buster began his line of questioning.

"So where is this shelter you mentioned? Are they gonna care that I am drunk? If that's a deal-breaker… No bed is worth people yelling at me. If so, I just gotta find somewhere dry to rest."

"The shelter is a few blocks past New Amsterdam. If you get off there, you'll find it north. I can point it out when we get close. I think they aa-aaarr-e used to helping inebriated people." During the bus ride, he sobered up a bit and his shame began to rush back. Autumn was being so nice to him, and he felt like he didn't deserve it. He deserved nothing. Autumn then continued to talk to break the silence. "You look like you had a fun night. Did you do some celebrating?"

"No, this night sucked. You know…like all of them. I just like to drink, and I seem to be pretty good at it. It makes me less annoyed." Something about her smile and her eyes made Buster open up to her easily.

"Annoyed? Anything in particular?"

"Had a fight with someone. Yeeeaahh—a while ago. Forgot how long, but yeah, whatever. I'm a monster…but they also suck. Who cares, life is eternal and a hellhole." Autumn was startled by how quickly he had turned dark. Her attempt to keep him engaged swiftly became morose. She didn't know what to say but that didn't matter because Buster kept talking. "I don't wanna talk about it… It's just that…man…why, man? Why do people do such dumb things?"

"It's unfortunate you can't control people, even when you know what's good for them. Especially when you love them."

"I know, right! Exactly!" Buster grew excited and grabbed the headrest of the seat and shook it. He then got a little dizzy. "Sorry, where was I?"

"Annoyed."

"Oh yeah! Annoyed! My mom, she just wants to die. Or is going to die. Why does she want to die? It's stupid."

"Sometimes wanting to die is a cry for help. I'm not sure what you mean but my mother was sick. Mentally. Though I never got to know how or why. She seemed set on destroying herself."

"That's the worst part. Other people are supporting her. No one but me seems to think she's crazy. They all think she's doing the right thing. If it's a cry for help, no one understands her but me. She's a priest. Apparently, that makes her death sssoooooo honorable."

"Priests don't have to die. I don-onon't think," Autumn said, confused as to how the two correlated.

"She's not trying to die but she's not taking her Rejuverron. I guess that means she's going to die slowly, but to be honest, I don't even know if she's alive still. She could be dead now."

"You don't know?"

"No, I haven't seen her since she told me she was going to die. Going to stop taking her medicine. I didn't take it very well."

"I'm not sure where mine went. I wish I could have at least said goodbye. It just makes it so hard to not have been able to say anything. To not know."

"She was just my best friend. We grew up together. She was going to take herself away from me for nothing. For some god I don't even believe is real. The worst part is that she didn't have to do that. Why would God give us these amazing drugs, give us the gift of eternal life, and then we just throw it back in his face?" Buster then made air quotes as he said, "To be wiser, and closer to god."

"So you left her because she chose to age?"

"I wasn't going to leave. But as we argued and debated, I got angry in a way I never had before. As everyone sided with her, my frustration grew, and I felt trapped. It was like watching everyone smile while someone put down a dog. My dog. Eventually, I couldn't take it. I felt mad and that's when I realized I was a monster. I couldn't help it—I pushed her. The fear in her eyes scared me and I ran. So, I'm a monster and a coward."

"Good people do bad things. While my father was sick, he had bad days. He was sick, sad, frustrated, and alone. While we shouldn't forget to control ourselves, it doesn't seem right to live to punish yourself. I realized we weren't guaranteed anything, even time. Even though most of us have been given so much. We are so lucky to have it. I saw my father age and it was hard, but I wouldn't have given up our relatively short time together."

Buster sat in silence with her words rattling around in his brain. "What scares me most is that I don't know what her face looks like anymore. I never got to see her grow up."

"Perhaps it's not too late. Also, not to break up our talk, but the stop for the shelter is two blocks away. Would you like me to inform the driver?"

"Umm, no. No. I don't think I'm gonna go to the shelter."

"Oh, I promise they won't yell at you for being drunk. Besides, you seem pretty sober to me."

"No, it's not that. I think I need to do something." Buster rode the bus and wandered for three days, debating his decision to go back.

The bench where Buster sat now was one of many that surrounded the southern and eastern exits of the compound. The fields that encircled the massive Gothic bricks were filled with wild-growing flowers; their exits were only mowed once a year. The fields were now mostly dead; only the browns, greens, and yellows of faded grass remained. He watched the land and took in the beauty as the grasses swayed in the wind. It was the first time he appreciated anything other than his pain. The compound stood several miles outside of the city, and in the distance, Buster could see the ant-sized cars moving in and out of it.

After taking the bus as far as he could, Buster marched his way up the unkept trail to the compound. The dirt road was sparsely lined with the occasional tree, which he used for shade and rest. He sat embarrassed by his lack of physicality, and though there were often cars that traveled in and out of the compound, none seemed to be there during his two-day hike. He would not have had the courage to ask them for a ride anyway. Between the heat and the exercise, he had plenty of time to sober up before he reached the gate, but it was not enough. As the vodka and beer sweated out of his system, his body began to feel better, but his mental fortitude began to drop—did he really have the strength to go back?

Markov's had begun as a safe haven for those who wanted to leave the crowded cities in hope of finding peace in a world of eternal life and constant stimulation. It started as a charity that evolved into a religious organization; the compound stood as an independent entity acting more as its own country than its own town. The ever-increasing structure was made within the confines of an old feudal castle and abandoned serf housing. The once large drawbridge was replaced by a welcoming arc.

As he gazed up at the entrance, Buster's eye could focus only on the one lively and well-maintained part. A polished golden statue of Buddha jutted out from the bust; surrounding it were the five symbols of the faith, the five human needs that could bring one eternal happiness. While not directly worshiped, Markov felt the Buddha's teachings were most in line with their ultimate goal, to no longer cling unnecessarily to this world. This meant something different to everyone, but each behind the walls hoped to find contentment and support in life. They were taught that Rejuverron was a drug sent by God to give people the time they needed to fully understand and purify themselves. Reincarnation made the process much longer; now they could fight to understand their souls in one long lifetime. The Buddha within the image was not perfect or smooth as he is often depicted in other cultures. Instead, this face was made to look old, to have wrinkles to show him aging as God had intended.

Buster had arrived at the compound as a child and those values were drilled into his head from a young age. Their ideas lived rent-free in his mind and were part of why he felt so much shame. The cult took the ideas they found best from each religion they came across and combined them. They viewed each ideal as a puzzle piece from God, part of a more grandiose riddle for humans to figure out together. Ultimately, the cult was about community and love, in whatever form that might take, as each person's soul was different.

One of their guiding principles was that humans began as a single beast, an organism with four arms, four legs, two heads, one heart, and one back. Something sinister separated the two, weakening humans and forcing them to wander through life trying to find one another. One way to leave the world was to find your perfect mate, through the connection of twin souls. That could take forever, so for the vast majority of people connection to a community was the thing they craved and needed first.

Humans as a society always tend to band together. Contrary to Buddhism where the idea was to lose connection to the world, they attempted to properly become part of the power of the universe through the special connections only humans could create. The first pillar, shown on the plate as two entwined souls dancing around one another, was love and learning to care about someone else. Buster had that once, but when he ran from his mother, he ran from that as well. The second pillar, passion, shown as a lit lighter, was one that he never had a problem understanding until he left; it was a dual-edged sword as one's passion for life could overshadow its intended brevity. The third, a weird and infinitely looping triangle, was acceptance in every form; we must accept things in the world, accept who we are, accept love, accept others, and accept those things you cannot change. This was the one Buster had the hardest time with. The fourth, a triple spiral, was knowledge and understanding. We all have to pull together all of the theories of the world; to learn to understand the world, understand yourself, and understand those around you. The final symbol was that of empathy, a key connecting the other pillars and making them all possible. As he looked up at them, each pillar brought a flood of texts and lessons to his mind. They played like an audiobook of his personal failings, and his heart sank in a way only sobriety could allow—fifty years without any progress. With a heavy heart, he finally walked in.

Buster walked through the compound and searched for a familiar landmark to orient himself. Though the large stone arches he came through were the same, everything behind it had changed. When he was a child, the area was less cultivated, and since then the small farms had been replaced with much larger greenhouses to sustain the higher population. Past them, the small shacks were now replaced with small two-story homes. As he looked around the now unfamiliar area, he was met with a mix of emotions.

With every step, he failed to notice anyone he knew. He thought there were dozens of people on the small, partially paved streets. At first he was happy everything was different because when he looked around, he felt nothing—his childhood was gone. There was no one there to judge him for what he was and the mess he had become. Soon, though, his joyful apathy was replaced with anxiety; with every unfamiliar building and face, he thought deeper about how it used to be. Then with every corner he turned, he was worried he would see his mother, not sure what he would say. He was looking for her, but a large part hoped he wouldn't ever find her.

His mother, Terra, had him when she was still very young, and thus they had grown up together. They fled an abusive and unhappy home life, one that Buster was not able to truly remember. His memories all came from being her confidant. Terra couldn't help but talk to him about everything that had happened in her life, *their* life. His mind was filled with fogged memories passed down by her of how his father had treated her, treated *them*. He didn't remember anything about his father except for his face and the burden of the information he was told.

When Buster looked in the mirror, he saw that same face; it was his father's, just with his mother's eyes. He had let his hair and beard grow wildly because it helped to hide the bone structure of a monster. He knew deep down his feelings of jealousy, rage, paranoia, anger, and distrust were all traits of his father; what scared him the most was how, though he had not been raised by him, he could still feel his influence—in his mind and in his heart. His genes were those of a beast.

Buster drank more to hide his feelings, and these realizations. He hoped to bury them, but of course, he couldn't stop himself. No matter how much he told himself that his feelings were irrational, it didn't stop him from feeling them. The older he got, the harder he found it was to control his emotions and the harder it was to hide them. Then when they boiled up, everything became rage. Once he left these walls, he only knew how to settle his feelings with fists.

Even after years of bar fights he was not a great fighter; in fact, he lost nearly every single one. When he drunkenly swung on someone, often larger and stronger, he generally hit them first but was hit back harder. He would then receive blow after blow before eventually being thrown out. The pulsating pain he felt was just the beginning of the punishment he deserved—tor his thoughts, for abandoning his mother, and for abandoning Fern. Every day that he spent outside of these walls was a day he missed with them and another day that proved he didn't deserve them. The harder he fought it, the tighter the knot in his heart grew. He knew that he was only another minute or moment away from becoming what he was most afraid of. On his last day there, he *knew* he had to leave before his mother could watch her pride and joy turn into her second greatest mistake.

Eventually in the distance, Buster saw a large cathedral attached to many smaller buildings—the convent. If he was to find her, it would most likely be there. The closer he got to the building the slower he walked. He didn't know what gave him the courage to come home, and at this point it was running out, but his body was still moving forward against his will somehow. A congregation of people was scattered outside. Half of them wore normal contemporary clothes, and the others were donned in religious outfits. He remembered that even before his mother had joined the convent, she had always enjoyed their attire. Terra found beauty in the simplicity of the tan garb and black accents. She found that removing something as simple as picking out your clothing allowed you to focus more on what you felt and what you thought throughout the day. In retrospect, the outfit should have been the first sign his mother was growing too close to God.

With each habit he saw, he feared his mother would be under one. When Buster reached the front of the chapel, he found a set of nuns standing outside. Their faces were much older than his. He looked over their faces. and with every wrinkle he noticed he feared for his mother. They like her, joined the convent, and decided to forgo their drugs to grow older, wiser, and closer to God. He was not sure he would even recognize his mother now.

"Good morning and blessings to you," the two spoke in unison before returning to their conversation. At first Buster walked past, but then he slowly turned back toward them.

"Pardon me, but do you know where I can find Terra?"

"Are you talking about Sister Terra or perhaps one of the other residents?" The sound of *sister* echoed in his head, and his heart shook with frustration.

"Yes…*Sister* Terra," he said through a clenched jaw. "Do you know where I could find her? Is she running around somewhere?"

"Oh, no dear," one responded.

"She has been bedridden for quite some time now," continued the other. "Her soul is as strong as an ox, but her heart and body are closer to God than we can imagine."

"Is she okay?" Buster's voice now rattled with fear. *Was he too late?*

"Mostly, yes, but we aren't sure how much time she has. You can find her in her room, but be prepared to wait a moment. She is still providing sermons and outreach from her bedside and many people still visit her every day. She has a *miraculous* way with words. The Lord truly speaks through her."

"Would you like me to show you where she is?" Buster nodded and the nun waved goodbye to her friend, walked in front of him, and signaled him silently with her hand. The two then made their way into the church. The structure of the church was much more elaborate than the other buildings in town; this one was built with love and experience. Giant stained glass windows were connected by dark, varnished wood and large blunderbusses. The altar was simple green marble. It was surrounded by small golden Buddhas and large candles that were never lit.

The two made their way past the altar and into the back hallways that connected to a larger set of rooms, housing for the nuns. At the end of the hallway Buster could see there was construction occurring as they added onto the building. After making their way down a few corridors, he saw a large group of people standing in line. The nun then looked at her Casio watch and back at Buster. "You happened to have missed Sister Terra's early morning sermon, but the next should be later this evening. You can wait for that, or you can wait in this line.

Depending on how long everyone's prayers are, you should be able to see her." She smiled, then bowed and walked away. "Also, if you're interested, we have a wonderful barber, Fern, who might be able to help you with your beard. That is, of course, unless it's part of your process."

Buster stood against the wall with the others. Each person in front of him, like him, was in plain clothes, commoners. Unknown to him, each person in front of him also felt the same uncertainty in their hearts, but each for a different reason. As he stood against the wall, he refused to look anyone in the eye. At one point, a man in front of him turned toward him and tried to make conversation, but Buster failed to hear anything. He in fact instinctually turned toward the wall and began to absentmindedly stroke his beard. After several hours, he was finally the next person to enter her room. He was met by another nun who guarded her door, controlling traffic.

"Thank you for visiting Sister Terra. May God be with you. Now, please try to keep your questions under ten minutes if you can. There are still many behind you." Buster again nodded and made his way into the room silently. The space was simple like the rest of the community, not nearly as elaborate as the chapel he had walked through. In the back corner, by the window, was a large canopy bed elevated a few feet off the floor. Though the frame and sheets were old and beautiful, adorned with golden lace, beneath it was an adjustable hospital bed. On both sides Terra was surrounded by health monitors that steadily beat with her heart.

Buster walked through the otherwise silent room, and the floor creaked with his every step. Terra gazed out the window at the outside world and admired the slowly setting sun as she waited for her next visitor. Her complexion was much lighter than her sons, both naturally and because she was so sick. Her face was exactly how he had expected it, wrinkled and paper-like. She was nearly eighty-five and looked it with a graceful beauty.

"Welcome, my son," she said in a gentle and loving voice. Her voice cracked as she forced her words through a deep exhale. The word *son* drew a rage deep from within Buster. She wasn't looking at him, so there was no way she could possibly know it was him. He knew she was calling others son. He knew it was part of her religious speech, but either way he couldn't help but be jealous. He could not help but think about how close she might have gotten to others while he was gone. He worried he had been replaced and that she now had a surrogate son. Buster knew he shouldn't be upset, but he couldn't *not* worry, or *not* be hurt. He did what he always did and swallowed it. It wasn't until he was upon her that he finally responded.

"Hello, Mother." His voice was raw and wavering. He had thought about how to apologize for the last fifty years, but no other words came out of his mouth.

"Buster, is that you?" she asked as she squinted. After all these years, his voice was still burned into her soul. Even though her vision was fading, and Buster was covered in hair, she could still see her son through it all. "Is that really you?" Terra then beckoned him to come closer by putting out her weak and shaky hand. "Why are you standing so far, Bustie? Please come closer. I'd love to see you. My eyes are not what they once were."

He approached but stayed at an arm's length with his hands in his pockets. He then turned away from her and looked out the window. "What have you been up to? Please tell me about your life. I bet you've done wonderful things out in the real world. Thank you for coming back. Did you hear I was sick? Is that why you finally returned?"

"No, I didn't realize you were sick. Maybe I would have had the courage to come back earlier if I did." After talking on the bus, he hoped that by returning he could finally speak with his mother and retrieve some lost time. Now he knew he didn't have that time anymore. He had truly lost all those years. He had left because he was afraid of seeing his mother like this, but now it's all he had.

"Why did it take courage? You know you're always welcome here. Please come toward me." Buster finally walked close to his mother's still outstretched arm. Then she put her hands up to his face. "You're as beautiful as the day I last saw you. Perhaps a little dirty. Why are you hiding your beautiful face under all that fluff? You should get it cleaned up." Terra smiled.

"You know me. Lazy as always."

"Why did you leave anyway? I awoke and your stuff was gone. You didn't even leave a note. Was your life that terrible here?"

"It wasn't about my life. My life was great." Buster fought back tears. Even in his drunkenness he hadn't cried in a long time. "I was so angry about pushing you. Even with all your help, I still turned into everything you ever told me about my father. I didn't and still don't deserve to be in your presence."

"I don't remember you pushing me. I only recall the sadness in your eyes the night before you left. I knew you were mad at me, but I never thought you'd leave forever. Over the last few decades, I have resided in that fact. Then I thought I'd never see you again, but I'm so happy to have you back. How do you know about your father? I thought I shielded you from him. My mind must be slipping in my old age."

"You. You told me. You told me everything he ever did to you. Why we left. Why I couldn't speak to him anymore. I've had it all playing in my head. Lessons to avoid. What I couldn't do."

"I'm sorry…I put that on you. I didn't mean to… You were so young. You didn't need to know truly how vicious your father was. The specifics of what he did. I was young and I think I didn't know what else to do. I didn't have anyone else, and you were my best friend." Terra lowered her hand off her son's face. "You could never be like him. I'm sorry to make you think otherwise."

"You don't have to regret anything. You never did anything wrong. You tried to raise me right, but I became just like him anyway."

"What are you talking about? I never saw anything of him in you. You were always the best boy, even until the day you left."

"I was good because I hid everything inside. I never spoke of any of the rage or jealousy I felt deep inside. Then one day it exploded. Inside me I still feel his rage and his anger. His jealously. Even with everything you did, you couldn't stop it. I was raised by a saint, and I still turned into him."

"Who have you hurt? What did you do?"

"You. Fern. I abandoned you both in rage. I haven't hit anyone I love yet, but I feel it. I could get worse any day. Otherwise, I've started plenty of barfights."

"My poor sweet boy. Your expectations for yourself are so high. I'm sorry I made you feel like you had to be perfect. We all feel those things. None of us are faultless. Even I was furious at first after you left. We are human and we have emotions. Is that why you've been so far from me for so long? I'm sorry to have put so much pressure on you." Buster's eyes became flooded with tears, which were absorbed by his beard.

It was then the nun guarding the door made her way back into the room to signal his time was up. "Sister Rose, this beautiful man is my son, Buster. Could you please take him to our old home and perhaps set him up an appointment for a haircut, if he wishes? I can't believe my dream was correct. I dreamed only a week ago that God was standing above my bed, and I thought I saw you in his eyes."

Buster spent the next two weeks traveling between his childhood home and the side of his mother. As she rested, he mostly sat in silence. It would be an entire month before he would make his way to the barber shop located in Fern's home. That day, he waited until the line had died out, as he knew his hair would be a project. That and he was nervous.

As Buster entered the small, converted living room, he sat in a chair against the wall and waited for Fern to be finished. Her olive skin was complemented by light brown hair and her deep brown eyes. She finished cutting the hair of a small boy with bright red hair and smiled as she let him up. She had a strong jaw, large cheekbones, and a bright round face.

As Fern ushered toward Buster with one hand to sit down, he wondered if she recognized him. The way she smiled as he sat into the chair made him realize she did, and his body was flooded with guilt once again.

"I wondered when you'd pay me a visit. Your mother sent me a message to keep my chair warm for you." Fern began inspecting Buster's matted mane. As she poked at it with a comb, she searched for how much she could salvage and how much needed to be removed. "Unless you are attached to this, I think it's mostly gone. This is the worst I've ever seen your hair and you never were too tidy."

He was a passionate man and not intentionally a dirty one, but his mind often wandered when his feelings took flight. He often forgot to think about the specifics of taking care of himself, but he had always been lucky to have someone else to remind him of such things, to get him out of his world, and that had so often had been Fern. As Buster tried to think about what to say, he thought about how nice it was to be back in her care. It reminded him of their youth when they would sit on the couch together after a long day. As they watched TV and talked, or sat and listened to music, she would groom his beard, pop his pimples, and clean his skin. The act was calming for both of them; it was a satisfying but absentminded process.

In her company was the most comfortable he ever felt. As she sat, listening and not judging, it was the only time he felt he could truly express himself—to let out the feelings he hid from his mother. His mind just flew, and he would sit speaking in a stream of consciousness. The understanding and complementary parts of these two very different people came together in bliss. Fern always knew that with just a little support Buster could be a great man. She always enjoyed listening and he was always willing to talk. She could space out, leave her mind, and enjoy the sound of Buster's passion. She got to know him better than anyone during those private sessions.

As he sat in her barber chair, it was like they had returned to their youth, but he didn't know what to say. "Cut it all," was all he could muster at the moment. Fern then pulled out a large pair of scissors; their hilt showed they were antique, but the blades were new and shiny. She used them more like a saw, cutting as close to the scalp as she could. It left him with only an inch of an afro. She then proceeded to slowly machete her way through his beard, able to partially reveal the face below. Even against his relatively dark skin, Fern could see the bruises from his fights that ran across his face and head. Fern gently touched them to test his pain.

"You must be quite the pit fighter. Doesn't this hurt?" She proceeded to gently poke each new bruise she uncovered with one hand while using her other hand to continue trimming him.

"My whole body still hurts, to be honest. So not especially."

"So where have you been hiding? Are you done having your tantrum?" she jested.

"I am not sure, to be honest. Sorry. Kinda everywhere. Really nowhere. I was…" He then quieted again and dropped his head.

"I'm happy you're being honest." Buster was embarrassed by how much he was apologizing, but he felt he needed to do it. "Why was it so important to be out there if you don't remember? I know you were upset about your mother but look at her. You've lost all that time." Fern had always been able to be honest with him, a bluntness he appreciated. "You're lucky that I didn't become a nun," she then passed awkwardly. "Not that you need to have missed me." A sudden shyness came over her. She hated it, stiffened up, and went back to cutting his beard. She was nearly done with one side. "Usually, you do all the talking. Forgot how to speak out there?" The subtle jab at him warmed him up more than any loving comment she could have ever made.

Buster began to ramble as he once used to, freely telling Fern everything she had missed. How he ran away, that he drank, and how he lost time. How he was ashamed and worried. How he saw things changing and how he got scared of who he was. He couldn't help but get angrier and angrier. How he feared being his father. How he wished he hadn't lost that much time.

"You don't need to have lost that much time. Your mother is still here. You can be with her at the end. Something she always talked about and wished for. She made her choice and she's doing what she thinks is right. What she has always done. If you love her, you have to support her." As she put the finishing touches on his beard, Fern continued. "I've been here, and somehow even with age, nothing about her ever changed."

"I feel like somehow nothing has changed between us. I just can't remember how much time I've lost."

"It really was a long time ago. Remember when we thought about doing the Trial? We really were in love."

"We never even got married but we were pretty adamant."

"We always understood each other. We never needed more than that. Besides, the Trial was a bigger deal…kind of like this knot on the back of your head. I forgot what a lumpy skull you have."

It was a beautiful spring day when the couple decided to take their chance at the Trial. On the compound life was slow, people were working on themselves, and so time seemed to pass leisurely. Buster and Fern had picked up where they left off and their relationship easily flourished. There hadn't been a day that Buster had not thought of her, and though Fern tried her hand at dating others, no one ever gave her the comfort he did.

In the morning, before their ceremony started, they both kissed Terra on the forehead goodbye. She wished them the best of luck, as they paid respects. Terra remained bedridden, somehow still holding on with too much to do. Buster and Fern told her about their Trial and how they decided they wanted to do it before she passed. The couple decided it had been long enough and they hoped to succeed like they would have done so long ago; they did it for themselves, for her, and for God. A few months earlier, the two had stood above Terra's bed as she used some of her remaining strength to marry them. A private ceremony between the three of them.

As they prepped for their Trial, Buster began to put on an outfit that Fern had laid out for him the night before. Both of them were dressed in nice but comfortable clothing. Buster wore a light undershirt and a large but comfortable teal sweater. His face and head were nicely trimmed, with a full beard and hair nearly the same length. Fern's shirt was a complementary but distinct blue with breezy laced sleeves, and she wore loose, tan paper bag pants. They did not wear anything elaborate and did not bring anything of value—no jewelry, only comfort. The event was about the connection of two souls, not showmanship.

"Are you sure? Do you think we're ready?" Buster asked his wife as he held her hand and stared forward. "What if we fail?"

"If we fail, we fail. We'll still be together. It doesn't mean that we are not perfect for each other. We can always try again. It just means we need more time to figure each other out."

"But no one has tried in what? Twenty years?"

"Thirty-five. No one has passed in even longer, but if anyone does it will be us."

"I believe in you. Thank you for believing in us. You have completed me in a way I could never have imagined, and I am sure now that God will usher us together into a place in his kingdom of heaven." As he fought back a tear, he continued, "I was raised that the purpose of life is to find love, and to provide that love to others. I can't believe I almost lost it."

Their ceremony started in the chapel only a few hundred feet from Terra's room. It was too dangerous for them to move her, though she wanted deeply to be there. It was done without large fanfare and no additional witnesses. The Trial was about them, and only them. The clergy were there only to enable the process. Outside the locked chapel, many people gathered and attempted to listen to the process through the door. Most had never seen anyone try the Trial; few were so confident and brave.

The couple began at the altar, where they were met by a shaman who would act as their guide. The priest, in contrast to the plain outfits wore by the nuns, was decoratively clad in royal purple robes with gold accents. Around his neck hung several sets of tassels covered in beautiful gems of every color. He wore a wig of salt and pepper hair, made from donations of clergy who had passed. The couple came together and said a greeting to the sage. Buster and Fern were motioned to look toward one another, and as they held hands, the ceremony began.

"Do you two come to this ceremony with your full hearts exposed to one another? Do you two believe that God has chosen you as a symbol of his love and peace? Do you two truly believe you are one soul, one disconnected and ripped apart by rebirth?" They lovingly stared into each other's eyes and could feel the comfort and happiness they each provided for each other pulsating through their palms. It was love that even after fifty years apart bloomed uninhibited. They squeezed each other's hands and nodded their heads.

They turned to the shaman and in unison said their rehearsed passages. "We, two souls, lucky enough to have found one another, put ourselves before God for judgment. We who have searched our whole lives for our other half have found eternal bliss in each other's arms. We submit before you and offer to show you the strength of our love, the deepness of our connection, and the truth behind our understanding." They then turned toward one another and began to recite their individual vows. Fern was the first to go.

"I, Fern Davis, vow to love Buster within the kingdom of God for all eternity. That I am content and overjoyed in the best friend I have finally been able to join souls with. I missed you for fifty years, and I am so proud of the man you've become. In a constantly changing world, you've always been my respite and I see the true gentleness of your soul."

"I, Buster Davis, vow to love Fern within the kingdom of God for all eternity. I am thankful for the confidence and joy you have provided me. How you always had the strength to never settle for something that didn't make you happy, and lucky that you found that in me. You have always been the sweetest and most positive person I know. You have helped me to cleanse my soul in ways you could never imagine."

The shaman smiled and said a small prayer under his breath. Then Buster and Fern were led through the western wing. They continued to hold hands with only their two smallest fingers. They were led to another hallway beyond the church walls and into a new building. Beyond the wooden church walls, the new section they entered was merely cement. At the end of a plain hallway stood a large steel door and beyond it a small room. The door was decorated in the same fashion as the Buddha that guarded the compound; symbols of the five pillars were connected in carefully drawn networks.

Inside, the room itself was decorated in very little. Only a few candles sat atop concrete tables that were built into the walls. Under them were many old, built-up piles of melted wax from previous trials as if they were allowed to burn uncontrollably. The walls were a mix of concrete and brown bricks with many small vents located along them. Within the center of the room was an altar, a bed, made of metal beams ordained with two pillows. The two were led to their resting spot and told to lay down in whatever way was most comfortable. Buster lay down first with Fern on his chest, so she could hear his heart. The two confirmed they were comfortable, and the ceremony continued. "Please, close your eyes."

As the couple lay there, the shaman sang in a language they did not recognize; his words and voice echoed in the silent room like a lullaby. The music of a kalimba played from somewhere in the room; its dreamy tune calmed their hearts even further. The shaman then lit the cane he had been using to walk and from its top, thick smoke appeared. He lit kyphi, an ancient Egyptian recipe made of sixteen ingredients; except for within the walls of the compound the exact recipe was lost to time. The room was quickly filled with rich, deep, sweet notes of wine, honey, and honeycomb. As he walked around the room spreading the smoke, he blew out the candles that riddled the room. The smells then continued, replaced by delicate middle notes of ginger, juniper berries, and vetiver. It ended with notes of exotic woods, sandal, and precious aloes.

After the priest had blown out all the candles and the room was sufficiently filled with smoke, he walked out through the steel door. Now alone, the couple opened their eyes, which adjusted to the dark. They could see that light was shining through small holes in the ceiling. The tiny patterns depicted stars, galaxies, and the entire universe. The pattern swirled in on itself so that everything came together in the center, right above them. As they held onto each other and as the incense flowed over them, the two fell asleep.

In the distance, Ligare's head began to hurt. He had recently fed and so was aware something strange was happening. There was an extreme pain in his nose that traveled into his brain, as if he was being stabbed. What began as over-stimulation led to an uncontrollable bloodlust. He began to run through the crowds of the city and toward the hill of the compound. He remembered this smell; it was an offering. He moved at an unnaturally fast speed, one he was incapable of doing normally. The pull of his nose forced his body forward. His hair was long and wild, formed into several long spikes in all directions, but his outfit was a fine three-piece suit.

Upon reaching the compound Ligare made his way over the wall and went directly to the ceremony building. He broke into sand and crawled up the side, then he rained onto the couple through the holes in the ceiling. Within it, he came together and wandered around the room, breathing in the smell of the smoke that beckoned him. It was a different smell from the imagination of someone passionate. Instead, it was an offering for free rein in their minds, two connected minds at once. As he stood above the couple who were peacefully sleeping, he was excited and happy. Ligare did as he always did and lit his lighter. The flames spread throughout the room, ignited the smoke, and created a sparkling fog. The demon then entered their dreams.

Ligare dropped into their thoughts as if skydiving, and below him he could see both of their dreams spread open like two maps side by side. Where they connected was a wall of light, and Ligare had to choose where to start. *Whose dream would be the most delicious?* The couple each sat in their own worlds, no longer aware they were lying together. Instead, it was their job to figure out they were dreaming, and to find one another before Ligare did; only, they had no idea they were being hunted. For Buster, his dream started as a nightmare. For Fern, it was the loveliest of days.

In his dream, Buster sat at a bar, a glass of scotch on the rocks in his hands. His beard was again long and matted, his clothes damaged and dirty. His face was grizzled and red from his buzz. The dimly lit dive bar was only large enough for eight people, but there were at least sixteen screaming adults. Buster sat calmly, but his back was being pushed up against by the crowd of people. Though it was already overwhelming, the noise in the bar grew louder and louder each moment. Then the drink in his hand was suddenly finished and he asked for another special, a shot and a beer. He pointed at the sale sign on the board as behind him the music continued to build, and the bartender ignored him. Buster's ears began to hurt from the noise, and he covered them, while still trying to signal for a drink. The bartender finally responded, but as he spoke his voice melted into the sound of the music. His face was confused, and whatever he was saying was a question. Buster struggled to understand what was going on.

In her dream, Fern strolled through the woods outside the eastern exit of the compound, searching for truffles with her mother. It was an activity the two would do many times during the season. It was a beautiful and breezy spring day, and her yellow sundress shined in contrast to the shadows of the canopy. Her mother was a short woman with the same hair color and eyes; the two looked nearly indistinguishable and could have easily been mistaken for sisters. As they strolled through the forest, their pet hog marched steadily in front of them and sniffed the air. Fern remarked at the beautiful weather, and the two giggled at the adorableness that was the hog's wiggling butt in front of them. It was another wonderful day in her life.

Elsewhere, Buster still held his hands over his ears and continued to yell at the bartender. The sound of the bar grew overwhelming to the point that his ears began to bleed. As the small drops dripped through his fingers and down his arms, he had had enough. With one of his bloody fists, he slammed the table and screamed for someone to "turn down the FUCKING MUSIC." Even through his aggression, no one seemed to respond; the bartender now completely ignored him, and he could feel the pressure of the patrons pushing even harder on his back. He screamed once again, "SOMEONE TURN DOWN THE FUCKING MUSIC." With another slam of his fist on the table, the music stopped.

The room disappeared and Buster sat alone in the dark, still on his stool. It was now silent. From a balcony above shone a red spotlight. He lifted his arm to block his eyes. "Is he going to do anything?" questioned someone in the distance. Buster could now hear the sound of people coughing and the creak of chairs. The light changed to a fainter pink, and he felt the rumble of the ground below him beginning to move. He remained in place, but a beautiful marble bar slid in front of him, a beer set on it. "HURRY UP AND DRINK IT," heckled someone from the crowd.

Buster nervously lifted the beer from the table and held it up to his lips, which was met with gasps and cheers from the crowd. Someone began to clap, and the entirety of the crowd joined in. As the beat continued, wind blew his hair back as if it were a fan. Instinctually, he began to chug the beer, too fast for his mouth to keep up. As the foam and beer flowed down his beard, the crowd began to laugh and the spotlight changed to a light blue. The lights on the stage then turned on and he could see the crowd of people in front of him, a sea of nuns and priests. They continued to laugh, and their faces began to distort, becoming long, stretched, and demonic.

"Drink, drink, drink, drink!" they cheered. The bar continued to slide in front of him, now infinitely long, lined with beer stein after beer stein. Like a conveyor belt, they passed, and Buster was forced to chug. He was now double-fisting, and the beer was pouring all over his clothes and then saturated his beard. His stomach was getting full and beginning to hurt. He had never disliked drinking so much; perhaps it was the first time ever. The crowd's continued laughter rang in his ears, and that is when he finally realized he was in a dream.

He struggled against his body, his mind, and his instincts to control his dream. The pain seared in his muscles as he fought it and slammed his glasses down, shattering the beers below him. Unable to let go of the shards of glass in his hands, he used them to smash the beers coming down the bar. His hands were once again bleeding. "Stop!" he pleaded. Everyone in the crowd began to boo him and they started to throw things at him. First, they were fruits, then they were books, each hurled at his head. He used his arms to block the barrage. He looked through his hands and scanned the crowd. "Fern!" he screamed.

The laughter of the crowd died out and the lights turned off. Buster ducked behind the bar and worked to catch his breath. He then tried to pick glass shards out of his hands. After a few moments of pain, they were gone, but his hands continued to bleed. He stood up and looked over the bar into the darkness. He felt himself fall forward, and when he tried to stabilize himself, he found he was suddenly walking through a doorway. Buster caught his toe on the sill of the door and stumbled into an ugly and ransacked home. His childhood home, whose memory only existed in his subconscious.

Past the decrepit living room, he could see a light from the kitchen and the shadows of two people. He could hear a fight and screaming. Buster rushed into the next room, and before him was the youthful image of his mother he had hoped would stay forever. In combat with her was a behemoth of a man whom he knew was his father. Emanating from him, Buster could smell cigars and whiskey. Even though she was significantly smaller, Terra was hitting him back as hard as he hit her. Buster rushed toward them but as he got closer, he shrank in size, and by the time he had reached them he was a child. He grappled at his father's ankle but was unable to move him at all. Buster then began to climb him like a scaffolding.

His father ignored him as he continued to throw his fists at Terra. Once Buster reached the top of his father's head, he grabbed his face and dug his fingers into his eyes. The man screamed as blood poured down his face, but he didn't stop. With one arm he grabbed Buster and threw him against the wall, then he blindly raged at Terra, swinging faster and harder. Buster's back was in pain, as he attempted to get up from the floor. He had hurt his leg and now hobbled toward them, ready to fight again.

"This is not your fight," yelled Terra to Buster. "This is your mother's. No matter what he says this is not your fault. I know you love me too much to stop, but there is nothing you could do. You are just a child. You don't need to feel guilty." Terra continued to brawl with the father, and the two exchanged blow for blow.

"But I love you. I can help! I'm not weak! I promise," Buster cried.

"It's not a reflection of your strength to hurt others. Using your power to care for those you love and to help others is a strength not everyone has. It's a strength you have. I have made my choice. You need to make yours." With her words, a door opened behind Buster. His mind was flooded with many thoughts—thoughts about overpowering his father, about beating him to death with his fists. He was an adult; he could do it. Thoughts that he could do it all—help his mother, help himself, help everyone. Then finally he thought of Fern. He finally remembered they were in the trial. He finally remembered he had to get over himself; he had other things he needed to do.

As Buster stepped through the doorway, he glanced over his shoulder at his mother one last time. "I am sorry I wasn't there for you. I missed you every day."

"I know," she responded while still fighting. "We all need to learn and go our own path. I love you."

"I love you too." With that, Buster stepped out of the house. He was once again an adult and standing in an open field, only now clean-cut and shaved. In the distance he could see the barrier of light that separated his dream from Ferns, though he had no idea what it was. He just knew he had to go toward it. Also in the distance, he saw a finely dressed man walking through the grass. It was Ligare. As he passed, everything turned to black, and the plants wilted and died. The incense increased his power and made his ability to absorb everything around him stronger. The world was melting at a much faster rate than normal; soon both dreams would be gone. The closer he got to the wall, the darker the sky over Fern's dream became.

Under the canopy of the forest, Fern gleefully picked truffles with her mother and pig. Then overhead the faint blue coming through the trees quickly faded to black, as if the sun had set. Then rain slowly began to fall. It started light but quickly reached monsoon-sized droplets. As lightning shot across the sky, the pig became startled and darted deeper into the woods. "Hampton," screamed Fern as she chased after him. Behind her she heard footsteps that she assumed were her mother's, but she lost sight of her.

Though the pig was sprinting in front of her, she found she was steadily gaining on him. Along the forest floor, water was building up, and as he sprinted, he kicked mud into her face and onto her dress. Their path cut through dense foliage and thorn bushes, which lashed out at her. Her once beautiful dress was now dowsed, ripped, and dirty. Even so, she found she was still gaining on Hampton. When she was close enough, she dove forward and latched onto him with both arms. For a moment he kept running and dragged her along the forest floor, then he grew tired and fell with an exasperated *plop*. Fern fought to catch her breath while she pulled a rope out of her truffle bag and used it as a leash. She then took a survey of her surroundings. She failed to see her mother anywhere, and the woods around her were dark and foreboding. The rain continued to come down. Fern contemplated where to go next as she grew cold.

"Mother!" she yelled into the empty woods. She listened as her voice faded into nothingness, and no voice called back to her. Conversely, Hampton began to gleefully roll in the mud they stood in. Fern looked for a landmark she could recognize. There should be one; she had been in this forest a million times. Try as she might, there were nothing but repetitive trees, banks of mud, and darkness in front of her. She pulled on the leash and followed her best guess out of the forest.

As she wandered, the path in front of her changed into dry dirt. On either side, rain fell but stopped as it reached the perfect linear path. She pulled Hampton, who fought to veer off the path and play in the mud once again. When she turned back to reprimand him, she saw lights in the distance; green and purple swirled around one another and grew brighter as they made their way closer. Fern had never seen anything like it before. She yanked harder and harder on the pig but he now refused to move. She attempted to lift him, but he was too stubborn and heavy. She desperately pulled at the leash, but it snapped, which caused her to fall to the ground. Behind, Ligare was gaining on them.

"Hampton, you stubborn pig. We need to get out. We'll get pneumonia," she shouted. "Wait, can pigs get pneumonia?" she questioned herself. Then she remembered Buster. He might know some silly fact like that. Then she remembered she was in a dream and the Trial was going on. *He's not real*, she told herself, referring to Hampton. *I don't have to worry about him. Those lights are also not real. I just need to find Buster.*

Her thoughts echoed through the forest in a way her words didn't. Now that she denied him, the canopy of the forest opened up and above in the sky she saw a giant eye watching over her. Buster watched as in the distance the eye opened up in the sky, and noticed rain fell from it like tears. He rushed faster toward the wall of light.

Fern abandoned her pet and began to sprint away from the lights. Her shoes were quickly lost. As she ran, a wave of water began to follow her. Behind her the trees vanished and a void appeared. She feared if she stopped running, she would fall into it. She continued to sprint but appeared to be getting nowhere. Soon she fell, and the wall of water stopped with her. From the waves emerged the lights, and she saw beside her Hampton once again. Ligare scooped up the pig into his body of lights. Within his vessel, Fern watched as Hampton desiccated, at first struggling but then quickly going quiet. Fern covered her mouth to mask her scream. The eye above her started to cry harder, and then the tears turned to blood. The rain was thick and sticky.

Ligare began to morph. His body shifted from lights into a large and monstrous boar of a man. His face was wide, his eyes bulged, and he grew tusks out of his face. His body was bulky but muscular. First, he stood on two legs but immediately he dropped onto all fours and continued the chase. Fern pushed herself up from the ground and broke out into a sprint. As she moved, Ligare followed closely behind her. His spit struck her back, and she could feel the heat of his breath on her neck. That was when she finally saw the light of the forest exit.

Covered in blood, Fern finally made it out of the woods, and in front of her she saw a deep slope into the valley. Down the muddy, bloody hill, Fern saw Buster running toward her, his image blurred by the barrier of light between them. She looked at the forest and it disintegrated behind her…all that was left was the pig beast and the eye above that watched and cried. She began her sprint downhill while behind her Ligare led a wave of blood.

Buster approached the barrier and attempted to push through it, but he was shot back. Then Ligare raised his hand, and when Buster approached again his father blocked his path. Buster struggled to get through and began to fight with his father once again. For a moment, the two men stood across from one another, their arms intertwined, pushing each other back, like reflections in a mirror. Buster's instinct was to push, to fight and punch, but then he thought of his mother. His father continued to strike at him, but Buster gave up resisting and put down his arms.

Buster looked his father in the eyes. "I forgive you, not for you but for myself. I know the greatest pain I could ever inflict on you is you never seeing me or Mother again. To be left alone. She was strong enough to do it. To let go and leave. I can do the same." Buster stopped struggling and instead gracefully walked through his father and the wall that blocked him. The man fought to grab hold of him but instead phased through him. He had no strength over Buster anymore. Buster turned back once more. "You didn't raise me. Just because you gave me your DNA, just because you hit my mother does not mean you get to control who I am and how I act. You're the past."

On the other side, he saw Fern sprinting down the hill, followed by a wall of blood. He sprinted toward her as she came tumbling down the hill and she fell into his arms. As the two embraced, they were submerged in blood. The couple stood still in an ocean of blood, somehow still able to breathe. Ligare swam toward them through the blood as naturally as a fish in the ocean. He reached out for them but as their souls combined, they emitted a beacon of white light. As he touched it, Ligare was shot back; their love made them invincible. He tumbled not only away from them, but he was launched out of their dream and back into the real world.

He loomed over their sleeping bodies, which also gleamed with light and repelled him. Ligare stumbled drunkenly from the intense and delicious dream he had just gotten to taste. Their love made every moment decadent. He smiled and stumbled away as he rubbed drool away from his mouth. It was a delicious treat, worth every moment. They had succeeded and he was full. Satisfied, Ligare turned into sand and exited through the holes in the ceiling. Outside, the particles of sand spread through the sky like a cloud and floated back toward the city. The shaman noticed the phenomenon he had only read about before. In his lifetime he never had the honor of seeing it in person. "They did it," he shouted at the other priests. "Start the ending of the ceremony. They are truly blessed by God. Two perfect souls entwined."

After a few moments the couple awoke. They stared at one another and started to cry tears of joy. Unlike most of Ligare's other victims, they remembered everything. Every moment, and everything they learned in their dreams. They started to laugh and kiss each other. Fern nuzzled her face into Buster's chest while he played with her hair and kissed her forehead. They did it, together. Against all the distractions, against their own minds, they had remembered one another and fought to get back in sync.

"I can't believe you ran so fast. You're perfect. I love you so much," Buster said as he kissed Fern's forehead.

"I saw you and I knew I had to make it down that hill. Even if I wasn't chased by a monster. God, I knew we were perfect for each other."

"I'm sorry for every time I failed to trust you. Thank you so much for waiting for me. For bringing me closer to my mother. For understanding, I'm an idiot."

"I only wish we had those fifty years back, so much time lost together. But we have forever in the kingdom of heaven. All eternity. We'll make up for it. Sometimes we need time to grow before we're perfect for each other, and I understand that. I wouldn't trade it for anything."

"We did it. We salvaged our families from our dark pasts, broke the cycle. I finally see that we are not mere creations of our parents but have our own futures to make. I love you so much. You're perfect. We're perfect."

As the two lay there, there was a ticking noise that echoed from the bed they were lying on. The final part of the ritual was about to begin. This was everything they had worked toward, their eternal reward. Tears of joy rolled down both their faces as they pulled each other in tightly. Below them a fire began to rise, and the vents that lined the sides of the walls opened to expose more flames. Under them, flames began to scorch the pillows they laid on and eat away at their covers. They cuddled each other's physical bodies one last time as the room was engulfed. Thus began the last part of the ritual, their transfer to heaven. They had earned their place in God's kingdom.

A fan turned on under their bed and pushed smoke up the chimney and out the small holes in the ceiling. Intense white smoke billowed as their bodies were cremated. Everyone in town, even those who were not standing near the chapel, could see the white smoke rise from the building in the distance. All over town, those who knew saw the smoke, dropped to their knees, and began to pray. If only they could all be so lucky.

Fern's family hugged each other and jumped with joy. From her window, Terra could see the white smoke coming out and watched as it joined the clouds. She too shed tears of joy. She was so proud of her son; he was finally able to find love—perfect love and a perfect connection.

She was overjoyed she would soon be able to see them in heaven and make up for lost time. The three of them would be together in the afterlife. She had a little more work to do on this earth but soon she would join them and see the beautiful couple in the eyes of the Lord. It should be any day now and she couldn't have been happier.

With a Steady Grip

With a Steady Grip

With a steady grip Cordelia held a gun to the side of her head, an antique service pistol she had purchased from a new and used shop. Unlike most people in this day and age, Cordelia was old and looked like it. Though she lacked many of the wrinkles a seventy-year-old should have, her complexion was patchy and her hair was dry. Her small and cute nose held up the thick glasses she needed to see anything around her. Cordelia's pain stemmed from a rare rejection of Rejuverron; it only seemed to slow her aging. She also had an underlying condition of fibromyalgia. While her body was mostly kept young and fit, something had continued to ravage her nerves. Her body burned with every movement, and her pills were beginning to lose their potency. She still felt everything, and she didn't know if she could go on. She pressed the gun to her head and continued to fiddle with the trigger. She just needed to just stop hurting.

She slowly rocked back and forth; a pulsating pain shot through all of her nerves. The only reprieve was when it was superseded by her nauseousness. Cordelia held her tongue against the roof of her mouth and pressed into it as hard as she could—it was an attempt to distract from the pain and curb her will to throw up. Instead, her body shook as she gagged with all the strength her throat muscles could muster. Luckily, she was merely dry-heaving. The fire in her stomach radiated into her back; a searing pain continued in her kidneys. As much as her body ached, it was eclipsed by pain she felt in her head. Her left hand was lifted, pressed against her left eye. Another application of pressure. Another attempt to hold back some pain within her head. Her eyes felt swollen, like tears had filled up her skull and were not just pressing, but actively attempting to push out of her eyes. A warm pain swirled and burned behind them.

In contrast, Cordelia could feel the cool metal tip of the gun pressed into her head. The gun was room temperature but in all the panic her body was on fire. Her head felt so warm she joked to herself the gun might melt. As she continued to rock back and forth, tears streamed

down her face, which provided another small way to cool her body. As she made herself laugh,

her smile contorted into a mixture of anger and despair. She had been sitting in this position for

over two hours. The entire time, the same thing—her body was burning, and her body was

shaking. While her palm sat cleanly against the hilt of the gun, her finger migrated between the

switch and the safety. She sat unable to tell herself to do it, nor to stop.

Cordelia had been awake for several hours already, fully dressed and ready for her day,

though she knew immediately this morning that she would be in too much pain to venture into

society. If she was lucky enough, she would be able to make her telehealth appointment with

Autumn. She had had the strength to get dressed, but as she continued to get ready, *her day went

to shit.* She found herself fumbling with her pills, dropping her glass of water, and then her joints

ached as she attempted to clean up her mess. Her already painful day became even more

annoying. As her frustration reached a peak that set her body on fire, her pain skyrocketed, and

she found herself sitting on her bed wondering if she could live with it anymore. There she sat

and rocked back and forth for hours, thinking about what kept her alive, besides pure

stubbornness. She was one of the few people in the world who knew her life would end without

question. Unlike others, she had to live knowing it was a matter of when, not if. She also had to

live knowing that the relatively short time would be painful.

As Cordelia felt her condition worsen, her mental health deteriorated as well. She had

made a pact with herself years before that she would not make any major decisions when she

was in this state. *I'm crazy right now. I can't trust myself. This is a terrible decision. I should just

go back to sleep,* she would tell herself, but her episodes had grown more frequent, and each time

it became harder to fight her dark thoughts. Her pain was now more severe, and though once she could hide in her dreams from it, the act proved less effective. At the forefront of the mental assault against her was her guilt and regret. On days she was able to go outside, she ignored these feelings as she attempted to mask her pain to make it through her day. She couldn't fight it when she was cycling, alone and undistracted.

Like many sick people, Cordelia spent much of her time asleep, attempting to escape the pain. Each time she hoped to wake up a little better, with a little more energy. She had not been awake for more than a few minutes before her daily pain, soothed by her sleep, had returned. The peace she felt was ended abruptly by an inability to breathe. She awoke to see a familiar shadow standing above her, a weight upon her chest constricting her lungs. The rising sunlight burned her eyes as it peaked through the blinds, and those tears joined the ones of pain that had been slowly leaking out through the night. She was forced to hold them shut, to lessen the pain in her head. By the time she had opened them, the shadow she reached out for was already gone.

She sat there with a self-loathing feeling of guilt, one she understood was not rational, but it didn't make it any less real for the voice in her head. She felt her life fading a little each day and she faced not being able to be normal. All of her friends had continued to stay young; their lives never changed while hers became more complicated and incompatible with their bodies. Though she aged slowly, her body still failed in ways science had no way of fixing or truly understanding. She found her guilt and pain were intensified by her isolation; the three fed into each other in a violent cycle. Her pain intensified the more time she spent alone within her house, and in turn she had less energy to go out and see others. She first started to avoid people because she was too tired for physical activity and felt uncomfortable not being able to pretend to be nice. She felt herself become a different person, one she didn't like. She was her harshest critic as she thought of what she once was and what she had now become.

Once the sweetest person, Cordelia began to get annoyed at little things, and in those moments, she began to care a little less about others' feelings. She did not have time nor energy. It was as if she was being rewired by the issues in her body. She felt disappointed at not being able to control her course, as if her genetics were her fault. She had talked through this many times in therapy and knew it wasn't, but she couldn't help but feel shame still.

It was especially bad in the beginning, as doctors always accused her of faking her illness and not taking her medicine. Her condition was so rare that they refused to believe it existed and provided her with no consultation. For years there was nothing she could do as each test came back negative, and her symptoms left no marks except in her mind. She moved from specialist to specialist searching for someone to believe her. Each day that she went home without answers she had to tell herself, "You can't convince someone you're telling the truth if they are hellbent on not listening." She grew disgusted with the number of times it was claimed her symptoms were part of her "personal responsibility," and told in brief that she must have done something wrong or she wouldn't be disabled. There was no exercise, superfood, medicine, or prayer that would make her able-bodied—she had tried them all.

She was rightly focused on her own pain, but she felt that took away from who she really was—what she always liked about herself, selflessness. When she felt herself begin to change, she chose to try and continue to be who she was for the times she could. This meant less time with people as her patience went down. She'd rather treat everyone nicely than treat some badly based on something they couldn't control, *her pain*. Even when she cared deeply it seemed her mind wouldn't cooperate. She would ask someone a question and the pain would start. Then she would feel the urge to yell at them to shut up, to leave her alone—the exact opposite of what she wanted. She would scream in her head while she smiled at their face. Cordelia hated that voice in her head and found it even happened with the people she loved most. She decided she couldn't subject them to that.

The voice in her head was a reason neither of her two marriages had lasted, both when she was much younger. They were always full of joy in the beginning, full of romance, picnics, and museum trips. Then they became routine as they settled into their space and time. They would do the same things, and become comfortable, albeit boring. Cordelia loved it. As she aged, she changed, wanting more of that routine and love. Her pain also made the deepest connections to her, the ones where they could sit in silence together—appreciate a calm evening without any pain. For her lovers, though, with their youth and energy, it never seemed to be enough. Cordelia was always afraid to tell them what she needed and hid her worsening condition from them.

Four years into their marriage, her ex-husband had a change of passions. The once homebody accountant found the call of the wild and changed careers to something more exotic. As he planned his life around travel, hiking, and exploring wooded areas, he moved onto a life she did not fit into. Her aching had started, and she couldn't make the long wilderness treks he had planned for them. He offered to limit his travels but the voice in her head wouldn't let her take that away from him. She knew if he understood the pain she was in, he would limit himself and she couldn't live with that guilt. She broke his heart to set him free.

In Cordelia's second marriage, her wife had fallen out of love with her as Cordelia grew bitter and addicted to sleep, then she found another she loved more. In her guilt Cordelia thought about her ex-wife, June. She thought about the moment her marriage began to fail, when Cordelia's body had truly begun to decay. One evening after she awoke from a night terror, June viciously shook her awake from a screaming fit. Instead of fear, Cordelia awoke with a rage she had never felt before.

"CORDELIA! CORDELIA! WAKE UP," June screamed. Her hands were firmly on Cordelia's shoulders, her legs straddling her waist. Cordelia continued to scream for a moment longer before she abruptly sat up, pushing June off the bed in the process. Cordelia's hands had been pressed against June's face and chest.

"What the fuck are you doing?" yelled Cordelia. Her hands gripped the bed sheets at her side angrily before she lay down again, slamming her head back into the pillow.

"Me? What the fuck are you doing?" replied June, who rubbed her face and played with her lower lip, which she now realized was bleeding. "You have been screaming in your sleep for the last ten minutes. I was trying to wake you up."

"Ugh, stop over-exaggerating. I was having a great dream. Why did you wake me up?! You know I'm in a lot of pain tonight." She ignored June's explanation and her voice trembled with dismissive anger.

"You…were…screaming…for…ten…minutes," repeated June.

"Stop over-exaggerating," she snapped again. Cordelia rolled over to face across the bed and away from June, who was still on the ground.

"I am not over-exaggerating! Besides, you hit me! I was only trying to help. You used to cry in your sleep—now it sounds like you're being tortured," lisped June as her lip began to swell. June stood up and sat on the bed beside Cordelia. She posted with her right arm and reached for Cordelia's shoulder with her left.

"I told you. I'm tired. Please. Leave. Me. Alone. We'll talk about it later," barked Cordelia, her voice growing sadder and less harsh with every word.

"Are you serious, Cordelia? You can't talk to me for a few minutes?"

Cordelia no longer responded to June. She had already fallen back asleep. June begrudgingly took her pillows off the bed and made her way out to the living room. Cordelia thought back to that moment as the night she fell in love with sleep. That was the first time it felt better for her to be asleep than it did to be awake, to be alive. That's when he first appeared. Unfortunately for Cordelia, people who are sick are closer to the dream world than the average person. As she spent so much time, weak and sleeping, attempting to bypass her symptoms, he would come to her.

As Cordelia lay in her bed that night, Ligare made his way into her home. As June cried herself to sleep in the other room, the demon made his way into Cordelia's mind. Despite the anger she was developing when awake, Ligare found his way into the deepest recesses of her mind where the kind and eccentric woman Cordelia used to be still lived. It was the subconscious of a woman whose early understanding of love was tainted by unrealistic romantic comedies which never mentioned the loss of love that happened in a world of eternal life. She was not naive in her understanding of the world, nor naive in her dealings with others, but perfect love is just that, unrealistic. Like her pain, it lived somewhere deep inside her, somewhere ineffable.

When Ligare entered Cordelia's mind, his often-crinkled, disfigured, and mangled human shape began to straighten, to reform. Within the ghost-like pits of his face now sat two beautiful and large green eyes; his black hair fell gently across his face; his bangs barely covered them— streaks of green ran through them randomly like lightning bolts in a stormy sky. He stared up and admired the endless warmth that fell on him, then breathed deeply. As he did, his body began to

expand and his thin frame formed a barreled chest. His body was not muscular; instead, he was

mildly plump. His tattered and broken clothing blew away, like a flower losing its petals, and

below it was a loosely fitting black suit and a matching skinny tie.

He looked upon his surroundings and found himself in the middle of a forest of evergreen

trees. The large pines raised above him into the sky. In front of him, a blue cloudless horizon lay

behind the needles and pinecones. They blew with the gentle wind. Around him, the world didn't

disintegrate; nothing died nor was absorbed into him. Instead, he stood able to enjoy the dream,

in a way he could never before—without feeding. Then his attention was taken away from the

beautiful scenery by an intense smell. He lifted his tiny and pointed nose into the air as he had

done so many times before. Only this time he did not smell any inspiration or dreams; he smelled

only dessert. Something new and deep in his body craved the sweet taste of pie.

As Ligare made his way toward the smell, it seemed to drift through the entire forest. To

navigate he wandered between trees, smelling in each direction to find the source. It wasn't long

before he happened upon a small white cottage with a bright blue door; it was loosely surrounded

by a well-loved, makeshift, and unpainted fence. The front and side yards contained a smattering

of large flower gardens. The plots in front of the house grew wildly with beautiful bushes of

flowers he couldn't recognize. Each was a different color; the most startling contained

alternating neon blue and pink petals. Among them, rows of wildflowers and weeds formed a

secondary barrier between the house and the surrounding forest. The gardens to the right were

more polished and ordered with an unrealistically uniform set of rose vines growing among

pristinely placed mulch and perennials.

Among the bushes he could see a body bent over, Cordelia, pulling small weeds from among the roses. Clad in a short-sleeved floral pink sundress and wearing a long, dangling golden locket, Cordelia worked in her garden happily pulling weeds, her body uninhibited. Something happened when Ligare looked upon her; as his body had changed when he entered this world, now so did his mind.

Cordelia had a truly miraculous brain. She shaped Ligare more than any other mind he had entered. As she lifted her head from among the flowers, he saw the crest of her chin and he suddenly released a tension in his chest he had been holding for years. Now the flutter of energy that always sat within his nose shifted to his chest. The world of her subconscious awakened something within his light. The energy condensed and a heart formed within his chest. His pale face became flush, and life returned to his skin. An electricity in the air alerted Cordelia to the presence of the Demon. It beckoned to her, and her head rose to meet the eyes of the mysterious man across the fence. Ligare was overtaken by a feeling of nervousness; his lights fluttered like butterflies. He waved at her and the two stood in silence for a moment.

"I am…I am sorry to bother you," the demon muttered in a raspy but gentle voice. *I must be near her*, his mind screamed. Ligare attempted to throw his legs over the short fence in front of him but caught his toe on the top. His body stumbled over the fence, and he used his long arms to catch himself. Cordelia reached out with one hand in a gesture of solidarity. "I seem to be lost in the forest," he explained while he cleaned off a few barbs of bramble that had gotten stuck to his coat. Cordelia smiled. She appreciated the awkwardness of this man's demeanor—she found it charming.

"I do believe you are oh so very far from home, sir. I'll have you know that all of the forest you just stumbled through is mine. So, what are you doing *lost* on my land?" she scolded with a smile. Ligare couldn't tell if she was baring her teeth out of friendliness or aggression—it was both. His smile back was half-cocked.

"To be honest, I have no idea how I wound up here. I seem to have forgotten. The last thing I remember is the smell of your pie. I'm so sorry to intrude but I am desperately hungry. I guess that is why I seem to have also forgotten my manners." He gestured for a handshake. "I am…" He paused and searched his body for an answer. *Not sure what to call myself,* he thought for a moment. From somewhere in Cordelia's mind came *Atticus*. The name slipped out of his mouth softly and smoothly.

"Atticus, what a beautiful name." Her voice was delicate and soft, like her dream self was trying to be quiet, as not to wake her. She reached out to shake his hand and took off her matching pair of pink gardening gloves. Though she was asleep, Cordelia could feel heat radiating from Atticus. It warmed her whole body in a way a dream sun never really could. "Well, I suppose it wouldn't be right of me to throw a lost soul to the wolves. Perhaps we can find out where you came from with a full stomach. Would you like something to drink while we wait for that pie to cool?" Her voice had returned to normal, and she never broke eye contact.

Not only did Cordelia not feel any pain or tiredness in this world, but now her heart raced, and her stomach was filled with butterflies. Awoken in her mind was an attraction far greater than even the most romantic beginnings of either of her actual marriages. He was everything her mind ever wanted. Sleep now meant love. From then on, the nights when he visited her were when her dreams were most pleasant; it was when her life was perfect. Each time Ligare would visit, the two would pick up where they left off. They always met in the same small house surrounded by the same flowers. Sometimes the seasons would change, but still the flowers remained vibrant—happily, they sat under fallen leaves or blankets of snow. Each time he arrived, he brought the same calming heat and Cordelia's body was comforted.

Something inside Ligare wanted to amaze her. In her dream, a part of his soul was born that didn't exist anywhere else. In her dreams, everything seemed new; the joy of her garden, her smile, and her laugh were things that lit up his soul. His mind when he was with her grew, as did his love and passion for her. Unfortunately, those feelings only existed as long as he was in her dream. When she woke up, and he exited her mind, his hunger was satisfied, and his soul was left in her subconscious; his humanity quickly drained. It was the opposite of his other victims; she would remember all of their experiences, but he wouldn't. His body would wander off back into the city and Cordelia would be left alone, again in pain. She didn't know how to do it but during every nap and every night she tried to call him. She knew he would not always come but that's why she had to try often. Her life was so much better when she was comforted by her sheets. Their connection was something special.

Eventually, Ligare discovered he could control parts of her dreams; he could create objects out of the air and change the weather at will. Something inside her put a song in his heart and he discovered he had a knack for many instruments, and as she worked in the garden, he would play music for her. Each concert was unique and soothing as he always chose a different instrument. The melodies drifted through the woods and drew animals to watch. Deer lay at the forest edge in groups and birds sat in the trees silently. Then Ligare found he could make creatures of his own. The creations were fragments from other people's dreams or monsters he had run into in the real world. They danced and jumped for Cordelia's amusement. Neither of them knew what they were but she loved it.

On mornings and afternoons when she was feeling strong enough, Cordelia would use her energy to recreate some of Ligare's creations. She would sit in her favorite chair and throw up her legs , slowly. Then she would pick up her crocheting needles, a ritual that helped to calm her hands and mind. She loved to keep her hands busy creating cute and strange dolls for those less fortunate. Though she no longer had the energy or patience to deal with children, she continued to make them toys. When finished she took them to the hospital, where they kept her dolls in a side room for any child or person who needed comfort. They sat in a box and the children would choose whichever brought them the most comfort. In cases where children were too sick, the doctors would bring them one anyway. Never was there a moment where the children were not pleased to be cuddling her incredibly soft and unique creations. Unable to be as nice and polite as she once was, she felt the service of her dolls and the little money she spent on others were all she could do.

What she missed most was when she was a teacher. Cordelia never wanted children of her own, but she was great with them for limited bursts. Even in her youth, she felt something was wrong with her. Then when she grew sicker, she didn't believe she had the patience to have a child full-time. She could, however, be a teacher, and during the hours of 8 to 4 she could show her students the love and support they deserved. She did so for twenty years, working with students ranging from kindergarten to middle school. She retired after an incident, the morning after a dream with Atticus. Cordelia went to work, right before summer break, with an especially painful migraine. The children were being exceptionally rowdy, and their voices cut into her like a knife. When they wouldn't pipe down, she shouted at them with intense distress.

Being sick her whole life, Cordelia was accustomed to groggy, painful mornings. There was a certainty about her condition. The weakness and the pain she felt after her dreams with

Ligare were the worst. It was really when she felt her age. From each beautiful romp with the demon, she awoke the next day a little less. It was after the first session that her doctors found the most severe nerve damage. Each time he visited, her condition worsened. Then the fog of pain would lead to her forgetting to eat, then eventually she became nauseous and she *couldn't* eat. With her on-and-off schedule, she lost track of many of her friends. It changed how she valued the world, and her personality began to change as well. Instead of draining her imagination and her dream, he was draining her body and her soul. Cordelia was no longer living for anything in particular; except she wasn't going to let her disease take away anything else from her.

No one could live up to the perfection that was Atticus. No one was as understanding; the patience she needed, and grew to demand from someone, was hard to find in a world where she was aging but no one else was. It was a place where people could party for life, their sexual drives never dropped, and their energy was eternal. Only in her dreams was she able to keep up with the young and be her old self. Only in her dreams was she happy. Though she tried to date others after her second marriage, she grew angry at their shortcomings. There was a lack of warmth and peace she felt they should bring to her. She hoped that someone would live up to this fantasy but was left with nothing but guilt when they didn't.

Cordelia was finally out of her own head, and she realized how weak she actually was. She still sat with the gun against her skull, but the muscles in her hand began to fail on her. The gun was drifting down, and her wrist was in pain. Her adrenaline from the morning was wearing off, and her hot flashes were dying down. She realized she had never gotten to eat breakfast, and her stomach ached in hunger through the pain of her nauseousness. Her body was now filled with chills. Without removing any of her clothes, Cordelia dragged herself to the top of her bed and slid under the covers with her gun at her hip, concealed. She faced toward the sun, which was coming faintly through her blinds, and got comfortable. Her eyes then became heavier, and she began to fall asleep. Through the pain, she smiled as she did.

As soon as she had awoken that morning, Ligare had tasted her desperation in the wind. He couldn't remember why but he was already on his way toward Cordelia's home. Like the smell of the first pie, her mind always left a trail that he could use to find her at her most vulnerable. When they were apart, he could not remember who she was. It was only once he had entered her mind could he really be awakened and remember who they were, *together*. The familiar tastes brought back familiar smells, and a part of his soul was reborn.

This time, it was only an hour into Cordelia's nap that the demon found his way into her home. He moved seamlessly into her room. He stood above her body, ignited his lighter, and entered her mind. Ligare was once again in that familiar evergreen forest, though this time the trees were covered with snow—gently placed on each leaf, pristine and untouched. Atticus was reborn; he wore a brown winter coat, and a large furry hood hid his face from the elements. He then found his bearings, and his heart once again appeared. Cordelia's love for snow and beautiful cold evenings flowed through him. A tear fell down his face as the beauty of the forest overcame him.

Ligare adjusted his hood and wiped the now-frozen tear from his face with his glove. He turned his nose up to the air. Instead of food, he could smell the sweet aroma of pine smoke in the breeze. He followed the smell, which guided him to Cordelia's cottage, where a beautiful cloud of smoke billowed from the tiny chimney. He stepped over the fence, as he always did, and looked at the flowers. All were frozen in time, not dead but merely covered in snow. Atticus walked to the front door, familiar and happy, and gently knocked. Without waiting for a response, he excitedly turned the doorknob and entered.

Ligare slammed the door behind him; a sudden burst of wind resisted him. After a few steps, he placed his hand on the doorless frame to the living room and peeked into it, smiling. There Cordelia sat in her favorite comfy chair beside a fireplace, her head back and eyes closed as she rested her eyes. The look of her peaceful, happy smile made Ligare's heart flutter. He walked into the room and Cordelia could feel his warmth and her heart began to race. She smiled as she opened her eyes and saw he was standing above her.

"It must be cold out there. You look like a bear," she joked with a snide smile, motioning for him to pull down his hood. Ligare reached his head down to her and pulled back his hood to reveal his short beard. There were sprinkles of green throughout it. Cordelia ran her fingers through it and played with the small curls between her fingers. "I have been waiting for you, my love," she muttered to him as he leaned down and the two shared a passionate kiss. Ligare removed his heavy coat and the two sat in comfortable silence by the fire; it was the kind of comfort that came from a long life together.

Cordelia sat with her arms wrapped around him. She rested her head on his body and absorbed his warmth that trounced that of the fire they sat beside. Ligare sat in her lap, with his head placed on hers and his arm around her neck. Ligare took occasional sniffs of Cordelia's hair, which smelled like almonds and honey. The room was festively decorated for the season with flowers from the garden placed in vases throughout the room and flowers hanging from the walls. The curtains were woven from long vines to match. "I wish you could be here forever," Cordelia whispered.

"If only. You know we don't even have as much time as we used to," Ligare said softly, breathing in her scent again. The two were only able to sit in that comfort for about an hour. Then Cordelia suddenly woke up; she had to go to the bathroom. Her body panicked and now her pain was back, and though barely, she was awake. Ligare was kicked out of her dream and stood above Cordelia. Her poor eyes left him as a shadow in her vision. As he always did, Ligare rushed from the room. He had an innate fear, and felt he had to keep his monstrous form from her. He knew she wouldn't understand. So, he hid.

Though her body ached, and her mind was weak and confused, Cordelia still opened her eyes with a smile. Though her dream had been pleasant, Cordelia woke up drenched in sweat. She looked out the window and saw it was still daytime. She used all her strength to sit up and lean her body against the headboard. She posted herself up in an awkward motion and checked her phone. *What time is it?* she wondered. *How much did I miss?* Luckily, it was only 3 p.m.

Cordelia then remembered why she had woken up. She had to pee. She slid her way off her bed and started her slow shuffle out of the room. She had to stop every couple of steps to stretch her back and arms. As Cordelia slowly waddled throughout her home, Ligare stayed a step ahead of her. His heart filled with joy as he ran his fingers along her dusty shelves and tables, admiring her photos and the memories that filled the home. Something forced him to stay; he couldn't get himself to leave. He made his way upstairs to the rarely used second floor and attic—the space was filled with memories.

Ligare followed rays of joy and grief that fractalized up the stairs and down the hallways. In each room, he could see trails of memories floating in and out. Down the halls hung photos, and guestroom tabletops were decorated with knickknacks. All of them were tied to Cordelia's mind. To Ligare it was clear that one of her lovers had lived with her in this home and fragments of her life with the other were still sitting on tabletops. Within him, Atticus got to see all her deepest emotions and past. Over their many meetings, he felt like he knew her entire life, her entire soul, and he loved it all.

In the bathroom below, Cordelia looked at herself in the mirror and adjusted her glasses. She had forgotten what she was wearing, having prepped for the day. Her outfit was wrinkled, and she was overdressed for napping. Then she noticed the sweat salt that had dried on her skin. Cordelia finally felt filthy, and now she realized her body was again on fire after her workout. She needed to take a cold shower, so she de-robed except for her glasses and a shower cap. Cordelia opened the door on her walk-in shower and stepped in. She waved her hand over a console and the shower turned on. Then with the wave of her hand she adjusted the temperature and sat down on the shower seat. She leaned forward and let the water hit the top of her shower cap and run down her body. The cold water helped to soothe her bones.

Cordelia sat under the water until her stomach reminded her that she didn't get to eat earlier. Then she quickly washed herself and got out. Instead of heading to her room, she headed directly to the kitchen with only a towel. On the way she walked past an open window and could see the city lights begin to turn on as the sun set. Massive tree trunks rose above the buildings; their branches only began above the building tops. Long ago, someone had discovered how to selectively breed beautiful redwoods whose branches would not start for stories and stories, so as not to block anyone's view of the street or the surrounding landscapes. Her view was a beautiful image she rarely took the time to admire. As she gazed up at the leaves flowing in the wind, she had a shot of déjà vu from her dream; the forest in her mind was far more beautiful, though.

Cordelia made a small meal, something that would be considered a snack for most, and carried it to her bedroom. With one hand she held up her towel, and with the other she held a plate. The walk back was longer than she remembered, and as she came to the hallway she leaned against the wall for support. She slowly dragged her feet across the floor with her shoulder pressed against the wall. She entered her bedroom and dropped her towel, using her now free arm to support her to her bed. She made her way to the head of her bed and sat down with a heavy plop. In front of her sat her meal of homemade sourdough bread and hummus. Something light and easy on her stomach. After she finished, she then rolled back into bed, throwing her shower cap onto the ground. As the blood rushed to her stomach, she was tired again.

After a few minutes, Ligare could smell Cordelia fall asleep below; these days were full of many small meals, as she fell asleep over and over. He walked downstairs and made his way back to her dream. As Ligare made his way into Cordelia's small shack, the interior was different this time. The small makeshift wooden door opened into a grand ballroom decorated with all manners of red and gold. In the center of the dance hall stood Cordelia. She was swaying to the gentle sound of strings coming from the distance. Her dress matched the room, a beautiful red gown with long, dangling gold tassels like that of a flapper—as if from a prom she didn't attend. The echo of his footsteps caught her attention and she turned to meet him. The two smiled as they always did, walked toward each other, and embraced. Then they started to dance and there they swayed to the music.

At 6 p.m. the sound of Cordelia's phone began to ring, and half asleep, her body reached to answer it. In her dream, Ligare could see she was distracted, her body flashed in and out within his arms. The call was coming from her doctor, Autumn. Cordelia lifted the phone up to her face and Autumn's bright smile took up her entire screen. She was wearing royal purple scrubs and had matching purple eye shadow.

"Hi-i Cordelia, how are you?! I see you're sti-i-ill in bed! I'm sorry to bother you. You didn't call to cancel your appointment…but you're not here…so I ca-al-lled," Autumn said as excited as ever.

"Darling, you know I love your enthusiasm and our talks, but I also told you not to bother me, if I don't show up." Cordelia was on autopilot. "I'm very tired. Sorry, I should have canceled but I'll talk to you tomorrow."

"O-ooh, do we have an appointment tomorrow?" questioned Autumn as she looked down at her desk. Before Autumn was able to follow up, Cordelia turned off her phone.

Like she had been daydreaming, Cordelia returned to the grand ballroom and the warmth of Ligare. Something had changed, though, and his face was now a scowl. The scowl of someone she did not recognize. It was the face of someone whose soul he brought with him. "Who was that?" he barked. Spit flew onto Cordelia.

"I am not sure. I think…I think it was the doctor," explained Cordelia. "I think she was checking up on me." She could feel the anger in Ligare's eyes as heat scanning her body; it was now the hottest part of the room. As he pressed himself into her further, his face began to contort.

"I thought we were not going to the doctor anymore. It's worthless, isn't it?" he questioned angrily. Without giving her a chance to respond, he yelled, "ARE YOU TAKING THAT MEDICINE?!!!!"

"No!!! You know I stopped taking it—that's why I'm here with you," said Cordelia, nearly on the verge of tears. She pressed her head against his body, and the two slowly began to meld—his body became more and more ameboid. "You know it stops me from seeing you. You're the one who hasn't been back."

"Oh, so it's my fault. Why are you even talking to that doctor?" His tone became defensive and harsh. He took a few steps away from her, toward the large glass windows, and looked out below at the beautiful valley. As he did, the beautiful weather outside turned dark and snow began to fall. He started to talk to her in a way he never had before. "We know people who *say* they love you will betray you…abandon you in order to avoid having their optimism challenged. They will openly admit that they cannot bear to live in a world as ugly as the one you live in. It's so *inspiring* to just get through the day as you." While she awakened something in him, Cordelia was not the only soul within him. She could not stop the other people he had become—absorbed—since she last saw him. He feared he could lose her, and that awoke something that lived deep within him.

"Why would you say that?" she retorted. Cordelia held her hand up over her mouth. She could not believe what he had said. She was now completely aware she was in a dream. She thought about her body resting on the outside; how weak and sickly it was and how alone it was, for so long. "Wait, how do you know that?!" she exclaimed with tears of anger in her eyes. "How do you know what I'm like outside of here? Are you real?" She took a long pause. "Are you the shadow I see above my bed? Are you a…coward?"

"Just like you're better here, so am I." Ligare's tone became soft once again, in contrast to Cordelia's anger. He walked toward her and held out his hand, which she recoiled from. Even still he pressed forward and grabbed her forearm. Cordelia pulled back but his arm began to melt with hers. "I'm sorry, my dear," he whispered but it somehow echoed throughout the room.

"You didn't answer my question," she said as she bared her teeth and pulled her arm away from his. Against her will, he pulled her in for a hug. He wrapped around her and like a leech he surrounded her body. As the two stood wrapped, Ligare swayed in place to the music that was still playing. Within his arms, Cordelia felt her body temperature rising. She was not just warm; she was overheating. Her body in the real world began to sweat. What began for Cordelia as a dream of joy and bliss ended in a darkness she couldn't wake from. The experience for Ligare was perfect and serene. As he absorbed Cordelia's time, he absorbed her soul, and he loved every moment of it. Like the amoeba within her dream, in the real world, Ligare lay in bed with Cordelia. He cuddled her tightly, something he never did to anyone else.

Cordelia sat comatose in her dream, taking in the blackness of her surroundings. Her heart pounded in her chest so intensely that even in her dream she began to feel it. She was having a small heart attack. Into the darkness she called out to him, "Atticus!" Her voice was forced as she fought the pain in her chest. "Atticus! You're hurting me. I'm dying…you need to stop. It's so hot…can you not feel it? My *love*?"

The darkness around her began to fade and she was once again in the ballroom with Ligare wrapped around her. "I'm sorry. You know I love you. I was so excited. I knew that I was hurting you, but I couldn't stop myself. Please do accept my apologies. We only have so much time together." He began to run his hand through her hair.

"We could spend more time together in the real world. Why do you hide?" Cordelia attempted to say sweetly, but her underlying frustration bled through.

"I may be there but I only exist here. When I am out there, I lose who I am in the world." Ligare made eye contact with Cordelia and his deep green eyes flashed and swirled. Something came over her, and her tone became passive again.

"I'll be there. I can be there to remind you. We can lose ourselves together." As Ligare continued to run his hands through it, Cordelia's hair turned gray and brittle. It turned into her real hair.

"See you're old and frail out there. You need me, here. It is where we can be whatever we want. There is no one else for you. All those others were fools. You know that. That's why you always came back to me."

"I always come back and yet you still hide." Cordelia attempted to move away from Ligare, but he squeezed her tighter. She could feel in his arms he was growing angry again. "Are you really some monster? Is that what you won't say? Why else would you hide from me?"

"I don't know what I am, out there. All I know is what I am with you, *here*. This is where I feel alive. I appreciate everything in the world. Through your eyes, I see everything as beautiful. You lift me up and give me a heart. You fill me with joy." He held her elbows and stared into her eyes. In the real world, Cordelia's phone went off once again. The loud ring pierced through the ballroom. Half-awake, she could see it was another incoming call from Autumn, but her phone was far away, and she couldn't move. The buzzing of the phone and its vibration on the desk reverberated into Cordelia's dream. "I wish these people would just leave us alone. You don't need to be fixed." Ligare grew angrier still.

Cordelia stared deep into Ligare's eyes. "That's not true." She began to choke back tears. "The doctors say my brain scans are bad, getting worse. My brain has been deteriorating at a strange rate. They said if I had taken my medicine, I might have been able to slow it…but now my body has suffered permanent damage. My time is growing more limited by the day." Instinctually, she hugged him again.

"And you think that's my fault?" Ligare responded, defensively. His grip on her lessened. "They are lying to you. They can't figure out what is wrong with you, and they are blaming you, the victim."

"It is my fault. I chose not to take it. I knew what I was doing." Cordelia paused and looked up at Ligare again. "But…you did suggest it. Initially…I think." Everything was slowly coming into focus about his silent influence on her life. "I just figured it was my own suggestion. That you were just some parts of me. But if you're real, then you tricked me." Something heavy dawned on her and the light left her eyes a bit. "Did you know you were hurting me? You're real. So, you actually helped lead me here. Then you hide. Do you know why I'm getting sicker? Are *you* why my mind is decaying? Is it you?"

Ligare let go of one of Cordelia's hands and he began to walk away. His arm tugged on hers to join him by the window. "I thought if you were here with me, it would help you. I thought I could help both of us. It's true something about me hurts you. I can see it in the details of your mind. Or the lack thereof. It's been getting grainer and cloudier by the year."

"You knew? And still you come here?" Cordelia's voice was fluctuating between sadness and anger. "I thought you loved me. I thought you were the little part of me that loved myself. Jeez, I wish I never knew you were real. I was content with thinking I had become this shell of a person. That it was all my fault. You were my getaway and my excuse to myself. But really, I was tricked. I was so desperate. I never gave it a second thought. I figured your shadow above me was just a trick. I thought I was making my own decisions, but you were there guiding me. For so long." Cordelia tried to pull her hand away, but Ligare's grip was suddenly cold and stiff.

"I…" His voice was shaking. "…was trying to help. Then when I knew I couldn't…I just couldn't stop seeing you. When you're there, I will just come. I follow you. There is something special. Feelings that only exist when I'm with you." His grip tightened. "I can't let you go. I couldn't stop and you love me. You said it yourself." As Cordelia resisted him, Ligare pulled her once again into his arms, and he looked into the distance. As he squeezed her, Cordelia felt her breath shorten as her chest was constricted. "This couldn't be bad. I know that much, in my heart."

Cordelia could feel her body heating up as Ligare started to drain her faster and faster, growing out of control; he was so afraid of losing her. She spoke through bated breath. "My life is not only for your pleasure. If you loved me, you would see that. I wish you weren't real; I didn't expect anything from you then. Now, I am so disappointed. Even more than I had been. Not just you, but so much in myself."

"Let's forget about all that. You said it yourself. We have such little time left. You don't know. But wouldn't it be perfect and romantic for you to die here? In my arms." Ligare continued to tighten his grip. Cordelia was beginning to overheat. Her heart was starting to give out and she didn't know how much longer she could breathe.

"You don't deserve me. It's my fault that I didn't second-guess your ideas. But whatever you are, you knowingly made it worse—you knew you were killing me. If you loved me, you would help me, try to save me. Not drain me for your own pleasure." In response to her words, her anger, his form started to change again. This time his look became less human and more animalistic. The streaks in his hair formed ridged edges, and the spikes and frills of a lizard emerged; his skin turned to green and scaley. Cordelia could finally feel *his* soul, not just the reflection of hers.

Ligare once again pulled her toward him, and she was moved by magic. Cordelia joined hands with him, and they began dancing. As the two spun, she could no longer control her body in either world, and though he was no longer wrapped around her, her body was still overheating. In her panic she tried to wake up, but because her mind was trapped by Ligare, she could not fully leave. With one foot in each world Cordelia attempted to jostle, but her body was paralyzed—half asleep. In the real world she could see Ligare, lying on her, clinging to her body. His body was phasing in and out as her consciousness did. Within her dream he screamed at her to keep dancing, to "stay with him." As he grew angrier his control over her fell. In the real world, Cordelia tried to move her body, and for the most part it too was under his control.

Then, finally, she regained some movement in her hand. In the tiniest tip of her finger. As she rubbed it onto the blanket below her, she stoked sensation back into her hand. Her body responded to the soft fabric even though she couldn't wake up. With a mind of its own, her hand searched the bed for the gun she had left there earlier. She hoped to feel the wood of its handle. With desperation she searched, as her mind spun in her dream. There was no longer any music, only his breathing.

With a sudden burst of freedom, Cordelia lifted her chest and pushed against Ligare's motionless body. She could only manage a single thrust but felt no weight from him on her. As if he only existed as tension *in* her chest. As she pushed against him, she phased through him. Meanwhile, her hand continued to search and she struggled to bend her waist the tiniest bit to the side. She looked at the monster above her, and he began to change, to flow over her and encompass her with his body. Again, he melted over her.

Cordelia struggled beneath her covers, but with her pinky she was finally able to feel the pistol. She slowly rubbed her finger against it, trying to get enough friction to slide it little by little. She just didn't have that much energy left. With patience and diligence, she worked it up, then put it into her palm. Then she began the task of moving her arm. She only needed the smallest amount of wrist movement to be able to position it at him. With every inch of her he covered, her heart felt weaker and weaker. "Atticus," she pleaded in frustration. "You're killing me. Don't you want more time together?" He was silent, absentmindedly feeding. He was lost in his own emotions. "Perfect…then. You're dead to me."

Cordelia pulled the trigger, and the bang of its antique round filled the room. In her dreams, the spinning began to stop. Ligare released her but she continued to spin on her own. Only slower and slower. His face became unstable, shifting between lizard and man. The emotion across his face was that of fear. His eyes trembled. He was terrified. "What?! What is happening?" he screamed. Cordelia began to be pulled away from him. She was waking up. "Come back! No!" he shouted. Ligare was pushed out of her mind and now only lay in the bed. He kneeled and turned toward Cordelia, who was covered in blood. She stared up at him with disdainful eyes and flashed a small smile as blood dripped from her mouth.

The round from the gun had gone straight through Ligare; his form offered the bullet no resistance. Instead, it traveled upward and accidentally into Cordelia. She had shot herself in the jaw; the bullet continued out the side of her face. Its final resting spot was in the headboard behind her. Cordelia could feel her body start to warm again, in a much different way, as she went into shock. With that false feeling she began to shiver. She could feel that her heart was slowing, even though Ligare had stopped feeding.

Cordelia smiled at him. "You scaly son of a bitch. You never deserved any of my time. I don't know who I would have become without you, but I deserved the right to know. You let me feel alone so I would play pretend with you. You're a pathetic parasite. You're just lucky I was too sick to see it before. I'm not sad. I've lived a long and frustrating but satisfying life. I hope you have to live forever seeing my face."

As Cordelia's mind began to fade so did the humanity in Ligare. With every passing moment he spent not in her mind, her soul drained, and he became more monstrous; each moment a piece of Atticus died and was forgotten. With his last remaining feelings, he knew nothing but fear, sadness, and desperation. He desperately rubbed his hands over her wound, attempting to put back together the puzzle, without all the pieces. Cordelia wanted to beat away his disgusting hands but was too weak to move. He pressed his palms against her and tried to stop the blood but there was nothing he could do. "This was your fault. You did this to us both, because you were afraid." Cordelia smiled and chuckled sadistically as she passed away. She may have hit herself, but she killed a part of him.

There, Ligare's heart broke. As he watched the light leave her eyes, a smile still on her face, something shattered inside of him—never to be reawakened. With her motionless body on the bed, he looked over her corpse and began to cry—the little part of Atticus still left. He had truly loved her. Once she was gone, the part of his soul she awakened would be gone forever. As he walked away from the scene and into the night, he continued to cry. Unsure of what to do with his arms, he flailed, and he accidentally rubbed blood on his head, clothes, and body. His lights flared with random colors. Within him part of her soul lived on but was lost in an uncatalogued sea of other souls within him; that connection would never be made again. He would never be able to call up her memory again, at least not on purpose. Someday, some part of her would flow into someone he was feeding on. She would come through him, but he wouldn't know it was her. In all ways now, he was alone, an aimless soul. As he stumbled out into a light rain, the beauty of her soul began to leave his body. It floated out and over him like a cloud of rainbow sparkles.

The particles bounced between the droplets and scattered their light throughout the evening sky, a rainbow in the dark; then he forgot her.

Cordelia's funeral took place a week later at a local community center. The ceremony was provided in tandem by Cordelia's parents. The ceremony was closed casket, a beautiful dark brown wood. On either side were large digital photo frames that stood several feet tall. As the patrons came in, they swiped on their devices and added pictures to a growing collage. After a few hours it became a beautiful collection of photos of Cordelia throughout her life. Unlike her friends and family in the photos, each of her wrinkles was documented.

The service was short; only Cordelia's ex-wife spoke. "Hello, everyone, thank you for coming. As we look at these photos we are reminded of the passage of time in our lives. A luxury Cordelia did not have of ignoring. But she did that to us a lot, didn't she? Bring us to reality…keep us in check…in the best way possible. I think Cordelia would be absolutely overwhelmed with how many people have come here today." June looked out at the sea of beautiful but sad twenty-five-year-old faces that lined the room. The small space was barely wider than the casket and only long enough to place three rows of chairs. The modest thirty seats were completely filled, and extra people lined the walls and spilled into the hallway.

"Cordelia was a stark reminder of how lucky we are. She was smart and original, fiery…didn't give a fuck what you thought. She was caring and a fighter, something we all struggled to be at one time or another. She was happy to be whatever you needed to better your day. I am sure I speak for many when I say that sadly I often lost contact for periods of time. Changes in work added extra distance…having a family complicates all matters. But no matter how much time passed between talking, our relationship was never hostile or awkward. I couldn't imagine our talks going any other way. I can see from the people in this room that many of you would agree. Even as she grew older and changed, as so many of us do…when her frustration began to show in *patient* pauses…you could also hear how much she cared about you. In her words, in her forced smiles, and the tones she attempted to take with us. She was in far more pain than she ever truly let us know, and all the time she only thought about how she could treat others better. Did you all know that forty-five years after our divorce, I still received a card for each important holiday from her? Was anyone else lucky enough to have been on the receiving end of her support?"

June turned her body to the casket and looked at the decorations that littered its top; small handmade toys, some made by Cordelia for the hospital and others brought in her honor. "It's the little things that touch us and keep us in each other's hearts. I was told that the hospital was Cordelia's newest family. I see toys she had donated. I was told she spent hours after her sessions in the pediatric unit, giving support and toys to scared children. Turning something scary into something fun for others. And there is it…another instance of Cordelia using all her energy on others. To care…to reach out…in the ways she could. I am not proud to say but I am honest when I say I am sorry I didn't realize it in the time. I didn't appreciate it."

June turned her attention back to the crowd. "Even in the hardest of times, in her sickest moments, Cordelia never gave up. If you did not know, her condition had reached terminal ends and she was estimated as only having a few years at most remaining. What she did was end her life on her own terms.… We can only guess a fraction of what she was going through. But I think in the end it was also an accident caused by our inattention. She cared so much for others that she was too stubborn to ask for help in return. I for one wished I had reached out more. I pray that each of us can fully discover everything she secretly taught us over the years. Pay it forward. I think that is the best way to honor such a wonderful person and how we can all strive to make a better world by keeping her alive."

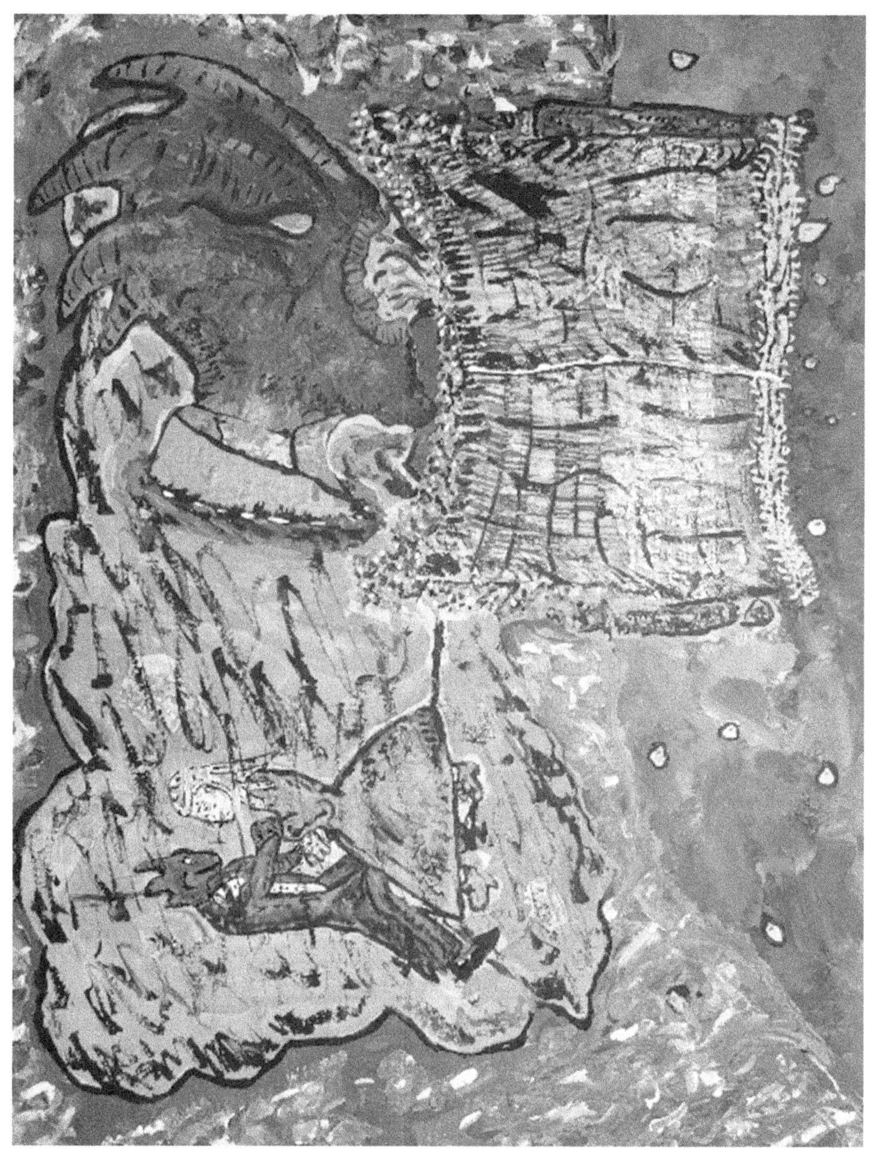

Going Home

Going Home

Ligare maneuvered through the sky in large, swooping arches and surveyed the land below. His current form was a large black raven, in stark contrast to the bright blue sky against his back. As he flapped his wings, small green flames rolled off his body like water droplets. As they fell off, they puffed into smoke, which gave his flight a small trail like a comet. Ligare was orienting himself as he searched for, then made his way toward, a large mountain. The mountainside was mostly bare; only a few scattered trees broke up the large brown and grey stone. The strange trees were thin and composed of two trucks wound around one another; this caused some of them to grow with a space or two in their bodies. Their branches were cluttered with crystalized fruit that dangled like bunches of grapes. The trees blew freely in even the lightest breeze, and they seemed to breathe as it took in sunlight. As they shifted, their trunks alternated between brown and rose gold.

Some of the trees stood stiff under the rising sun. They were impervious to the light that woke up everyone else on the planet. In the light their bark glistened with the purest and brightest gold, far shinier than the others. However, as the sun shifted over it or when it was covered by a cloud, the gold faded to show a deep black. Below the black trees sat rancid earth. The ground was soft and squishy, as if flooded with water but still completely dry. The land was being poisoned by the dying trees, making it soft and fluid.

Ligare arrived at the mountain and swooped down to land just outside of one of the circles of blackened earth. His head turned back and forth as he scanned the tree for its fruits. A few were still attached but most of them had fallen into the liquid earth and sat floating on top. Ligare dipped in his toe and caused a ripple to travel along the ground. It bounced off the tree and back to him. Meanwhile, the fruits in the water bobbed up and down. The rancid earth stuck to his toe like tar and only with much effort did he rub it off.

Ligare pumped his wings and began to float just above the ground. He then flew over the rancid earth; his toes barely missed contact with it. He honed in to the location of the cherry-sized fruits scattered about. Under the sunlight his feathers turned iridescent, much like the trees around him—shades of emerald green. The crystalized fruit on the ground was different than those that grew happily on the other, healthy trees. The fruit that sat among the soil had lost its shiny and solid exterior. They appeared more like real fruit, soft and rotting. They were slowly returning to the earth.

Ligare shifted through the soil and found several gems whose light was not completely faded, not completely rotten. After he gently picked them up from the ground with his beak, he placed them securely into a phantom satchel that appeared on his back. Like those still on the trees, the crystals varied in color between shades of green and purple. At each petrified tree he was only able to salvage a single gem or two, so he had to travel between many. Ligare continued to do this until his bag was filled. Then he perched on a nearby healthy tree and from his pack he dug out gem after gem, each of them green. Then he gently placed the fruit into contact with the healthy fruit on the tree he sat on. It fused and glowed bright and healthy like the others; he was cultivating them. The raven flew around the tree decorating the various flowers with new gems until his satchel was nearly empty again.

Then Ligare landed on the ground and dug through his bag one last time. He made sure he held onto only eight small gems, each only the size of a marble; one was green and the other seven were various shades of purple. He took to the sky and flew away from the mountain. Behind him the mountain was becoming active. Its peak gleamed with a bright beam coming from inside, like a volcano of light. The rays outshined even the sun behind it; they were a distinct and almost thick yellow and fluttered into the sky.

Ligare flew a few miles, his strong wings flapping only on rare occasions. Below him the trees began to change to pine. That signaled he was close to his destination. Their large trunks were ordained with thick branches that were dotted with pinecones. The large number released a scent that gave the region a distinct atmosphere. After flying a bit farther, the trees began to clear out and the forest became less dense like before, but the variety of trees increased. Leaves, flowers, and fruits painted the ground in a rainbow of colors. The raven began to soar downward, in a deliberate slow spiral. As he lowered himself, his body began to shrink, slowly becoming the size of a canary. He made his way toward the body of a man who was asleep among the tall grass of the field. His body made a distinct cut-out in the grass, he had folded the long stalks over as a make-shift bed. On it he was wrapped in a dark brown cloak, sleeping peacefully. Ligare landed on the man and dug his way into the man's coat. Within the small area, the raven moved his gems from his satchel into the man's inside coat pocket. Then he nuzzled into the man's chest and joined him in sleep.

Marshall awoke with the sunlight shining on his face, the warmth beckoning him. As he slowly shivered himself awake, the morning dew rolled off his cape. Ligare began to roll around in his coat, starting to wake up himself. The two yawned and stretched. Marshall extended his knee-high boots out onto the dewy grass around him. Their white base was tarnished, covered in dirt and scuffs from many hikes. His pants were green, and his shirt was white and slightly less dirty than his boots. He was awake and now realized he was *actually* a little cold. His shivers did little to warm him. He picked up his pillow and unfolded it into a leather vest that he then threw on. From the ground he picked up his green leather wrist straps; their color matched the grass and trees around him. His straps doubled as impromptu weapons; each had three leaf-like blades extended off them. Marshall strapped on a belt and tightened it to bring his cloak and his vest closer to him.

Marshall's hair was thin and cut into a loose bowl cut. He had a trim but patchy beard, his hair brown with small strips of gray. He was not especially tall, only five-foot-nine, but was so skinny that he looked quite lanky. He itched his well-defined nose and began to inspect his surroundings. He was standing directly next to a small fire that was still smoldering from the night before. Also, he was in a small forest clearing with densely packed trees to the north, and less densely to the south where the ground became sandier. It dawned on Marshall that he had no idea what he was looking for. Unaware of what was happening or where he was, Marshall looked around, confused, in search of anything that might spark his memory. The first thing he noticed was the medium-sized backpack at his feet. He bent down and picked it up.

Ligare emerged from his pocket, still tiny, and began to hop up Marshall's arm to his shoulder. When he got there, Ligare rubbed his head against Marshall's. As he did, he grew a little larger. The bird brought no new memories to Marshall's mind, but upon seeing it, a warmth grew in his heart. Marshall smiled and the two of them looked up at the morning sun. It was still not warm enough for Marshall, and he pulled in his cloak closer. He then tried to decide on a direction to go.

Now that he concentrated, he could feel a vibration in the ground traveling up his legs. He placed his backpack back on the ground and kneeled. Loose soil was bouncing around at his feet. He lowered his ear to the ground. He could hear a low vibration, a trembling and stomping. He jumped to his feet and spun, looking for the source of the sound. He turned left and then right…nothing. Finally, his attention was drawn back toward the northern forest. The vibration was getting heavier and the noise louder.

To the north the trees rustled, and Marshall could hear the bending of the wood. Birds scattered from the trees as something moved through them. From the forest edge emerged a large tree trunk that dragged itself across the ground, past the other trees. Behind it, tenacle-like roots pushed against the ground and wiggled the tree forward. Marshall could see the tentacles wrapping around trees and shifting through the dirt like snakes. He began to run south, away from the rapidly approaching mass, but it gained on him. As a root approached his leg, he dove out of the way, among the less dense trees. The wiggling tree rose from the soil and now pointed its bare trunk to the sun. Its body opened and a loud roar was released that sounded like the bending and rattling of wood. Marshall covered his face with his gauntlets and pointed the blades toward the tree, bracing himself for a blow. Ligare grew larger on his shoulder and squawked.

Instead, Marshall only felt the cool of shade—the sun having vanished from above him. He unclenched his fists and moved his arms from in front of his face. He looked and saw that the tree was splitting open. Starting at the tip and along various layers of its body, the bare tree split open, revealing an evergreen set of leaf plumps, small bushes, and branches. The creature now looked like a small menagerie of plants. The tree extended its trunk farther into the sky and now shaded the once-open field. As the tree basked in the sun, it wiggled under the warmth, like a cat basking in a window, comfortable and quiet. After a moment the tree then drooped slightly, as if it had fallen asleep.

Marshall placed his hands on his knees and caught his breath. He was already sweating, and it was not even hot out yet. He turned east and began to walk, but Ligare swiftly came off his shoulder. He blocked his path and grew larger, effortlessly hovering. Marshall turned his body south and that choice agreed more with the bird, who then landed on his shoulder. Ligare then nuzzled into his face. "Okay, okay…not so…little buddy. This is the way you want us to go?" Marshall asked gently. He then began to pet Ligare, who had shrunk down. "I'm trusting you—don't let me down!" he joked.

Marshall turned his attention away from the slumbering tree and walked as Ligare directed him through the sandy forest to the south. The area was much less dense than the fir forest but significantly more colorful. The simple green pine trees started to be joined by taller palm trees and thin, winding trees of different shapes and sizes. Pops of color were provided by the dramatic increase of mushrooms on every tree. Large sail-like appendages branched off of the trees, creating the appearance that bright red, blue, and yellow arms were reaching out to you. It was only a few hours into their journey that Marshall noticed something strange that Ligare already knew about. Sporadically through the forest was a black infection that spread through the ground. Streaks radiated through the earth and followed the roots of the trees. They flowed through the ground like bulging veins. The infection traveled up trees, which began to harden, becoming metallic in appearance. On those sick trees even the mushrooms changed; they became purple and rainbow, somehow even more beautiful in death.

Even so, whether it was the presence of his friend or the beauty of the world around him, Marshall felt comfortable to simply wander. His direction was set by his feathered friend, tapping him on the shoulder whenever he ventured too far off the path. Their walk wasn't tiring, and he felt like almost no time had passed, but eventually the sun began to set. That is when Marshall's survival instincts kicked in. The unfamiliarity of the forest grew creepier as the sun began to drop behind the trees. The moon was nowhere to be found as clouds filled the sky and the forest turned into a dark tunnel. Marshall decided he needed to make camp.

He dropped his bag to the ground, and for the first time started to look through his belongings. At the top of the bag sat a large green and blue feather pen, some clothes, a small satchel, and some food. Stuffed into one of the side compartments was a leatherbound book and thin sheets of paper neatly pressed together. Instinctually, having not eaten all day, Marshall picked up the small box of food, which he opened to find a thin piece of flatbread and some strips of fruit jerky. He lifted the tough jerky up to his mouth, but after biting down he realized he was not actually hungry. He spit his small piece back into his hand and placed it into the container with the other food. Then he began to wonder why he was in the backpack in the first place. *Oh yeah, the darkness.* That's when he realized there was nothing he could use to light the way.

"I guess we should start to make camp, bud," Marshall said to Ligare as he patted his head. Then he began to clear off a spot for a fire; he dug with his hands while he searched the diminishing horizon for suitable sticks. That is when Ligare started to obstruct Marshall's view once again. Marshall playfully swatted at the bird. "Could you wait a minute? I'm trying to get this done before it becomes too dark to see." Ligare then began to glow. His green flames emanated from his body, and a light brightened the area around him. As Ligare attempted to get close, Marshall tried to dodge in fear that he would be burned by the bright flames.

"Ahh," he yelped prematurely but as the bird landed on his shoulder, he felt nothing. Once it touched him, he realized he was immune to the fire. It flowed through him without any resistance. It brightened his path, but no warmth came from it. "Wow, that's amazing," Marshall said in awe as the flames rolled past his vision and over his body. "Well, I wasn't tired anyway, so I guess let's keep walking. Thanks for being so helpful. It probably isn't the safest to sleep in an unknown forest anyway…as beautiful as it is."

Ligare continued to direct Marshall south until the peaceful silence of the forest was broken by the sound of music. A most unnatural music could be heard throughout the woods. Its exciting and rhythmic beats clashed with the surrounding darkness, silence, and malaise. The tune sounded funky, played on drums with a leading beat made by a collection of horns. Their noise was distinct from what he imagined of traditional instruments; in a way he could not describe. Perhaps it was *raspier*. Through the breaks in the trees Marshall could see light flickering in the distance. "Hey, can you turn down your flame a bit? I don't think it's safe to be seen just yet. We don't know who else could be around," asked Marshall of Ligare. After they broke the forest edge, he could see the light was coming from a large bonfire taking place under an oddly shaped tent. Smoke rose from the fire and was pulled by a mechanical fan toward the top of the tent and out a makeshift chimney. The tent was protruding out from a large caravan beside it.

Marshal could see that in its prime, the caravan was once bright red trimmed in gold but now it was well loved. The red was mostly replaced by dark rust, and chips of gold were missing through its use. At the front sat a cockpit. Large glass windows showed a dark space filled with more levers and buttons than he cared to note. He then noticed that the top of the caravan was fitted with an umbrella on a long retractable neck, and that was where the tent was coming from.

As they got closer, Marshall began to crouch down, slowing his motion toward the caravan as he looked for signs of life. At the edge of the lights, he saw large boxes of provisions, stacked up as a small wall between the action happening under the tent and the forest. He slid his body against the boxes and pressed against the makeshift wall. He began to move around it. It was then that Ligare leapt from his shoulder, extended his wings in full flight, and darted under the tent. "Come back," Marshall whispered, at first a little too loudly, his voice dropping out by the end. He searched above him for the bird, but as he could no longer see him, his heart began to race. *Whoever was there must have seen the raven*, he thought. *I can't just sit here, now.* Marshall began to sweat as he continued to move along the wall. As he turned a corner he was met with another wall of boxes.

He continued to move in stealth until the sound of music was overcome by the sound of voices. There, Marshall peaked his head over the wall, and he could see the music echoed out of a cavity of the caravan, from a built-in speaker. In front of the amplifier was a short individual, wearing a thick military coat, half red and half purple; it had large shoulder pads and straps where many small tools hung. An attached hood provided a magical darkness that entirely obscured his face. The only thing that came through was his eyes, which shined a bright yellow. The hood was also red and purple, but on opposite sides and on them he wore goggles. On his hands he wore large metal gauntlets ordained with large crystals, again purple and red. Marshall watched as he began to tinker with several control knobs on the side of the caravan. The music changed; a more folkie tune began.

"How dare you change the music? I was just about to dance," a feminine voice hissed from elsewhere.

"You have never danced *once*, Matilda! Have you really had that much wine?" the short creature yelled back. Marshall looked to the side and saw Matilda. She was much taller and skinner but also in a two-toned outfit. Hers was a thick, heavy cloak and hood. Like his, her face was completely hidden, and only two bright yellow eyes shined through its abyss. Like him, her hood was opposite colors from her cloak, half light blue and half tangerine. The cloak ran down the length of her body to the ground, and each side was embroidered with symbols of stars, moons, galaxies, and other celestial bodies. It was open in front to reveal her simple outfit below.

She wore a long black and gray dress that was split into layers as it expanded down and out. Its texture was seemingly fluffy and hung over her large brown boots.

"Mind…your…*own*…business, Revolocat," snapped Matilda, a sudden playfulness in her voice. She then sat down, a little heavier than she'd expected. She raised her hands in the air to balance herself, and she caught herself on the arm of a small wooden piece. She slid into her seat and laughed, splashing a little wine as she carried it to her mouth. Her goblet disappeared into the darkness. Marshall continued to scan the area.

To the right he could see two more figures sitting at a table, both on stools, their hands and arms entwined. One was a large man, the sides of his head shaved. His remaining hair was a large brown and gold mohawk. The man's face was surprisingly soft, with a large, thick, and flowing mustache. Over one shoulder sat a golden belt, which traveled across his chest to a large metal crest within the center. It continued and attached to another golden belt at his waist, where a medium-length kilt hung. The man's feet were pushed onto the floor and the bottom of the stool, causing him to almost stand. His face was angry and red, and his veins bulged as he clenched his jaw with force, his teeth shining.

"Ahhhhh," strained the man. Marshall looked at his partner and realized the two were arm wrestling. Across the table sat a large humanoid creature; its face was long with a wide nose, and layers of armored plates covered its body. It had fine hair covering its face, and its hands had only three fingers.

A giant…armadillo? How strange, Marshall thought. He could see that the armadillo was showing no emotion and not straining nearly as hard as the much larger man across from it.

"YOU'RE CHEATING AGAIN," screamed the man. He started to strain even more—new veins burst around his face. He was biting down so aggressively that Marshall feared his teeth would shoot out. The armadillo chuckled before slamming the man's arm down onto the table. Their goblets of wine bounced, lifted by the force. The man rubbed his sore arm and then began to windmill it. He spoke exhausted and annoyed, "I know you're cheating, you rat. Don't you creatures have any shame, Nmu-tua?"

Nmu-tua chuckled. "Oh, come on, Piper. Just because you can't beat me doesn't mean I'm cheating."

"What's the problem? Why is Piper being a big baby?" asked Matilda from her chair. Her long legs were draped over the chair's arm and her head hung over the other side as she attempted to carefully pour the wine into her hood. The wine too disappeared behind the darkness of the fabric.

"Nmu-tua! Locked her plates! I know she was cheating. That's the only way she can beat me," barked Piper.

"It's not cheating, just because you don't have armor. Get stronger." Nmu-tua laughed again and took a drink of her wine with one arm. She then stiffened and loosened her arm plates. They made a clinking as they slid to lock and unlock. Then, Ligare flew out of the darkness toward the group. In his mouth he carried a large yellow fruit. As he circled over the group, they all yelled. Ligare began to swoop in and out of the tent past them, and they each gave an unenthusiastic swat at him. He then dropped the fruit onto the lap of Matilda, who caught it and coughed from the impact. Piper stood up from his seat and ran toward the bird, grabbing it out of the air.

Marshall gasped and instinctually stood up, but was not sure what he was actually going to do. So, he didn't do anything; instead, he froze in place. Ligare had shrunken and was now in Piper's palms, trapped. Piper looked up from his hands and smiled. His gaze now caught Marshall, who quickly tried to duck down. Too late. "Hide and seek, *huh*?" Piper shouted. Marshall attempted to skulk behind the boxes and wondered how he could free the bird. He was in over his head. As he darted back around the corner of the wall, he met Revolocat. His large, gloved hand grabbed Marshall by the ankle. As the stout creature waddled back toward the music, he easily dragged Marshall around the corner and into the center of the room.

Piper stood above him and threw his arms into the air. Ligare flew straight up and grew larger before landing back down onto Piper's shoulder. Piper then reached down toward Marshall while flashing a smile large, his massive teeth glaring. He grabbed Marshall by the collar and effortlessly lifted him until their faces were even. Marshall's feet dangled above the ground. Still smiling, Piper leaned in and kissed Marshall on the cheek, then threw him into the air. As he came down, Piper rapped him in a bear hug. "Where have you and Sabin been?" he asked, talking about the bird as it nuzzled into his head. Marshall tried to speak but he could only whisper under the pressure of Piper's hug.

"I…*uhh*…got lost," Marshall forced out.

"Oh, I'm sorry, friend," responded Piper, who now realized his grasp was *too tight*. He placed Marshall onto the ground and quickly helped to straighten out Marshall's outfit. "We haven't seen you in a few days. We were about to pack up and continue the survey without you." Piper's smile grew even larger.

"Great! We can finally leave in the morning. We're running out of supplies," said Matilda.

"We have plenty of supplies," responded Revolocat.

"We're almost out of wine," said Piper.

"Urgent enough for me," giggled Nmu-tua, who was still at the table.

"We'll continue our survey until we have something to report, then we can get more wine," reprimanded Piper. He then grabbed a goblet seemingly out of nowhere and took a jar off a nearby crate and emptied it into the cup. He then handed it to Marshall. "Happy you're back."

As Marshall drank the wine, he felt effortlessly comfortable about the strangers. Why could he not remember who they were, when they knew him so well? He sat and joked with them all night, losing time. Marshall awoke the next morning once again in the dew, only this time under the caravan tent. His cloak was once again wrapped around his body, and Ligare slept in his pocket. Scattered among the space were the other travelers. To his left, on the chair, lay Matilda and Revolocat piled together, cuddling. Up against another wall sat both Nmu-tua and Piper, sleeping while sitting up. A finished jar of wine lay tipped over on the ground between them.

Marshall stood up and stretched and admired the light bouncing in the morning mist. From his pocket emerged Ligare, who began to squawk an upbeat but annoying tune. He flapped to the adventurers and gave them each a personal wakeup call. Revolocat rolled off of Matilda and fell to the ground. Matilda yawned, "Everyone get up, so Sabin will shut up. Let's do this survey and then hurry back to town. Marshall, you mentioned something creepy and black in the woods. We'll start our investigation there." It was amazing how quickly she turned on.

Piper and Nmu-tua helped each other up, and the crew got themselves ready. Marshall stood awkwardly with his backpack over his shoulder, unsure what his job would be. He wanted to help but had no idea what to do. Each person except for Revolocat grabbed their own small bag of supplies and gathered by the front of the caravan. Then they began to walk. Marshall followed the group as they made their way back toward the direction he had come from. "Do what you need for the survey everyone. I'll just be here packing up the caravan," Revolocat begrudgingly yelled at them.

"Isn't that a lot of work for him just alone?" Marshall questioned the group. "There are so many boxes, and we made a mess."

"No, what are you talking about? He's actually so lazy," Matilda responded. Behind them he hit a button and the caravan began to pack itself up. Its body shifted and returned to a car, two wheels in the back and one in front. From the side came a large mechanical arm that quickly stacked the boxes and pulled them inside. Revolocat pressed a few more buttons and pulled some levers before the tent folded up and turned into a smaller umbrella. The carpet rolled up and tucked the car. Revolocat then climbed a small ladder on the side and took a seat under the umbrella shade. He pulled out a book but immediately placed it on his stomach and fell back asleep.

Piper and Nmu-tua led the party as they made their way back into the woods. As they traveled, Nmu-tua and Matilda each made notes in small notebooks about the trees and other life they encountered. They hiked for several miles before they found anything of interest. In a clearing of sand was a congregation of drag-plants. When closed, they were shaped like a large reptilian face but fiercer. Its nose pointed at the front like a dragon. As they bathed in the sun they opened their various folds to reveal beautiful iridescent scales, and like the tree he saw before they raised their bodies like a sail to absorb sunlight. Now that he was closer, Marshall could see that the scales were leaves and colorful veins ran through each one. A group of five circled something on the ground, a dead one. They shifted and moved their bodies as they communicated, and the creaking of wood made it clear they were distressed.

Nmu-tua approached them, her voice shifting from English to the same creaking noises that the plants were making. When she made it to the circle, she could see that there was a drag-plant. Its roots looked dry, and it was lying on the ground. Its thick wood managed to look wilted; it was dead. Nmu-tua reached down and placed her hands on the plant. A small red aura radiated out of her and began to heal it, bringing it back to life. The plant stood up tall and stretched its leaves. It then used one of its roots to give a small hug to Nmu-tua. It squeaked in joy and shook its branches, dropping a few twigs on the ground. She picked them up and threw them into her bag.

"Thank you," she said in plant. "They told us to head over this way," she now yelled at her team who were still at a safe distance. "It seems that there are more sick trees over there. This might be what we are looking for." The herd of drag-plants made their way west away from the group, who traveled deeper into the woods. Ligare flew in front of them, surveying for sick trees.

"That was amazing what you did with that creature," complimented Marshall. "It really looked like it might have been dead."

"It was," Nmu-tua confirmed. "I am a necromancer, but I've always felt a special connection with plants. So, I'm a botany necromancer."

"Wow, well that would be amazing for the plants I fail to keep alive in my house," he responded. Marshall didn't truly remember that, but it felt like a common experience.

"Well, I couldn't do anything until they were actually dead, and I'd rather help to professionally grow them and keep them alive in the first place. They don't need to suffer. Anyway, I can't really control them.They are fairly strong-willed, even after death. I can't really help living plants, but I can bring back dead ones. *For instance*." She reached into her pocket and pulled out a dried and shriveled fruit. As it sat in her palm it began to glow and grow larger, eventually becoming full body and ripe. She handed it to Marshall. "See, it was dead and now, it's delicious. Have some. It will keep you from getting dehydrated. It's a cactus fruit. It's quite quenchy."

"That's not a word," responded Matilda.

"I made it a word."

"Well, until it's published in one of my textbooks, let's use 'refreshing.' They store a massive amount of water within themselves, in case of severe drought. They are kind of like eating a water balloon." Matilda kept taking notes as she condescended.

"What exactly are we looking for?" Marshall finally asked.

"You have the worst memory. This is a recognizance mission. We were hired to figure out why the water in town is arriving tainted from this direction. We are also trying to figure out why trees are dying in seemingly random places," Matilda responded.

"The water comes from that mountain in the distance, but we were hoping to find something before we make it all the way there," Piper said as he pointed at the horizon.

"We still haven't found anything strange. Some dehydrated or dead plants here or there but nothing out of the ordinary," Nmu-tua continued. "I assume if it's in the groundwater we'll find something in the river coming from the mountain. Should be only a few more minutes away." They then arrived at the river, where along its edge they saw a series of dead trees leading to the water. Along the ground they saw twigs thrown everywhere, as if they had been attacked. She made her way past each one of them, using her powers to wake them up. Before she was able to speak to any of them, they sprinted away from the river and back into the woods. Matilda continued to take notes on their reactions, until they made their way to the river edge.

Below, they got their second indication that something was wrong. At the base of the water lay another drag-plant body, black and tainted. It was lying in the water and slowly dissolving into it. A bright blue liquid bled out of it and into the stream. Like the trees Marshall had seen earlier, it was stiff and shining silver. "Come see this, comrades. I think we found our first real clue," Nmu-tua called out. One by one Piper grabbed the arms of each crew member and lowered them down to the river's edge. After they had all gotten down safely, Piper jumped from the cliff—down six feet, landing loudly but firmly and with ease. As they peered over the body, the group noticed the wood was not rotten but crystallized.

Nmu-tua placed her hands on it and attempted to bring it back to life like the others. As the light flowed out of her paws the tree remained unresponsive. She tried again and concentrated even harder. The light flowed out of her and all over the tree in a bright light, nearly blinding everyone. Then Nmu-tua fainted from exhaustion, but the tree failed to move. As she collapsed, her body folded in on itself, rolling into a ball and snapping her shut.

"Mmmmyyyyy turn," Matilda sang as she approached the remains. "My…my…so beautiful really." Piper and Marshall sat next to Nmu-tua, who was slowly waking up and opening. Matilda pulled a large rapier out from under her cloak; its fancy hilt wrapped around her arm and hand, and its long, thin blade resembled a scalpel. She stood perpendicularly to the tree, and she rapidly slashed at the corpse. Her actions were swift but calibrated, much like a surgeon. The sound of clanking radiated from the body, as if it was the clash of metal on metal.

There was a sound of bending metal as Matilda used her hands to open up a cavity she made in the tree. She then peered deeply into it; her head disappeared. The three stood up with Piper and Marshall holding onto Nmu-tua in case she fainted again. They gathered closer to see what Matilda was staring at. As she leaned back and began to write some notes, they could see a shine from within the corpse. Just below the bark, within the veins of the plant, were thousands of small crystals—like grains of salt in a wound, but they shined like diamonds.

"This is the first tree we have found that I was not able to bring back alive," said Nmu-tua, who was back on her feet.

"Uh-oh. Look at the mountain," Piper advised. From the mouth of the river, they had a clearer view of the mountain. On it they could see large clumps of black upon the hill and within it dead silver trees. "I am afraid that whatever this blight is, it must have come from there."

"I think the tainted water is traveling along the river and underground, infesting the roots of plants," Nmu-tua concluded.

"Our best bet is to take back the body and show it to the king. Then we can get supplies before we go to the mountain," Matilda explained. "Then again, perhaps simply showing them this creature will be enough to finish our mission."

"Look at the water! There is a black vein running through the earth. I don't think it's coming from the plant. It must be coming from the water source of the mountain to the north, past the city. We've got to fix this," Nmu-tua pleaded.

Piper picked up the body and, with great strain, threw it to the top of the cliff. Afterward, Piper helped each adventurer back up. Nmu-tua, specifically, asked for a roll. She turned into a ball, and with one arm Piper picked her up onto his forearm. Then like a bowling ball, he tossed her and rolled her to the top. She popped open as she blasted off the ramp and subsequently landed on her feet with a happy squeal. Once they were settled, Piper tossed the tree over his shoulder, and they all walked back to the caravan. On the way, they passed the wild drag-plants again. They hissed and ran away, scared of the tree that Piper carried.

When they returned to the caravan, Revolocat was still peacefully sleeping off his hangover. He was woken up by the shaking of the vehicle as Piper threw the metal corpse into the back storage compartment. "Hey, be gentler with the car. She's been through a lot!" he yawned, not actually caring. For the first time, Marshall entered the caravan with the others through a small side door. Though it looked much smaller from the outside, like magic, the inside of the caravan was massive. Within it was a long hallway filled with rooms. Each was labeled with a small wooden placard; they each had their own. At the end of the hallway, he could see the entrance to the cockpit and off to the side there was another hallway that led to a grand dining room. From upstairs, Revolocat came down to meet them. "How did the mission go?" he inquired. He was clearly sleeping the entire time they were gone and *still sleepy*. "I'm awake and ready to drive back to town. It's going to take almost a day's drive anyway, so let's start now!"

Exhausted from the day, everyone dispatched to their rooms. Marshall, followed by Ligare, slowly made his way down the hallway looking for which one was his. In the dead center he found his placard, in between Matilda's and a spare room. Marshall entered his room and dropped his bag onto the ground. Like the rest of the caravan, this room was much larger than he had anticipated, though it was only modestly furnished. A small mattress lay on the ground, and a closet was built into the wall. In the center of the floor were engravings and markings he did not recognize. Their design radiated out to the walls and climbed them like vines. Marshall felt compelled to drag his bag to the center of the floor, where he sat down. He surveyed his room and saw that only a small flame light kept the room lit.

Marshall lay on the ground and stretched out before he began to riffle through his backpack once more. His soul was drawn toward the notebook and beautiful quill. The lighting was still very low, so he searched for something to help him read. He found a candle on a small table near his mattress and picked it up. Almost immediately Ligare used his green flame to light the candle, and it too burned with green fire. The room was then filled with light, half red and half green. Now able to see, Marshall inspected his quill more closely.

He ran his finger over the vane of the feather and felt the barbs click back into place. While it appeared natural, it had a strange mechanical feeling to it. It was much heavier than you would expect it to be, and as he searched over its body, he saw etchings and symbols carved into its stem. At the bottom, Marshall saw two distinct pieces. The first was the tip that resembled a fountain pen, and the other was a small, round bulge right behind it. He held the quill as he would a pen and moved it in his hand. That was when he noticed the small bulge was actually a compartment. He twisted it to reveal a small hole. He placed his finger into it and moved it around, wondering what it did.

Ligare shrunk and made his way into Marshall's coat again. "Hey," Marshall muttered. "We're not going to bed yet; I'm still trying to figure this out." From within his pocket, he could feel Ligare moving around, fidgeting. "Get out of there," he said as he reached into his pocket. As he went to grab Ligare, he instead found the stones the bird had placed inside the day before.

"What are these?" Ligare pulled them out of his pocket and let them roll onto the floor. Marshall examined the eight stones and admired their beauty. Then Ligare motioned them toward Marshall, who picked one up. Ligare danced with excitement. Unsure of what he was supposed to do, Marshall rolled the rocks in his palm before bringing one with his fingers near the quill. Ligare got even more excited. "Here?"

Marshall took the green gem and slid it into the hole in his quill. Automatically, the cylinder closed, and the pen pulled from his hand. It slid across the floor to the center of the room, where the glyphs were positioned. As Ligare flapped his wings, flame once again bounced through the air and landed on the quill, which began to spin. A light burst from it and projected an image, *no* a video, onto the wall. The small clip was a father pushing his daughter on the swing. She was wearing a judge's costume, and after he performed a "duck under," her fluffy white wig bounced off her as she laughed. The short scene resonated with Marshall. A tear of joy began to form in the corner of his eye—he didn't know why. Marshall was so confused by his emotional connection to the image that he failed to be astonished by the magic that was bringing it to life. "Wow," he said out loud to himself. He shook his head and walked over to the quill.

As he picked it up, the projector turned off and the compartment opened. Marshall carefully dumped the gem into his hand before placing it in his pocket. He then rummaged to find another gem to test. This time he selected a light purple one and popped it in. He let go of the quill and it floated back to its spot and projected onto the wall. The light that came out of the quill was darker in tone and energy. Even before the projection started, Marshall felt a guttural reaction to the light. It felt as if he was being stabbed in the heart, and he grabbed his chest. In the image, a young man sprinted toward a taxi in the rain. In one hand he carried a duffle bag. In the other he led his pregnant wife. Marshall could feel their hearts racing and the rejection they felt. After the video played for the second time, he finally had enough and kicked the quill with the outside of his boot. His hand was still over his heart.

"Purple…*purple*. Means bad. The negative emotion was so strong. Not going to look at any more of those," Marshall said while pouring out the contents of his pocket. "All purple, huh? Strange." He picked back up the quill and notebook and began to take notes on what he had just seen and felt. After he finished his synopsis, he turned to a blank page and began to doodle an exaggeration of the pain he felt. In it he drew a small man grabbing his chest and a large fire coming out of the cavity. As Marshall put the finishing touches on his flame, the page burst into fire. He dropped the book but quickly realized he had to stop it. He proceeded to stomp on it to muffle the flames. "What the fuck?" Ligare began to dance in place. "I have magic?"

Marshall bent down and ripped off a small corner of a page. He then once again drew a flame. This time, however, before he finished the image, he began to throw it. As he released, a small fire ball launched across the room. At first he was stunned, but then he remembered he had to stop another fire. More stomping commenced. Excited, he spent the entire night determining what he could draw to life and what he couldn't. He learned the potency of the spell was based on the size of the paper, not the size of the drawing. Over the course of the night, he was able to make it snow with paper confetti and chill his drink with a few ice cubes. He was unable to make anything living such as a plant or rodent. Electricity never crossed his mind.

Overnight, as nearly everyone slept, something stirred from within the contaminated tree, a small blue blob. Like an amoeba, it crawled out from the storage department and slid under the door. It then pulled itself down the hallway toward Marshall's room. It began to slide under his door but quickly realized he was still awake tinkering with his magic. It retreated and made its way farther down the hallway, where it found Piper's room.

"Evening, everyone! We've almost arrived in town. Get ready!" Revolocat shouted through the intercom, a few hours later. His voice echoed throughout the vehicle through sound tubes connecting each room. "Almost there. Good thing for us the city only comes to life when the sun sets! Can't wait to see them lights!"

The announcement woke up Marshall, who then looked out of one of the small porthole windows in his room. In one direction he saw the forest in the distance, and in the other a city slowly being surrounded by darkness. As it grew darker, more and more lights turned on, magical beams of light shot up into the sky, and large torch beacons were lit across the walls and at the top of tallest towers, like lighthouses. The city was surrounded by large walls on all sides and only two breaks allowed traffic to move in and out. The outside of the city was littered with parked vehicles that were too large to navigate the city's small streets. Their car would be one of those.

Piper pulled out their tree, and the group made their way through the front gates of the city right as the sun finished setting. "Welcome to Beacon," announced Nmu-tua gleefully. The group made their way down the cobblestone streets with Piper carrying the petrified tree over his head with one hand. The streets were filled with people selling and buying as well as the occasional cart and horse-drawn carriage. People jammed against one another, pushing in both directions. Some of the stands had clearly been there forever, and others were beautiful and new. The food vendors were the most distracting to the group. The first to stop was Nmu-tua, who stared with joy at some grilled BBQ insect kabobs. To the vendor's dismay, Revolocat slapped the food out of the armadillo's hand. "You can't eat yet. If we don't eat all our meals at the capital it will look disrespectful!" he warned.

"We're just getting a snack," complained the armadillo, to which Matilda joined in.

"Don't worry about it—we have time. There is always space for a *little* snack," Matilda said while she purchased several different large fruits on a stick.

"I wouldn't want to be you guys…very disrespectful," Revolocat said as he chugged a pint of beer. He then placed his glass back on the table for a quick top-off. He drank three before catching up with the rest of the group. By that time Marshall had wandered off. Ligare led him through the crowd and down an even smaller alleyway. He caught his breath in the cool provided by having broken from the crowd. Further down, a sign caught his eye. A group of symbols he could not recognize were burned into wood. Ligare beckoned him down the alley and flew into the shop; he tucked himself into a hole between the roof and the door. The shop appeared in an alley only a few feet wide. On either side were extra-large stone skyscrapers. The simple door was surrounded by old wood.

Entering the shop was a surreal experience. Marshall pushed open the door and somehow entered a small temple. Behind him the door slammed shut with a much heavier thud than he'd expected. It startled him and set some creatures in the garden in front of him scurrying. Then he noticed Ligare sat on the arm of a small tree, set among several large pits of sand. Across the area was an old Asian gentleman with long white hair, beard, and mustache. His clothing was red and decorated with silver accents. His legs were wrapped around a pole that was dug into the earth. With his arms crossed, he balanced on stiff legs in a stoic trance. Ligare returned to Marshall, who then stepped forward into the garden of flowers. The rustle of the grass drew the old man's attention. Without opening his eyes or moving his body he asked, "Did you come here for silent meditation and self-discovery, or did you come in search of an answer?"

"Hey, I'm not quite sure why I am here. I suppose it's by accident," Marshall said, scratching his head in the process. "I've been led here by my familiar but now as I stand here…

now that… I am speaking to you… I feel as if perhaps I have been here before. Or maybe that we've met before?" The man let out a coy smile, then laughed, and stroked his beard. He gracefully leapt off his post and landed among some flowers.

"Welcome back, my friend. I see you're nearing the end of one of your journeys. It's a pleasure to see you again." Then Ligare flew over to the old man and sat on his shoulder. "Did you bring me anything?" Marshall looked confused and thought for a second. Then he remembered the crystals in his pocket.

"Do you know anything about these?" he asked while reaching out with a palm filled with gems. The distance between him and the old man vanished. His hand reached out and grabbed a couple; he made sure to pick the green one.

"Wonderful, you are asking the right questions. These gems and the blight on this land are one in the same problem. But like you have done before, I believe you can fix it all. At least for a short time." He began to roll the gems in his hand. Then he picked out two, one green and one purple, and held them in between his thumb and fingers. He then looked through them. "These are your memories. They are powerful concentrations of your mind. Soon, you will need to sacrifice them for what you have come to call the purification ritual. By sacrificing your own thoughts, you'll be able to heal this world."

"Why me? Why do my memories look so distant? I'm not even in them." Marshall didn't understand.

"You will know soon, when the ritual is complete. You will see. It's not my place to tell you. I found in the past, when I did, it only stifled your quest." The old man grabbed a flower from the plants in front of him and brought it up to his hand. He took two of the gems and placed them into the mouth of the flower. He closed it and shook it, and a small ray of light burst from it. "You will need to combine eight in total to complete the ritual." The man grabbed another gem and placed it into the flower. A larger burst of light shot out. "The flower is merely a vessel for your own magical strength. I will only be able to combine so many for you. My power is limited." The man placed together five gems and each exploded larger than the last. The final one sent wind throughout the small garden. "You will need to protect it and when the time comes, combine the last gem." The old man poured the combined gem into his palm; he rolled it around as it steamed. It was now a dark and deep purple. "True memories are combinations of feelings and moments. They do not exist independent of what happens before and after." Marshall took the flower and the gem from the man, placing the gem with the others and the flower gently in his backpack. "I'll see you again, friend."

Ligare flew from the old man's shoulders and at Marshall. He got too close and caused Marshall to step backward. His foot gave out on the ground, and he tumbled. His momentum took him out the door, and he found himself lying on the hot, dirty sand of the city. Above him the doorway and shop vanished; all that was left was a blank alley filled with trash. As the sweat filled his brow, he realized it was morning. Though it had only felt like a couple minutes, Marshall had lost the entire evening. Unsure of where the castle was, Marshall asked Ligare to direct him back to the caravan. There they found the crew packing up.

"Where were you? You completely missed the meeting," Piper yelled as he tied down some supplies.

"More importantly! You missed dinner! The king was furious. I told you!" Revolocat scolded from under the caravan. He was doing some maintenance.

"We had to pretend you died!" Matilda announced in a very monotone voice. She was sitting in the shade of the car, fanning herself.

"Oh, yeah…so next time we're going to have to pretend you're a zombie. Or you're not getting paid," said Revolocat as he slid out from under the car.

"Isn't that a bit dramatic?" Marshall questioned, making his way into the car.

"No seriously, he would have killed you," Piper confirmed.

"I'll make up something about you being half plant or something, and that I brought you back. It'll be fine," Nmu-tua reassured.

"Either way, we left the deadweight tree with the king…. He said he was interested in making jewelry or something out of it? Maybe an ottoman? He was all over the place," Matilda said as she stood up and made her way into the cabin.

"We have some supplies for collecting samples and some potions made by the alchemist. But most importantly, food and wine," Piper cheerly announced. "The potions are supposed to help to cleanse anything negative. Sounds hokey but we'll see. He, nor anyone in his court, really had any idea what they were doing."

"I had a vision and I think I know what to do now. When we find the source of the corruption, you can leave it up to me," Marshall said with a confidence he had yet to show.

"Thank God, you're back. Let's get this venture going," Piper cheered.

"What?" Marshall said, surprised.

"You are always the one who has a plan. The leader who helps us take care of every situation. It's not fair to always put that pressure on you, but we are all happy you're back."

Nmu-tua placed her hand on Marshall's back. "Besides, we think something is wrong with Piper since he started to take over. I think it's causing him to be a little…forgetful."

They loaded the caravan and began their journey to the mountain. By going around the forest, they were able to reach significantly closer to the mountain than they did previously, before they had to journey offroad. As they approached, Marshall marveled at the beautiful view of the mountain. The large gray and silver volcano had a large cavern in the front that water readily flowed from; a small tributary that connected to the larger river system below. The volcano was part of a range, of which it was the largest. At one time, all the trees that littered the grass and moss-covered rocks were gold and pristine. The mountainside was once littered with glittering and wiggling signals of life. Now many of the trees were black and—though still shining and silver, and beautiful—dead. The ride grew bumpier the closer they got to the mountain; the ground became rolling hills.

During the trip, Marshall began trying his hand at combining gems. As he sat on top of the caravan, he dropped two in and held the flower in his hand. The blast shot out and blew Marshall off the roof and onto the floor. He stood up and sprinted after the car. Revolocat had it in autopilot and was napping, so it took a moment for someone else to stop it. When they reached the base of the mountain, Marshall was finally able to see the trees up close and could see the landscape of fruits. Most of them were much larger than the gems he held in his pocket; then he saw the ones that were rotting on the floor, corrupted by the tree.

The grounds near the base of the mountain were flooded; they traveled over the shallowest region, a bog. As the caravan trudged through the mud, it began to stall and the tires became gunked, slowing their progress. By the time they reached the base of the mountain the caravan was on its last limbs. Revolocat parked the caravan on a ridge, out of the water, precariously upright. They each climbed out of the cart and dropped into the mud. They would have to make their way up the river that was the mouth of the cavern entrance. They made their way up the slippery slope, hopping along as much dry land as possible.

"This place used to be so beautiful, especially now when the geyser is active," Matilda commented. The center of the mountain shot light into the sky that drifted down like pollen. The little balls of light floated in the breeze, making them look like they were dancing through the air. Marshall attempted to catch one and realized that when they hit something, they popped and disappeared. The sun was again setting as they made their way toward the summit of the river. The light was even brighter against the sunless sky, and the pollen of light floated throughout the air and drifted into the cave, lighting the way, gently.

Even still, when they entered, the adventures readied their torches. They would need more light. Each of them but Marshall grabbed a sturdy wooden device, with a metal cage at the top. One by one, Marshall used his paper magic to cast small fireballs into their scepters. For himself, Marshall had an idea and it just so happened to work. He drew a sun and crumbled it into a ball, then he threw it into the air. The ball burst into flames but stably as a little sun; like the pollen, only brighter. The ball of light led in front, just in arm's reach away from him.

The group then marched into the darkness, and as they did they continued to watch their step as the water continued to flow, somehow faster inside—they were now ankle deep. Only a few yards into the cave it opened up, and the large mouth gave way to an even larger chasm. Ligare flew across the ceiling and weaved between giant stalagmites, showing the crew where they really were. The rocks that surrounded them were all large crystals of varying sizes, most of them transparent. As Ligare flew throughout the room, the light from his flames bounced everywhere, creating a kaleidoscope of green-tinted rainbows. For Marshall, he could swear the lights were an image, that of two bodies dancing across the room. What the group didn't know was that creatures dark as a moonless night were in fact running across the room. Following them, the intruders.

After a trek through a few more rooms and across the chasm, they made their way into the source, where both the light and water were born. In the center of the room was a beautiful altar carved out of the stone of the mountain, and below the altar, and surrounding it was a pool of water—the birthplace of the stream. It flowed toward them quickly, going from a few inches wide at their feet to the river behind them, always picking up speed. Above, the altar light shot into the sky and the pollen drifted through the air. Once they were no longer stunned by its beauty, they quickly saw the problem—well, several problems.

Many dark-bodied rodents soaked in the water, using their long pink tongues to lap up the light. From their bodies leaked blue and black that soaked into the water and flowed down the river. "We need to stop them, get them away from the water," Marshall commanded, as he rushed forward eagerly. His team followed swiftly and readied their weapons, but then behind them they heard a noise. A second group of those creatures crawled across the walls and out of the dark. They were nearly impossible to see as they scurried across the ceiling. Their position was only given away by their occasional hiss. Then all at once they readied for a strike. They hissed and they growled, and as they did spines shot out of their bodies. Like porcupines they became fluffy and jagged, except as they screamed their spines flooded with light on and off, as if it were pumping out of its body. Then from both sides, the creatures lunged.

They all readied their weapons and Matilda was the first to go on the offensive. She lunged at the closest one and, like when she dissected the tree, she swiped at lighting speed. Those that came too close were sliced to pieces. As they were cut, they disappeared into a burst of light. Revolocat made his way to the side and pulled from his pocket two dice, and off his belt he grabbed a large wrench. He threw the dice behind the monsters as he charged. The dice rolled for only a moment before they popped open and formed two much larger turrets; they began to fire on the creatures, drawing their attention. Revolocat swung his wrench at them with great force. Nmu-tua rolled into a ball and bowled her way through some of the monsters. After popping open she pulled some dried vines and fruit from her pouch. One by one she gripped them, then threw them at the monsters. The vines grew and traveled across the ground and swam in the water, wrapping up the creatures and constricting them. The fruits grew into large spiked bombs that burst and pinned monsters to the ground and wall.

Marshall aimed his attention at the monsters that were actively feeding from the light. If he was supposed to purify somewhere, it would probably be there. He ran forward with his notebook in hand and his quill in the other. The pages were cut so they could easily be torn, so as he ran, he used his quill to draw a spell—say a fireball—then he used the same hand to flick it through the air, shooting the spell. Marshall dodged, ducked, and jumped, as he used ice to stick monsters to the ground and send others floating down the river. He used fireballs to illuminate the area enough to send a shot of wind to knock monsters against the walls. Marshall made his way to the altar and then began to try and combine the seventh gem. As he tried to squish them together with both his hands, they fought him, like the same sides of a magnet.

Close behind, Piper fought the monsters with his dual shields. Monsters bounced off his arms as he spun. Then as he charged one into a wall, smashing it in a pop of light, he hit his head a bit. From his ears, a blue goo began to drip down his face. He grabbed his head, and he was suddenly overcome by monsters. It was only for a moment before Piper broke out, somehow covered in more blue goo. He charged toward Marshall and from behind lifted him in a crushing bearhug. "What are you doing, Piper?" screamed Marshall. He continued to try to put the gems together.

"You do not deserve those memories. You do not understand the power of them. Their potential. Hand them over to the darkness and forget with us. This is a waste." The voice that came out of Piper was dry and high-pitched. On his final breath and under the cracking of his back, Marshall was able to combine the gems. A giant explosion occurred, pushing Piper away and into the river. Marshall too fell face-first into the water. The gem fell out of his hand and into the pool. As it splashed into the water, the creatures all turned their attention toward it and charged. From Piper's face the blue goo crawled out and charged the gem as well.

When the mass of creatures got onto the gem they began to meld and push into one another. They formed one large creature and absorbed the crystal into their body. Ligare dove down and attempted to swoop and attack it. His body burned through the monster's arms and torso, but as swiftly as he cut through it, the creature formed back its pieces. The creature made its way toward the altar and began to drink in the light once again. As it did it grew larger and larger, and below it so did the trails of black that flowed down the river.

The adventurers converged on the beast. "Help me up!" shouted Marshall. Nmu-tua placed some vines into her hands and slammed them into the ground. They grew and spread through the water and grabbed the monster's legs. It screamed and turned toward them. As it spun, it ripped the vines with the strength of its legs—only momentarily slowed. At the same time, Revolocat and Matilda swiped at the monster's legs with their weapons; the entirety of them simply bounced off. Ligare continued to dive at the face of the monster, who swatted at him. "Up," Marshall yelled again, and Piper made eye contact with him. Piper lowered himself and placed his shield on his back. Marshall ran and jumped off the shield. Piper stood up as he did this, shooting him into the air. Marshall then used a shot of wind to push himself even higher up. He flew in the air toward the face of the monster.

Even through all the harassment, the monster was keen on Marshall's movements. As he flew through the air, the monster watched him and waited. As Marshall approached, he readied a full-page fireball, but the creature grabbed him. His friends continued to wail on the creature to no avail. "All that matters is that we get the gem," yelled Marshall. "I know what to do." He dropped a piece of paper between him and the monster and created a fire. The monster's grip loosened for only a moment but Marshall once again used wind to blow himself forward and he dove into the monster's mouth. The rest of his team screamed in confusion and began to attack the monster even harder. They released a loud "No!" together.

The monster began to turn away from them; their blows were doing nothing to stop him. He returned to ingesting the light, and as he did, he grew larger still. Within the monster's body, Marshall dove down, searching the creature's insides for the lost gem. As his mind faded from the powers of the monster, he dove farther down. Then a rumbling echoed through the cave. The sound grew and grew until it reverberated in the chamber, shaking everything. Then with a flash of light an explosion came from within the monster. The monster was vaporized, nowhere to be found, and Marshall with the finished gem fell through the air and into the water below.

Marshall and the gem splashed into the semi-tainted water, and a white magic began to spread throughout it as well. It flowed down the river and encompassed all the black and blue that was there, purifying the water as it did. Marshall floated, unable to move along the pool, away from the current and away from the gem. He then floated to the altar and began to ascend. He was now being pulled through the air and into the light of the volcano. As Marshall floated away, his friends waved to him from below. The light grew brighter and brighter as he was pulled out of the top of the volcano and into the sky—and Ligare followed.

Marshall's dream had ended and so Ligare exited his mind. Marshall stirred in bed, not paralyzed but merely groggy. Ligare, in his humanoid form, smiled as he walked out of the house and left Marshall to go about his day. Marshall awoke in his bed, in his home—the one he was always disconnected from. He stood up and got dressed. A smile and tear both graced his face as the sun drifted in through the window. It was early but he was excited. His body had changed, his skin was wrinkled, and his hair was gray. His face was completely clean-shaven. Marshall made his way out of his room and down the hallway. He went to his daughter's room, slowly opened it, and peered in. Sound asleep in her bed was Autumn. He hadn't been able to remember her for a long time. Marshall made his way to the kitchen and began making breakfast. After the pancakes were done and the eggs were cooking, he made a slow run back to her room and sat by Autumn's bed.

Marshall dropped onto the bed the best his old body would let him. He placed his arms over her and shook her awake. "Good morning, Autumn. We don't have that much time…before the food gets cold. I've made you breakfast and a glass of chocolate oat milk." Marshall kissed her on the head and slowly got up and ran back to the kitchen to check on his eggs. At first, Autumn was groggy, but she quickly sat up, realizing what was happening. Her father was back and last time it was only for a few hours—she mustn't waste time. Autumn bolted from her bed and into the kitchen. There she found Marshall, dancing while cooking. A small radio on the table was playing one of his favorite songs.

Autumn's green eyes complemented her olive skin, but the bags under her eyes begged for her morning skin care routine. She pulled up a chair to the bar counter and watched her father enjoy life for the first time in months. "Is your mother around?" Marshall asked while cracking another egg into the pan. "Need to know how many eggs to make."

Autumn gulped, not sure how to remind her father. "No, I haven't seen her in a very long time. She is out, somewhere." Autumn got annoyed for a moment and she blushed. "She walked out."

"Oh, well. That's okay." Autumn was noticeably bothered by her father's defense.

"No, it's not you…" Autumn was interrupted by her father's gaze. The one she remembered would always remind her to breathe.

"Don't judge her too harshly. Your mother had a lot of people try to put a lot of negative things in her mind. She was told she was nothing from a very young age…. She never was the best at being her own cheerleader. Deep down she is the sweetest person, but she has a hard time…finding time to show it. I hope…she is happy." Marshall handed Autumn a plate of food. Her sunny side eggs were eyes on her pancakes. Some strips of bacon acted as the mouth. She let out a sigh.

"I hope the same. I still really never got to know her. I wish I could make up for lost time." Autumn took the bacon off her pancakes and placed it on a side plate. "What would you like to do today? Maybe we can go to the park? Or would you like to draw?"

"I'd like to do whatever you'd like to do. I just want to spend the day talking to my daughter." Marshall placed a plate down next to Autumn. He stood while he ate. "Also, tell me about your life." He started to shovel eggs into his mouth.

"You know me. I don't do much, mostly reading. I've been taking classes online. Working on my medical degree to help patients with mental disorders. I've been working with AI patients and…" She paused, unsure if she should tell him that he was her other patient.

"You should get a real person. I'm sure it would be much more applicable. Hell, use me. I'll be your little lab rat." Marshall laughed while he cut into his pancakes.

"You're right, I'll ask them to use you. Thanks for being so sweet." Autumn kissed her father on the head. "But don't worry, I won't start for a long time, and you'll be around for a long time."

"Well, don't hold yourself back on my account. I'll be here when you get back home from work, and I'll be proud." Marshall pointed his fork and knife at Autumn before using them to drum on the table. Marshall then paused and spaced out for a moment. Then he repeated, "Tell me about your life." He smiled, not knowing that he had just lost the last moment. The repeat meant that he was slipping again. Autumn knew they wouldn't have time for the park. They should sit, draw, and talk while they could—it would only be a few hours.

Autumn picked up both of their empty plates and brought them to the sink. "I think it would be great if we spent the day doing what we used to do all the time. Let's have some tea, draw, and talk nonsense." Marshall got up to do the dishes, but Autumn stopped him. "We'll deal with them later. I have tons of crayons and oil pastels and other stuff. I'll grab the paper." Autumn signaled to him, and Marshall sat down at the dining room table. Soon Autumn returned with all the art supplies she promised. Marshall began to draw a picture of his friends from his most recent adventure, as Autumn went and prepared tea.

She returned to him, furiously drawing with a huge smile on his face. While they drank tea, Marshal told her all about his friends and the amazing abilities they had. Autumn was just happy to be joking with her father once again, for things to feel normal. They sat there for hours, until it became evening. They only got up to get a snack. Perhaps they could have gone to the park, but Autumn loved this so much more.

Early in the evening Marshall grew tired. His voice began to slow, and his laughter was longer and more drawn out. "How are you feeling, Dad? Are you getting tired?" Marshall smiled and yawned but tried to deny it. His vacant stare meant he was exhausted; the biggest sign, he was too tired to draw. Autumn helped get her father ready for bed and lay him down once again. Autumn tucked Marshall into bed and gave him a kiss on the forehead. "Good night, Dad. I love you so much," she whispered.

"I love you too, darling. Thank you for a wonderful day. I'll see you tomorrow." Marshall closed his eyes and got comfortable in his bed.

"I hope so," Autumn responded. As Autumn turned off the lights, Marshall fell back into his mind, and he lost himself again. His body drifted through the floor, and he fell into the abyss. As Marshall fell his clothes changed, and returned to the white boots and cloak he adventured in earlier. As he fell through the air he fell asleep, and as he lay in the air this descent slowed. By the time he reached the ground, he gently loafed into the grass like a feather would. He was asleep and waiting for his next adventure and his next chance to go home.